SURRENDER TO
A STRANGER

Jeremy Reed is the author of over fifty books of award-winning poetry, fiction and biography, and also a celebrated performer of his work with Itchy Ear as The Ginger Light. Concerned with writing from the visionary present into the near future, J. G. Ballard described Reed's talent as "almost extraterrestrial in its brilliance." Controversial, edge-walking and propelled by luminous imagination, he has for both his work and looks been described as "British poetry's glam, spangly, shape-shifting answer to David Bowie." Amongst his recent books are the poetry collections *Sooner or Later Frank*, *Candy4Cannibals* and *Psychedelic Meadow*, and two non-fiction books, *The Dilly: A Secret History of Piccadilly Rent Boys*, and a biography of Lou Reed titled *Waiting for the Man*. He lives in London.

SNUGGLY BOOKS

jeremy reed

SURRENDER TO
A STRANGER

THIS IS A SNUGGLY BOOK

ISBN: 978-1-64525-103-3

SURRENDER TO
A STRANGER

1

MR. W.H.

What's my type: amoral, atypical, a third-culture individual, a rogue escapee from history, or an online male escort lubricating the rich? You tell me. You can run across a Tudor meadow with driving rain at your back, or trek over desiccated moon regolith where it hasn't rained for 400 million years; you can download your DNA on to a USB stick, conceal your nominal identity through a hack-proof quantum satellite, hide under a stairwell at Waterloo Bridge for five centuries, but none of it adds up to the oddity of me. You'll find out.

The error is in assuming I'm dead, whatever that means, by incinerating body mass into gritty ash as the conversion of 140lbs into a dry 5. There's no official record of my death, there's no Mr. W.H. listed, and no documentation of my ever having existed under initials synonymous with the dedication to a book of Sonnets published in 1609 by Thomas Thorpe, and sold at Paules Church-yard at the sign of the Crane by Walter Burre. The book that made my name into a biographical enigma continues to time-travel down the centuries, rehabilitated by mass-market paperbacks and downloads, with my initials coded into its sustainable exhaust.

Do you think reading this you can get to know me as someone who isn't a guess? I mean be familiar with the colour of my hair, skin tone, pigment and eyes, my blood-type, birth sign, diet, speaking voice, health, education, interests, sex-life, the drugs blowing through my system, the underground garage that's my memory. Are my eyes the same shape as my lips, does that get you coming from a man?

My story as a missing person—I'm always thrown by their photos—has of necessity to be chopped up like DNA or mushrooms on a board. It covers six different centuries and is still happening, otherwise how could I write this book. My building blocks are the fourteen-liner sonnit: Sonnet: derived from the Italian word sonetto. Traditionally written in iambic pentameter, it includes the octave (two quatrains) that forms the proposition and the sestet (two tercets) that proposes a resolution.

You imagine getting celebrity from a sonnit. I'm not part of literature, but used by it in ways I never asked by a writer who got known first in muddy bear-pit theatres, and later in the ubiquitous dialectic of global theatre. From Shoreditch to Mars he's the word mogul whose reputation has never dipped in bankability. And I'm inextricably a part of this man's biography, a no-colour like Absolut Vodka or London Gin. Whoever got more famous under the foggy corona of a grey London sink by the river? Those theatres were swamps in which people fucked, died, robbed each other, grew old in the process of watching, went in with blonde hair and came out grey. The Elizabethan plague was retroviral, it was sent into the future to remake its unstoppable profile as AIDS in the 1980s. This man, my lover, W.S., didn't do condoms, not like my favourite Okamoto 002 filmed like an air-kiss on the skin.

I've got a lot to tell you if you believe in me as undercover resource and an insider to MI5 and intelligence. I've got a feed to those guys who go into the darknet and access poten-tial terrorists, human traffickers, Russian Mafia dishing out polonium, arms-dealers and Tony Blair's golden handshake;

and the ultimate terror imported from apocalypse—Isis stockpiling depleted uranium.

Why am I me; and why was he, the man, the language greaser, the one who caused words to pop out of his brain chemistry? There's no explaining individual destiny, it's just chromosomal, and whoever you are you just go with it, as it's you. You don't really know you're you; you need other people to tell you. There's been so many literary historians looking for me, some of them good—Leslie Hotson, A.L. Rowse, Robert Giroux, they've all thrown shapes into biography, pinched up traces of my DNA, but the sequence never fits. Just look at the proposed list of possibilities. William Herbert, the Earl of Pembroke. Henry Wriothesley, the Earl of Southampton, William Hall, a printer, William Harvey, Southampton's stepfather, William Haughton, a contemporary dramatist, William Hart, William Hatcliffe of Lincolnshire, William Hughes, William Hole, all listed because they were somebody known in society, rather than a rogue gene who lived on the edges of reality with no consistent ID.

Let me tell you, maybe 150,000 people worldwide die each day, and we don't usually know any of them. Their identities are simply rubbed like a Starbucks table with an anti-bacterial wipe. But he's different, I mean the man who came into my life and who was simply writing what was normal to him, and got taken up as a frontline academic brand, and still remains that today. At the time of our relationship he was concerned like all of us with living, money problems, an acrimoniously collapsed marriage, taxes, health, the whole business of daily survival. If he'd thought his name was going to fly down the centuries, he'd probably have turned his back on the idea, like a blinding rainstorm. He came to the capital to use and exploit people necessary to him: he was too self-regarding to have real friends, and so much of his life was eaten up by writing, there wasn't much else to offer, just sex and greed.

He kept me defensively secret, all punters do that to rent, have you in subtitles at the bottom and if questioned deny your existence. But with me, he landed a big mistake. How could he have known that my initials, his fuck-boy, would become the subject of persistent enquiry, the sonnits he'd never dared give my full name to, the gateway to his own bi promiscuity. If you sell sex you can never be equal to the punter. Even though he's degrading himself by paying, he'll have you as loser for selling. There's no way to ever redress the balance, the user takes precedence over the used. It's like a ministerial getaway in an armour-plated Humvee that's an automotive fortress. The people left behind melt into the explosion. He was always like that, quick to get back to a life in which I wasn't included. I was peripheral to his real motivating thrust of work, but pulled into his life by a mutual need—his to launch sex on a man—and mine to be part of someone who didn't want love in return or for me to stick. Whatever our chemistry, it suited him to be transitioning between lives he mostly damaged in the process.

2

20 MAY 1609

Tho. Thorpe. Entred for his copie under the handes of master Wilson and master Lownes Wardenes a booke called *Shakespeares Sonnettes*.

Weren't no authorised manuscript, as I kept it, as the only thing he ever gave me. The printer George Eld worked from an unauthorised copy. In my job I had eyes and ears all over the city and saw things like a sighting dashcam. You need to know, but it comes later, that it wasn't just the black skinned Lucy Negro, who seriously compromised our thing, but this punk called the rival poet who was more in on my life than out. And to me, on my senses, he was the better poet—the rogue pundit so far down the road you couldn't see him for his word hoard in Cloud, a quantum Cloud, which fetches us up to meet tomorrow, somewhere in the mirrored sky-scraper jungle, under the street, talking of a great reckoning at Deptford Creek.

And me, I preferred Kit. He was punky, lived ahead of himself, didn't grease authority, and wrote out of his balls as well as the poetic shape of his thought mixing the street with a language so loaded it still has the exhaust plume of a Yamaha bike getting off a red light.

You need to think of time as a sequence, like the visual frames the brain cuts to process info. Most people get stuck in one frame in which their biology systematically corrodes. Will, the other Will, the one who gave me the Sonnits, fuck the e, also switched on the facility to time-travel, maybe it was a generational thing, I don't know. I learnt how to get out of time and back into its river, and once I'd learnt how I've kept on repeating it. You can arguably biohack me, but not time—nobody's got into its central nervous system to manage its workings. I used to tell Will that time is like consciousness; you can't locate it because it's what you are. There are moments when the space between what you're observing and you the observer completely dissolves, and you get a sort of hint as to what it could be, but mostly the distance is maintained, and you're set back looking. There's this pot of Farrow & Ball black paint, and there's you reviewing the dribbles on the can, and that's where the two of you remain. It's got something to do with subverting biological closure, and the carriers are left freakily isolated like a red Japanese sun flag masted on the moon, while a tractor operated by robots kicks up a dust cloud for the space-mining economy.

You go find Lucy Negro, the Clerkenwell prostitute who was part of our triangle; I can, as she's still around. When Will had used me up too often, she was his destination, the red light walk-up in a streaming alley to which he went because he couldn't nail me. Lucy claimed the river as her mother because it was black as her skin. She said someone had fucked Limehouse Basin and she'd crawled out on the shore, got a pimp and set to work selling sex to men attracted to her pigment. He took up with her because she wasn't the least interested in his celebrity. He was just another punter with a deviated psychological twist. It was I told her he wrote, when we got stoned on black spice, or opium, imported from India, getting blissed out in a sleazy riverside hole. She said he treated women backwards as though they didn't have a front or he couldn't work it out that way. I'll never know about Lucy. Sex workers look out for themselves and downsize punters into types, and not people. Black Luce, as she sometimes called herself, and Gilbert East, her pimp, their business was brothels, and they drank together on London's hub to talk business. You know what Luce said to me one day: 'He's cold, he steals from me, like he's sort of inside my skin for info.' What she meant was he lifted aspects of her personality for real, and he did it to everyone and put it back in your face as words. And of course he wasn't personally connected to the work he wrote, it was depersonalised like the way Lou Reed phrases 'Heroin,' cool as black ice on a highway. If ever I dared read back a line he'd written, he wouldn't recognise it, he was that far removed from the content, and that much ahead of abandoned work.

I go back to Farrow & Ball house paint. Put one coat on another, you still got black, not Vanta black, but black on black. It's on the door I'm facing in Hop Gardens London WC2, like time peeling under its gloss. If I look at it long enough, distracted from writing this book, I'm ten, twenty minutes older in my blue-cuffed Levi's and black suede desert boots. Lucy worked northeast on the London compass and fifteen minutes with a client could stretch her a year on, like a snapshot of the future.

The first mention of the sonnits, stacked like one fridge on top of another on the page, was given away by Francis Mere's mention in 1598 of 'his sugared Sonnets among his private friends.' Sugared, like gay speak, or sugaring the rim of a glass before pouring a pumpkin pie martini, only the coating in this case is scratched to reveal an emotionally twisted interior. There's nothing we do doesn't carry self-interested traces of our own bacteria cloud. Poetry isn't Lego to be taken apart, it's more like spooning a yoghurt pot for the plump blueberries. The one thing that attracts me to the sonnits is of course me and my little circle coded into the contents—street trash licked over by the veneer of language.

Am I hard on his celebrity? Should I show more respect for his ability to network social media, drink himself into the bottom of his glass with actors, and climb above them all with his 24-7 facility to turn words. Thing is he could do it cold, effortlessly, anywhere, write like it really didn't matter, but it did when you weren't looking. This was someone who left his wife his second-best bed and me the sonnits. I didn't want anything to do with his work, I just happened to be the subject of his climacteric. Off-page he lacked small talk and filled in cold spaces with speculative business, he was always on about money, his company, his rivals, the infrastructure of theatres. It wasn't my world, but we had something going like an emotional apple core, a sort of pixel stick glow that was always there, like you know you're standing back to a door by the awareness swimming around you. But him, the man, my absorbent, he was forensically analytic, his protein dug out of burnt meat and lodged in his gut like a Big Mac. I mean, he wasn't sensitive like you'd expect, he was coolly voyeuristic and hard in that means were an end. He faced into contractual writing like the paint job on a wall—Farrow & Ball for high-end gloss.

He wasn't secret about it, like those moodies who write in an exclusion zone, he'd do it around me, one draft only; he never rewrote anything, it was either right or it wasn't. Altering it only made it different, not better, he said. Anyhow, the reader doesn't know of the changes, or have any method of comparison. He simply couldn't care, because it was right.

Everything about our relationship was like a room full of mirrors. I had this casual on/off thing with Lucy, a bit sexual as a source of revenge; but also to wind her up so she'd bitch something terrible about him, skinning him like a tomato. It occurred to me she'd probably infected him, or he'd picked up an STD on Turnmill Street, because something in him was suddenly turned down at the corners, like he knew he was sick, but didn't really want to know. And I picked up on it, and at the same time brought her more regularly into conversation, something that turned him defensively cold, resistant, until he abruptly took off into the London rain. It wasn't in him to talk about it; he kept the visceral for the stage and illness as buried data.

We were both Will—and who cloned who? If I spoke to him I was speaking to myself, same name sharing does that. It's like drinking from the same glass, only you don't change sides. Like we in part shared Lucy, principally to make each other jealous, as emotions too have quantum entanglement. Lucy was our fuck compass to being bisexual; and he, the other Will, used to quote his doctor, Thomas Cogan, who advocated frequent sex as the best way to modify 'sadness, madness, melancholy, anger, fury.' If you're looking for the source, it's *The Haven of Health*, 1594.

He travelled a lot with his company on the theatre circuit, he liked money and it came as dollops of tainted cash—I mean the others in my life had wealth too, but with him it was like an adhesive, it stuck. Nobody else saw any of it, not his wife, the actors he employed, or me. He paid only when he was pinned up against an alley wall by some vicious punk with a knife and a slouching hoodie. When he came to me one day there was caked blood all over his left hand where he'd been slashed by a blade, and of course he wouldn't call a paramedic; he made out with it and had me dress the cut. He was too intrinsically preoccupied to call doctors; he said he didn't have time, and that the future was too full of things he'd never get to see ever, even though he was one of its principal tourists. He felt he was ahead and behind at the same time— he couldn't catch up with his life and that for him time went both ways. Writing, he said, locked him into time because it so occupied the present. It was like taking blood and doing your own analysis in screening for genetic disorders.

I'm sitting on a wall in Hop Gardens, writing this, a cut-through from St. Martin's Lane to Bedfordbury, Covent Garden, eating a hummus and falafel wrap I bought at Eat, spiked with red cabbage and peppers. I'm a picky vegan who like Morrissey thinks meat is murder and steak-men cannibals, like R.T., the capital's most influential meatman who turns Galician beef cooked in a computer-controlled Thermodyne oven into semi-rare. The other Will, he didn't prevaricate over hunks of cholesterol-rich flanks hacked off a body heavy as a car.

I'm a transient in this alley, like the people who transition through in the trancy street-daze you get in London, where you're constantly expecting to meet someone or something that changes your life. I write there a few hours in the afternoon, sitting out with workers from the St. Martin's Lane Hotel, having cig-breaks in their white shirt black trousers contrast. If they notice me they don't let on, I'm just this anomalous energy cone, self-absorbed, but distractively sharing the same light, the same London B-side alley to collect my life in a sequence of snapshots that interact with words.

Food: He was always eating, me never. I've told you the carnivore slashers would have supplied him from an abattoir with stacked offal. But it didn't stop there, mutton, rabbit, veal, game, boar, venison, but beef with its dietary sell of vitamin A, vitamin B12, folate, selenium and zinc was his big bite. Poetry from pathogens, like the wrong day of the week for sex. And he liked salty squid, oysters like detached retinas, skewered mussels, eel, marzipan, cheeses—no lactose intolerance, bread rather than seasonal veg, pears in nutmeg and saffron, yams and difficult angles on stews and soups.

It wasn't that I was ascetic; it was also that I was self-conscious of weight, like I still am, rarely posting above ten stone, as the thin ideal of being taken up by strangers. Will, the other Will, regularly got stoned on black cannabis, the psychoactive THC helped shape his work, give it a druggy architecture, a drag of India on a wet sullen English afternoon. He didn't know nothing of the brain's biology in processing cannabinoids, and more to the point tetrahydrocannabinal THC that produces the high—I mean I don't know his work, but centuries later I picked up a cheap paperback of *The Tempest*, lit a joint and it all came together, the floaty hallucinated schematic, the drug directing the build of imagery like marshmallow blocks.

He was permanently stoned in London, and one gin-clear day when we went out to Pawles Wharf to sit and tidy up our relationship by letting our thoughts mix like paint with the reflective green water, he prepared a pipe and we shared it, as a means of mentally sorting and climbing up into the drug's heady, euphoric chemistry. And it was sexy; the weed went down to my balls and up to my brain's limbic system. I too began an on/off habit and started buying the drug on the docks and dealing him black Indian hemp. They all used it knowingly, Ben Jonson, Kit Marlowe, George Chapman, the whole gang were doped on psychoactives that fed into their inspired visionary writing.

Another time, another century, I got onto heroin, smack gunned like diesel into my veins—you know it—the Lou Reed mythology. The black on black wraparounds, or the Pete Doherty middle-distance look that's always some place he is cooking into, I was there too, but that's another story, hiding in a Portobello cellar, but doing bespoke drugs as my body was sold as property to a man whose Edward Sexton suit with its tone-on-tone buttonholes dusted the Commons. Politicised sex that cost him everything in the translucent teat of a condom.

You know I like long haul with teleports, not the pretence of linear chronology, the pushing of an artificially constructed story to find a fake resolution. After William Burroughs and his deconstruction of the formal novel, why go back to convention as cheap? *Naked Lunch* nuked an assembly line of retrograde novels that persist today as Waterstones cake-filler, like millefeuille with custard and not cream. You wanna buy Barnes, Amis, Hilary Mantel, you're digging yourself into a mainstream pit, no GABA uptake, just flatline impulses for a writing shade between unredeemed grey and charcoal.

Let's get back to trouble and the man. My man. Of course he wrote all that without the exhaustive Bacon conspiracy theories—the pathway to apocryphal fake. With his sort of expansive imagination all you need is archival data and you can reconstruct history cold out of your brain cells. He wasn't a global tourist, just back to Stratford for a break, or touring the provinces with his company. The idea you have to be mobile like Hemingway, Fleming or Bruce Chatwin isn't necessarily attractive to those who write on nervous exhaust, and he didn't have time to travel, but just listen in pubs to those who came back from slave continents. His conception of the globe was that of a 4D six-sided casino dice. He wasn't writing to be remembered, it was work he flavoured with style, like a strawberry ice-lolly, or bitter, orange.

Go into this salty Thames warehouse; change the subject, the office pinned with dozens of brown paper patterns for handcrafted jeans for a small denim company, the fabric imported from North Carolina, the 125-year-old Cone Denim— just outside Greensboro. I met this man who wanted me to come look. A WWII-era buttonholer for pewter rivets, two computerised looms and rows of clattering analogue counterparts operating on shock-absorbing wooden floors rather than standard concrete. The room I'm told by Ted needs to be damp; the river provides this, as humidity keeps the fabric supple. It's a small, customised label, the retro looms producing quality selvedge denim for themselves and premium brands. There, I've told you what occupied 20 minutes of my time today, 20 minutes having a Tea Pigs break with Ted, and most likely he won't see me again. I'm like that; I don't stick. I'm who I am as I transition through people, who in turn are built out of time in their DNA base pairs.

I'll do it again at Leicester Square, sitting out in the accidental Chinese, Islamic, Euro amalgamated foot traffic; the heat solid blond like some urban desert shimmy. I've a feel for a tourist returning from the future, and an eye on a Chinese street performer doing fireeating with orange torches. He's so present he creates the time in which he performs, like W.S. when I saw him writing with total preoccupation. You can't ever do it the same again, only different, he'd say, by stretching your imagination. Me, I'm into the dystopian physics of J.G. Ballard—I mean tech hassling lit off the page.

Met this man there, in the square, focused on the fireeating act, but tangentially on me. His identity kept slipping like the separation between spirits and juice in a glass, or the thin divide between blue atmosphere and black space. There were three Asian girls grouped next to us in breathed on skinnies, sharing images and clips on their phones. Told me coldly with no intro that he had a benzo problem, and he'd clearly sneakily observed me crumbling granules from a popped Diazepam blister pack on to my hand. Told me coolly you can die of Valium withdrawal and that he'd buy from me. I could feel his need and time starting to gel; things were that sticky. I'd been through the whole benzo withdrawal syndrome many times, wrung-out, bleached of all context, panicky days of collapsed purpose.

The man, dusty blond, white cotton shirt and blue jeans, rotated the cap off a bottle of water. 'You don't know who I am,' he said, fixing me, 'but we've met before.' And I thought the same, 'you don't know who I am,' with my exhaust plume of condensed time-travel. 'Kit's the name,' he said, 'Kit Marlowe.'

I didn't answer, just looked at him, sort of knowing this would happen, discovering the blue pigment in his eyes, and intuitively quizzing the rate of absorption of the drug I'd just swallowed.

'I know what you're thinking,' he said. 'That I've stolen the name, that I'm delusional or something; you've every right to.'

'It doesn't matter,' I said, thinking how closely he must have observed me to be aware of the drug foil I'd lifted from my pocket to scramble maybe 2mg from a cracked tablet for the micro-dose I needed.

He stood off. One of the Asian girls was adeptly piling her hair up and securing it with a purple band, before tucking a black bra strap under. Kit, and for some reason I didn't doubt it was him, looked like he'd dropped out of tomorrow, or belonged to a dawn on the other side of the Earth. I could see withdrawal in him like the fade in jeans. He was looking at me as abstract, and the drug as real.

'My doctor won't do it any longer,' he said. 'He wants me to go into rehab, and I won't, the Priory's like a mausoleum. Doctors think benzos are like some sort of alien mind virus.'

I'd known it too, the need to go private or get Indian whites from a friend who returned from Goa with hundreds to sell on at a pound a pill. I was never without strips of them in my pockets as the sign of an unhackable habit.

'My Doctor Faustus is on again,' he said, with no hint of personality disorder; just the same cool drug-focused detachment that he wasn't going to leave me without pills. 'I can't prove that I wrote it, or that I'm around again to remember, but I did. And I know you; you're the elusive W.H. Think I'd forget?'

Thrown as I was, I didn't doubt him; nothing to me was strange, given my implausible time-slips of biology. I knew only too well that it's possible to transport a human brain across the galaxy and end up in Leicester Square as your backstory. There's nothing local about geography, unless you're subject to ordinary mortality and can't go connect with the future, that space into which Boeings climb out as a window on the hyper-real, and that's where it starts.

'You've got blues haven't you, not whites,' he said. 'The generic does it for me, although I'll do the copy.'

'Let me see what I've got,' I said, stalling. 'I'm not a dealer you know, I need it as much as you—I'd kill for a fucking grain.'

He looked over a boy in the crowd like he was skinning a banana, throwing a hot look at his crotch. I got there too, but he was first. I didn't need confirmation of his sexuality, but his thrown look did it. Raiding me for Valium was psychologically like hacking my bank account, hijacking my pin; and inwardly I resented the intrusion; but I dug into my pocket feeling for a loose tablet, and dug up a second.

He'd pulled his phone out of a pocket and was skimming text. It was alarmingly clear he'd picked up on me as another time-jockey and that something made us conspicuously alien. I shoved him two generic blues in my palm, as though I was giving him back his life with 20mg of blue dust.

'Look,' I said, 'I know what this drug does when you can't get it, I'll see what I can do for you and phone around.'

'It's the nausea,' he said, 'gets me. Withdrawal sweats the stomach onto the tongue. I can taste my need.'

I threw a peeled look at him. 'Did you really recognise me?' I asked, shocked, guarded, not letting on. 'Who is or was this Mister W.H.? You're a complete stranger to me, and apart from pills I don't know what you want.' I looked away at a busker trying to remake the Beatles' 'Here Comes The Sun' without that dose of whatever it takes. Then suddenly I underwent a blinding time-slip to Kit Marlowe living in Holywell Lane in Norton Folgate, a room in which he wrote, drank and smoked dope. He was suddenly there; centuries back, a presence, like a dark object at the edges of reality, and his copy, if it was that, confronting me now.

In a confused state I agreed to trade numbers on our phones, and he stuck to me, like I was the first person he'd recognised in centuries, but it was me thinking that so as to try and sort it out for myself.

'What about the Starbucks on St. Martin's Lane,' he said, as a black hatted, wrung-out, redhead singer journeyed out on a cover of Dylan's 'Wheels Of fire.' 'We could go there and talk if you have time.'

'All right,' I said, questioning his invasion of my time. I'd never lost my youthful looks as part of my transitioning identity, and was currently spending time at Charles Street, Mayfair, with a Market Leader from the private bank Coutts, who was recreationally obsessed with proving the historic identity of Mr. W.H. Oxford educated, with walloping mood-swings that left him a reckless impulsive mess lubed on gin, inherently taciturn, frustrated he couldn't write, he'd moved up the Coutts curve with rehearsed talks of exteriorising costs onto future generations as still another portfolio theorist.

Together, we walked across Leicester Square, not saying very much, the precinct streaming with quizzical, trancy tourists, Japanese girls carrying Fortnum's and Selfridge's carriers, hijabs in numbers, a French school visit, everyone filming geographical reality.

We took window seats at Starbucks, opposite the St. Martin's Lane Hotel, with its Philippe Starck appointed, funky, minimalist style shepherded by a taxi line outside showing their orange welcome signs. It was starting to rain and Kit looked less alienated, now he'd got the drug into his system, and settled to a blueberry muffin and Americano.

'What do you do?' I asked him outright, confronting the enigma of déjà vu.

'I snoop on the future,' he said. 'It's like running time both ways. I'm a tech spook, if you really want to know, part of a secretive intelligence agency designed to create ways of staying ahead of cyber criminals. Does that sound strange? It's not so very different from what I started out doing for Francis Walsingham, in our time.'

I couldn't quite take this in, it was like light from the galaxy suddenly telling me where it came from on its journey through space in reaching me. I looked out the window briefly at scintillating splinters of rain and the hotel doorman jumping in and out on call. I didn't tell him, but my life was about allowing people at a price to own what they wouldn't otherwise possess. My body.

'I've gone back to the Folgate streets,' he said, 'with Heron Tower as its mast. It scares me a bit, vertical, cladded economy. It's not so far from where my friend Tom Watson killed a man called Bradley on Hog Lane. The blood was like smashing a bottle of wine against a wall. That bad.'

I was on to it with near enough perfect recall. 'You mean the murder of William Bradley, who used to drink at the Dolphin near St. Botolph's. Strange as it is, I know more than you think, even if it is a bit like stretching a spaghetti strand across five centuries. Murder doesn't change; it's undoable.'

Out the corner of my eye I noticed a black girl throwing us inquisitive looks, as though she'd picked up on something said. I noticed her burnt orange eye shadow, the orange colour pops repeated on her lips. She was wearing a zip-through leather skirt as part of her wraparound curves, looked at us hard and went back into her phone.

'What do you know that I don't?' Kit quizzed. 'I mean about your lover sharing Southampton as our mutual patron. I'm going back now, but your Will was rotten jealous of my sponsor, but it went deeper than that, the way counterintelligence gets into the cracks of thoughts. Do you follow me, or think I'm mad, crossing centuries?'

Distractively, a couple came and sat down next to us, the new merger of a-nationals with modern, a youth who really didn't own to a nationality but transitioned across frontiers as mobile adventurers. She could be retro-punk French, and he another ratty knee-holes in his jeans tech kid. The black girl was still looking at us periodically, as though she meant business.

'I don't know why, but we seem to be attracting attention,' I said. 'It's not the place to talk what we may have in common, and anyhow, you could be anyone. Leicester Square's the place where you can't trust your own shadow. Believe me. I know.'

This time he came back at me unnervingly full on. 'I think you know who I am, independent of benzos. You remember Jack Poole? The counterfeiter I met in prison, after the murder charges. Remember, and think hard, I brought him to your place and he parted with a fist of money for sex. He broke into your flat later looking for a manuscript given you only I'd got in first and was waiting for him in your wardrobe. You came back and found me sitting in your chair writing.'

'And you were sitting reading the manuscript,' I said, 'as the only other person ever to do so, until its publication. Now I almost believe you. The sonnits: the story of two years in my life made into history. 154 of them shaped like mortuary fridges.'

I felt that together we were processing strangeness, building a meta-reality to which I had no reason to commit; but inwardly, I was certain it was him, Kit, as the unnervingly exact detail in my domestic life wasn't to be found in any biography I'd encountered. And all the time I was thinking simultaneously of Farrow & Ball black paint for use on a floor at Charles Street. I mean Pitch Black Blue with its eggshell finish, Black Blue, with a perceptible blue pigment, when spread in larger areas, and Off-Black, much softer in tone than Pitch Black. And I wanted to tell him in our awkward silence of Vantablack, a superblack made from carbon nanotubes , so saturated that when the light gets in it can't get out.

'If we're making sense,' I said, 'then who else in our circle is still around? The big player, Shakespeare, Lucy Negro, Henry Wriothsley, Thom Walsingham, you tell me? It sounds like madness, us being here by default.'

Kit was looking at me like his habit was nagging, working on me like undercover, his intelligence getting into me insidiously as a virus. This time, without his even asking, I pulled out a foil of ten generic blues and handed them over for him to pocket. He was always masculine gay, tough masking soft, and it hadn't changed, and the leathery scent he was wearing was like my partner Howard's, an atomised citrus lick on tight layers of presumed masculinity.

When my phone alerted me with its faux-mechanical ring, I was suddenly flipped back into the awareness of now, and the realisation we could both be psychos, delusional strangers picking up with all the risk of homicide in the potential. On impulse, I thought of just clearing off and leaving him there, but I knew he'd stick all the way to the tube and down.

'Look, we can't resolve this here,' I said, feeling increasingly unnerved. 'I'll put you in contact with someone who regularly brings back benzos from Goa. Let's meet up again when we've had time to think this through. We can't bounce centuries down into minutes, if there's any truth in all this.'

He looked me over this time like a hardened operative. His white shirt cuffs were blue and red check on the inside, as a colour split, a bit like his mind. I could see his hand fitted over the drug foil inside his jeans pocket, as the addict's true math. Our big ball of context was still up like an angry red sun that wouldn't set. I thought of us as escapees from history, who'd simply never cooled into any process as mundane as death. I wondered what this would mean to the punky black girl who threw us a disquieting look as she got up to leave, earbuds in, as a sort of mixed reality.

'We need to talk at length,' he said, outside. 'It was your sugar daddy put out the word to have me murdered, as his rival. Nobody has ever dared implicate him, but you were his partner at the time, and his wife too dumb to know. I call him Mister Cold. It's not without note, that there's a photo of Lou Reed in 1979, appropriately called Cold. You may know it. He's cradling a guitar upright against the zippered leather skin in which he lived. I've a print in my flat. You'll see the likeness.'

I watched him peel a dark-haired boy with a retro-future look, as the rain came on, as a London constant. The boy snapped round, but hurried on into a dissolve with the crowd.

He looked at me with chilling dissociation. 'You know, it wasn't me that got recognition for the plays; it was the actors. My celebrity was on a lower rung. I could be murdered because outside our circle nobody knew me. And today, it's no different. I'm a name on a book, a Penguin edition, or a device; and to the reader I'm an abstract concept.'

And standing there, doorwayed out of the rain, I had this intense flashback, like a brain zap, to seeing him differently. We'd both lived in Southwark, the disreputable side of the river, the lawless Bankside warren of alleys like Fishmongers, Ram's Rose, Mermaid Bar, and the Kit I'd known was loopy. He'd rowed across the river at night with an armed gang and committed robberies in Westminster, just for kick of it. It all came back to me, money he'd robbed as firsthand experience for writing about the underworld he dipped into as his adopted own. He'd never cared, and it was this won me over; the fact he lived by lies, a blade, and plays put on in muddy sinks by the river.

I let him go off into the night to pull a taxi outside the Gym Box. I kept telling myself I wasn't alone, and that if I could run time backwards to my youth, then why shouldn't he, if we shared the same reconstructed history. I watched the rain build to a slow silver dazzle before I walked off into the West End drench.

I'm back in Hop Gardens, the walk-through in which I write and think on a ledge opposite the Friends House. What do you make of this story, the rehabilitation of two synchronised Elizabethan young men coming together in Leicester Square? It's a fact London invites altered or manipulated timelines, a quantum math that can entertain tourists from the future, as well as the past, like different epoch aircraft checking into Heathrow simultaneously—a BA 1940s de Havilland landing on a parallel runway to a Boeing 747 Airbus in suddenly thickening weather.

What I can't readily do is reverse time. I'm continuously referred to the future, like someone trying to dodge round a sleeping pill to get there first. Writing still remains for me the smartest form of decoding experience into approx verbal equivalent. You know, we start seeing things that aren't there to wipe out things that are. Like one afternoon walking back to Howard's Mayfair flat I saw Graham Greene in a Burberry trench coat, pushing fists in his pockets through the rain. I was convinced in my mind it was 1955, *The Quiet American*, his depression flat in his brain, and betrayal of his wife uppermost in his mind to endorse his conviction you have to break something to strengthen how it works.

In ten minutes I'll go back. Howard usually brings wine from the Bottle Queen, and something expensive from Jermyn Street, a shirt or jumper in pastels, and the re-loop of his trading day. He doesn't know who I really am, or need to. He's probably unaware that someone called Mr. W.H. ever existed as historic enigma, or rent to Shakespeare.

3

BIOGRAPHY 1570

Star Sign Aquarius
Height 5ft 10"
Weight 140lbs
Birthplace Bankside
Parents Not credited
Occupation Escort
Hair Grease Black
Eye Colour Blue/Green/Grey
Diet Vegan
Blood Type A
Scent Hammam Penhaligon
Brush With Greatness David Bowie
Books Jake Arnott *The Long Firm*
Music Marc Almond Pete Doherty
Artist Francis Bacon
Epitaph: 'Not marble nor the gilded monuments
Of princes shall outlive this powerful rhyme'

4

MISTER T.T.

He's the one who started it, T.T., Thomas Thorpe, the lugu-brious publisher of the sonnits—we're modern now sonnits, after I personally loaned him the manuscript. You can't im-agine, even then, how much I hated being the subject of these formal wrung-out blues, let alone the highly cryptic dedica-tion glaring at me like red neon.

But we had history, T.T. and me, and the sort of sex for which we would have swung at Tyburn on a blood-plaited hemp rope. He was the first person came on at me with the offer of tainted cash. He was learning to print with a guy called Richard Watkins at a shop in little Conduit Street at Cheapside. His ambition covered air miles, he wanted them all, Will, Ben Johnson, Kit Marlowe, George Chapman; he wanted his logo to travel down the centuries attached to ce-lebrity, what else do you call these men who pan-fry their words on the page, so the chemistry spits like a greasy fry-up of elevated Inglish.

Thom, like Thom Gunn, and not Tom, was from Barnet, but never went back there. He had two gold teeth and some-body paid. He was hyperactive, like he was impatient to get out of the present into another time zone. Conspicuous for his lipstick-red hair—he pulled you into his centre without any awareness it was happening. He drank like we all did, grew manic afterwards and the next day flat. He was someone who lived under the radar, snuck in the corner of things and went away with the plot. He knew books and stacked his on the floor, like intelligence was always rectangular, and weighed more than the coconut-shaped human brain.

It was Thom introduced me recreationally to hemp seeds as a psychoactive. He knew the notorious Kit Marlowe and a Thames waterman, John Taylor, who operated an early river bus, transporting people across the river's skin at a time when London Bridge was the only north-south pathway between the two shores. It was Taylor told Thom a grain of hemp grew in size to a mountain, a hallucinated gold cone he sat in front of on the river, a stoned rude boy in a boat. Today, the architecture he imagined is real. I look out at a cluster of islanded mirror-glass skyscrapers built into low cloud, like powerbrokers get smarter in towers. My neighbour's so fucked up on crack he sees holo ghosts issuing from the steaming London sink.

Anyhow, we'd get expert on distinct strains of hemp and cannabis, each with its unique biochemical composition and uses. Being on the river and meeting dealers Taylor got to know that hemp has lower concentrations of THC than cannabis, but higher concentrations of cannabidiol CBD. We bought off him, and the city around us changed with our chemistry, and Kit was a part of it too, building vision into a hallucinated tower.

Times don't change much, only the available tech, and cloud storage of data owes its origins to drug architecture—I've got the overview on it—it's simply a virtual tool that suggests offworld, rather like enhancement by psychotropics.

Thom advanced by living secretly and cultivating few friends, mainly fellow printers and booksellers, and I can see now his policy that the fewer people you know the less gossip if you're same-sex and ambitious to succeed in pushing literature with a gay basis. Kit promised him books before he was murdered at Deptford, and he went on to publish his translation of the first Book of Lucan in flown English with a blood bank of Roman atrocities tracking the narrative of the atrocious butcher war between Caesar and Pompey.

Thom was always black with printer's ink and burnt by industrial metal a lot of the time. Setting a book he'd say is like re-ordering the universe, you take it apart and reset the pattern and get lead poisoning in the process. All this was done letterpress; you can feel the raise of printer's ink on the paper like a ribbed condom.

Thom kept me because he said I was too beautiful to work, and that's how it's always been, men looking after men in an exclusion zone from heteronormative society. It's this allowance that works in the interests of creative time, rather than being shuttled on the Jubilee Line towards the Docklands Railway for inclusion in the big financial diamond in the sky.

Nobody outside our circle knew we were together, and we never appeared so in public. I modelled, and on/off worked with a jeweller to review the light inside a ruby, emerald, or tourmaline, as part of my aesthetic. I wasn't precious; I'd walk barefoot through black Thames mud to feel the city soak into my feet as bacterial slush. I had issues, and periodically self-harmed as a consequence, a pattern of self-repeat stayed with me through the centuries, right to the time of living with the Liberal politician Mister J.T. They're all mister, like degraded status. Strip them of privileges, and they end up lower than the street toughs they attempt to buy.

Thom got alienated from me by work. So much of him went into setting he missed my exclusion. I would have needed to turn into print to have him notice me. He spent a lot of time squeezing Ed Blount, a publisher who put books his way, when he finally started out accidentally or deliberately as publisher to the greats. Go into Foyles today, into book aisles as big as mews passages, and they're still there, Marlowe, Johnson. Shakespeare, Chapman etc., as part of his original stable of ace choices. They're being read electronically in skims at tables in the rooftop café, the industrially designed Leaf concession, as a postmodern loft for phone-preening manga girls with black bangs or red ponytails simultaneously immersed in social media.

Thom comes at me, (think I can forget?) like a grainy black and white photo bleeding into colour. He's red eyed from type and drink and throwing shapes into the future. I tell him no one wants to live in the present; we're all ahead of ourselves in some imagined space that's an alternative reality. He's got a scam going with a paper merchant, something to do with weed in exchange for 175mg stock that he's hoarding. His face is getting carved out from drugs, but he's sold on language blown around his mind like cornflakes. He doesn't know if it's Tuesday or Friday, or that I'm starting to see some-one else, because multiples are in my genes.

Thom was indomitable routine. He took the bus across the obsidian river each morning—John Taylor didn't charge him—his mind raging with the pissing rain and new writ-ing. You know anything that starts out in English poetry is a mixture of W.S., the Romantics, Ezra Pound, Ted Hughes, Sylvia Plath, J.H. Prynne and Jeremy Reed. Write in your own substitutes. What about Kit Marlowe, Cyril Tourneur, William Burroughs, Anna Kavan and Pete Doherty? Now I've lost you, the names don't add up even into accidental. They're prejudicial idiosyncrasies.

Amongst my acquaintances Kit wasn't rich, but he plun-dered cash from theatre companies and players. He'd say to me, 'Put your hands in my pockets and it's gold.' He made money to get rid of money, unlike Will who invested in real estate and lived off his tenants. I think Thom knew I was seeing Kit and did nothing. Language occupies the left side of the brain and he lived immersed in that process. Neither of us wanted to trip him—he was devoted to Kit's work, and out of character he'd started seeing a Chinese girl imported for sex work, and got her a squeezed room in Norton Folgate in return for a bit of black opium paste. Thom, if he wasn't seeing Yukio, largely hung out with Ed Blount in the theatre bar scouting for talent. Books to put into Foyles in four or five hundred years without the T. T. logo. Blount was the first to do Cervantes' *Don Quixote*, Marlowe's *Hero and Leander*, John Florio's translation of Montaigne's *Essays*, all that stuff now shelved as classics in stores.

Thom started to get boils at one stage from lead poisoning, all those toxic metals that got into his bloodstream. I looked after him, got him detox remedies like Milk Thistle, and Yukio came over with solid soups. All he wanted to do was smoke and stare at fonts, frontispieces, rubrics, title pages, the weight and grain of papers, in a stoned, marginally unfocused way. It took weeks out of his apprenticeship and, and when he got back to work he put in all the hours he'd missed, coming home blackened from ink and red-eyed from his habit. He always smelled of the Thames, the fuming river air that walloped him on his bus over.

Today, Kit the cyber-snoop showed me his beefed-up BMW 4 garaged in the Devonshire Place Mews where he lives as incognito as a toothpaste smear. He'd got a 100-pack of benzos from Johnny and was back to regulating his dependency. The car seemed the physical extension of his work in intelligence analysis; his type followed Bond into arch-filling alloys and an exhaust emitting a menacing rumble at idle that built into a cultured howl on output.

Kit had something sexy going with his smiley supercar sprayed aircraft paint aluminium, like a BA Boeing. Partially exempt from policing by his links to intelligence, he told me he'd pushed 150mph on the Westway in sleek highway drizzle. 'At full throttle,' he enthused, 'there's scarcely time to click the paddle shifter before the tacho needle plunges into the red paint.' He slapped the car's skin and turned on me the force of his knowledge. 'I've always liked tech, because it's cryptic. With this freak, adaptive dampers react instantly to changes in the road surface, or your driving style, creating edginess and wonderful throttle-adjustability. I'll take you to Deptford in it one day. I've got a disused floor in a warehouse by the Creek. When I go there, I still feel the place tense on my skin, like I'm about to be set-up all over again.'

We talked and it grew easier, despite the awareness of our continuing afterlives written into us like jetlag. If we'd been lovers once, then this time we shared a habit, a degrading search for Valium saints who sold fake pills on the street. Kit was like me, addicted to need through habituated receptor sites.

Devonshire Mews, a top-end rehabbed alley, was famous in the sixties for the Stephen Ward scandal, the osteopath turned sexual entrepreneur at the heart of the Christine Keeler scandal, who'd committed suicide rather than face trial, after a police raid on his flat implicating government ministers. Kit's BMW was the substitute for the suave oyster-coloured Bentleys and red E-type Jags parked up conspicuously for Ward's sex parties. Now the alley appeared sanitised and washed by laundered money, characterised by portfolio mafia, mostly transient ghost property owners snuck in the Marylebone heartbeat.

Inside, it was all minimal: racing green cushions on a lived-in tan leather sofa, everything digitally stored, and a device he pointed to, a portable compact 10cm cube, the sort that will project images from a phone onto any surface like a table or wall. The only physical giveaway was a shelf full of the Elizabethan poets and playwrights—Christopher Marlowe, Thomas Kyd, Thomas Nashe, Robert Greene, George Chapman, together with what looked like all the Marlowe biographies ever published, right from Leslie Hotson's seminally investigative *The Death of Christopher Marlowe* to Charles Nicholl's superb *The Reckoning*. I made no comment on this biographical glue, assuming only it validated the fact he'd been researched, factorised and kept historically updated by academics investing in the elusively dodgy myth surrounding his name. And I was no different in reading my assumed life and the whole futile attempts to decode my name as the apparent inspirer of poems that lived like space vitamins.

'It's crazy,' I said, 'if we really are who we think we are. Meeting like this, if there's truth in it, is bigger than Homer, China, Coca-Cola or the Beatles.'

Kit looked defiantly away, and in that moment I recalled the disputed portrait found protruding from a pile of rubble when it was discovered by chance at Corpus Christi College, Cambridge in 1953. The painting restored by the London art-dealers W. Holder & Sons, and authenticated as a genuine Elizabethan portrait was returned to the college as most likely the double-dealer Kit Marlowe. I'd often studied it, the sensitively expressive eyes looking more inwards than outwards, like the creative do, and always trying to maintain the dissolve as a defensive frontier to establishing a resting-point. It was the eyes remained as I looked over Kit's facial expression.

Someone suddenly beat loudly on the entrance door, omitting use of the unmarked buzzer, and to my surprise Kit in avoidance of biometrics, spontaneously opened it, admitting a skinny guy in a black wool knit hat, wearing a grey suit, his black hair raffishly deconstructed to look artfully messy in a punkish way. He sort of fell in, wired, stringy, other-dimension like a geekish crackhead.

'You fucking owe me man,' he jerked out. 'I'll do you if you don't pay. You want crack, you go get it, right.' Kit dug his hand into a jeans pocket, pulled out a wad of twenties, and peeled off what looked like a hundred.

The guy grabbed it, and looked hurt over something. 'Why donch you wanna see me anymore? It used to be good between us. You got somebody else? I'm not just drugs, I'm sex.'

This was the Kit I'd known in times used up centuries ago, the dodgy one pinching up rough trade by the London docks and drinking in corners where you shouldn't go south of the river. He didn't look like he'd learnt, but continued to repeat the pattern, perversely self-destructive and unafraid of the consequences of street toughs like this one, scrambled on crack and digging for money.

'I've been so busy,' Kit said. 'I'll call you when I'm through with a job. Now's not the time, as you can see I've got some-one here.'

'Don't believe ya,' the boy said, looking to make the door, and with Kit following him out to the yard. I could hear them heatedly talking for at least five minutes, before Kit came back inside, sewn-up, prepared to say nothing, uncapped a bottle of Gordon's and poured us each a blue-tinted dollop in chunky tumblers, and as a footnote fizzing tonic.

'Sorry about that,' he said. 'I met this guy back of Camden in a crackhouse. Benzo withdrawal does strange things and I was looking for anything to knock me, and we sort of got together in a mad state. I made the mistake of bringing him back.'

I smiled. 'You haven't learnt,' I said. 'I mean about mixing with lowlife. Remember what happened at Deptford, if we're really who we think we are. You don't want to get murdered twice.'

Kit came and sat down next to me, almost unintentionally, clearly confused by mixed realities. He dissociatively placed his hand in mine, the one that had driven *Tamburlaine*, *Dr. Faustus*, *The Jew of Malta*, and was still charged with reckless electricity. We sat silently sharing a reflection on time that didn't exist to others, but was still condensed in our memories as accessible reality. I spontaneously remembered getting up at dawn to prepare T.T.'s luncbox: XL cheese sandwiches, an apple, beer and two or three packed joints that he smoked while he worked to enhance concentration.

Kit poured a second wallop of gin and collapsed back into the cracked sofa. There were times, I observed, rather like me, when he looked like a tourist back from the future, before reconnecting with the present. He threw a look at the bookshelves, before saying, 'They're still no closer to the truth; I suppose all biography is modified fiction. There were plays I wrote like *Commodus Gladiator* and *Nero*, big epics probably destroyed or lost in house fires after I was rumoured dead. Secret Service don't leave traces even for investigative crime journalists. I'm still looking to complete my story, as presumably you are. By the way, I'm told W.S. is currently working in London, and like me some sort of spy, and into cryptocurrencies.'

'Who told you that?' I asked, shocked by the casual reference to Shakespeare.

'It seems that some people, including ourselves,' he said, 'can't die. He works for a closed intelligence group which last year floated on the London Stock Exchange with a market capitalisation of more than 1bn.'

All of this fitted, but didn't, like our lives that lacked adhesive to ends. Sometimes all I longed for was a closure to this mad cone of continuity; everyone apart from zombies collapsed into normal biological death, but for some reason I and a group of associates were continuously catapaulted back into a singular identity that kept updating itself with the awareness of always being the same.

Kit was on a third gin, clearly rattled by the crackhead coming after him at his buried mews. I'd noticed the one city hatchback parked up in the cobbled aisle, a smart navy

Peugeot grimed from disuse, but otherwise the row seemed typical London ghost homes. I didn't doubt this was Kit's reason for living there.

'I've always been a snoop,' Kit continued as the drink loosened him. 'It may not be your field but we learn from research into DNA. Bacterial spores deliver snoop-proof storage. Key-bearing spores are almost impossible to intercept as they are mixed with decoys. It's how we work, hopefully as a preventative to being bio-hacked.'

'Do you still write?' I asked, working on the theory that something of the spy's sangfroid was always in the back of Kit's poetry as the personal chill behind its epic pitch, and that one provided material for the other.

'Of course,' he said, testily, 'only I need to know you better to tell you under what name. I've always come through; it's the resource natural to me. Poetry's simply a more imaginative form of espionage. Fuck it, it's always been like that.'

'You mean it's the virus of the demimonde,' I added, recalling his lowlife entourage when the capital was like a swampy sewer. Will on his back for clues, posting an ear in the room to hack into Kit's outrageous angles on writing. The sort of plots he wouldn't dare entertain, writing always in the reflection of this kickass punk with a banker's math as financial incentive.

The windows walked in as we talked, and the dull reverberating rumble of an explosion somewhere central pushed its shock-waves in on us, as another dirty bomb from some radicalised psycho's asymmetric terrorism rattled the capital. This time it was a big one, the mushrooming noise cone expanding before collapsing back on its fallout.

Kit didn't look fazed, as though history's stuffed channel was backed up with so many human atrocities, they no longer merited recording. 'Done it again,' he said, 'another slab of the city down, just like it's Lego. It's the jackal they're looking to pop. Blair.'

'You know where he is presumably,' I said.

'Of course, he's wormholed his way into St. Petersburg, into the warren of criminal czars. Warlords stick to each other like spaghetti.'

There was the ubiquitous noise of blue light sirens tunnelling through the city on rapid response. I could tell from the sound they were vectored east in a convergent pattern.

'It's obvious to me,' Kit said, ignoring the background noise, 'that we're improbably here to solve the Shakespeare mystery, or my murder, if you believe it happened. It's this sharing of intelligence keeps us so radically different.'

Kit's statement had me do a fast take on my own continued life as Mr. W.H. one of history's great enigmatic outlaws, like every Soho Johnny I'd been to date, as patronised rent.

'Pete, that's the kid who just called, is still around,' Kit said, looking worried. 'I've got a drone on him for facial recognition. He's outside a pub on the Marylebone High Street. Crack fries your brain, and his has holes in it, believe me.

'I'll take you in the car when you need to go. The blue hatchback you saw in the yard is also mine when I want to use an unmarked vehicle. But I'm curious. Tell me a bit about your life with T.T., the one who effectively immortalised you with the dedication. Was it his idea or Will's to give you celebrity?'

'Oh Will's,' I said. 'Thom wasn't quite sociopathic, but he didn't mix, as I'm sure you remember, outside of a couple of publishing friends. He was a perfectionist who worked with his writers. You can see in Chapman's *All Fools* and Ben Jonson's *Sejanus*, from the excellence of the text and the marginal annotations that both authors oversaw the printing themselves. He did few books, but good books, the two of yours and the sonnits—126 directed to me, literally handcuffing me to his page.'

'And how did T.T. come by the sonnits?' Kit asked. 'From my researches, and of course I'm curious; I believe he pirated them.'

'All the best books come out like that,' I said, determined at this stage to hide the truth that it was me owned the original manuscript and that it was still in my possession. 'He probably picked it off Will in a pub, when they were stoned.'

'There's more to it than that,' Kit said. 'Remember I'm a snoop. I go for the sensitive infrastructure. I'm a cyber-criminal for ransomware and malware cocktails that need to be decrypted.'

'But now you mention it,' I said, 'I remember Will's wife turned up one afternoon when I was there at St. Paul's Yard, and started shouting at Thom to get the book out of the shop. Fortunately he only had a few copies, as two booksellers called William Aspley and John Wright had bought up most of the available stock.

'Anyhow, Anne really laid into T.T., she tore at his hair and kicked him about, spitting at him that he'd published a book about her husband's gay life that was dirty. You know Thom's existence as a printer was day to day, he didn't do po-litical stuff or thrillers, just the writers in who he believed. The sonnits earned him nothing, despite the author's celebrity. I think looking back, after I left him, he changed. Ambition was lost for commitment, acquisitiveness became ambition: he continued to smoke too much often out on the river. I did it with him recreationally a couple of times. When you smoke on the river's back it alters the drug's spatialising effects, vision seems to expand vertically, like it's skylined on a momentary viewing platform.'

'Naturally he knew things about me you never did,' Kit reflected, as a second explosion somewhere in the city's navel rocked its subterranean axis. A dull, muffled reverberation like a bomb going off in the underground somewhere central like Oxford Circus or Piccadilly.

Kit went into his iris recognition thumbnail minutes later and pulled up news. 'It's Oxford Circus,' he said. 'A bomb in the underground.'

The random terrorisation of London was increasing, mostly by solitary unaffiliated Islamic State individuals walking into the underground wearing a suicide belt as death-kit. Captured by CCTV their images invariably followed a pattern of hoods, faces masked by beards, their brainwashed martyrdom written into interchangeable features like urban replicants.

Kit kept tapping his wristpad to access updated news, before throwing me an ambiguous sexy look. 'Go on,' he said, 'you need to prove your historic identity. Back then, as I remember, we were lawless bandits immersed in London grime, mostly strapped for cash, and expected like magic mushrooms to feed on our own shit.' He laughed.

'You're right,' I reflected. 'For what we did, we could have been bundled into carts and strung up at Tyburn for sodomy, just near the big Primark.'

Kit emitted a frozen laugh, rechecked his update and swished another botanicals sniffy gin.

'Why don't you think the sonnits were authorised? You know, when people are near to death, they often want to make something scandalously private public. So you make it known to the world that your big hard-on affair was with a pretty boy.'

He reviewed the translucency of his drink like clairvoyance and continued. 'The clues to my murder are in those poems, some of them are codes. I've had a long time to study them and analyse the bits.'

There was another loud perfunctory hammering on the door, each smash louder than its predecessor, as though someone was skinning a fist. I could hear Pete shouting, 'Open up Mister, fucking help me.'

Simultaneously Kit pulled a handgun from a fake Sony cube, and went into indomitable cool. He authorised the biometrics to open and Pete fell face forward through the door, bleeding heavily from an obvious stab wound. The reddened shirt stain was upper chest, like a popped doughnut of an artery.

'What the fuck?' Kit exclaimed. 'What's happened, who did this to you?'

He laid Pete out flat on his back on the floor, fetched towels to compress the wound, and together we tried to stop the bleeding.

'Thank god it didn't stick your heart,' he said. 'The wound's superficial, but we'll need a paramedic to stitch you up. Who jumped you, was it a crackhead you were selling to?'

'Guy outside the Mews,' Pete forced out on his breath. 'Shouted in my face, something like "Will sends this to Kit," and slashed me. Fuckin hoodie on crack, I'll find 'im.'

'I've got a private app,' Kit said to me, 'I'll do an emergency video call for advice.'

He went into the adjoining crypto-kitchen throwing Pete a concerned look, while I handed him a bottle of Evian water. The bleeding seemed to have stopped, and coagulated, and he was fully conscious in his own jerky uncoordinated way, pleading for a dirty cig.

Kit came back into the room and said, 'There'll be somebody here in five minutes. They'll take you to be checked out in a private clinic near here. I told them I found you in the yard. You understand. I'm not part of this. I'm just saving your life.'

'Fucking bovver boy,' Pete spat out breathlessly, 'I'll get him. Fuck it, it hurts,'

'Just hang on, you'll be all right,' Kit said, placing his hand unexpectedly in Pete's bloodstained one, as his phone lit up with an incoming call.

'They're here,' he said, 'two medics with an unmarked carrier.'

They came in noticing nothing, put an oxygen mask on Pete, and stretchered him out and into the vehicle, as though it had all never happened.

Kit slammed the door shut and reset the biometrics. 'Sometimes it pays to be in secret service,' he said. 'No questions asked. Private treatment. No police enquiry. He'll live; it's not life-threatening. The bigger mess is that he's more drug than person, more crack than haemoglobins.'

This I thought was the old Kit from Walsingham's espionage updated into tech native. Cyber criminals ruled the capital through digital assaults, and he was somewhere involved in counter-defence. Only a week ago, according to my partner Howard, Coutts had been victim of a distributed denial of service (DDoS), in which a computer server is swamped by trivial requests that make it impossible to serve legitimate ones. Coutts according to Howard was threatened with crashing, the noxious pings coming not from one location, but from computers located all over the world that have earlier been hacked and organised into a botnet which can then direct thousands of millions of requests at a targeted server in order to bring it down. Coutts survived, bringing in Brian Krebs, the world's foremost investigator of online crime, who trawls the dark underbelly of the net for rogue cyber bandits.

Kit I noticed lived with nothing on view, other than a personal library of books. It was like he'd arrived from the future, a three-pounder brain, and the schematic of the whole city's malware compressed into smart cells. Some people just had it, this ability to hack the brain's bilateral functions, like a keyless car thief accessing a BMW.

'I'm on a job,' he said, 'but principally my own disputed murder, and that's why we met. I've been tracking you for sometime. Actually, I've been inside your brain. Think hard,

Will. If Pete was right, the man who created your celebrity is still looking for me. And it's a knife again. I think we're establishing our linked identities. You know as I do, time's tricky, like an object travelling faster than the speed of light returns to the past without the event ever having happened. Neat, if you apply it to the body.'

I felt unnerved and crept up, finished my drink and got up to go, turning down Kit's offer of a lift back home. 'I've got a device to temporarily suspend cameras in the Mews,' he said, 'so it's like you and Pete never happened. Understand?'

I understood only too well, as I went back outside and faced the drizzled scattering of dark pink sunlight focusing in from west London. People like me walk, the better to make sense of history I've arrived at like a tourist from tomorrow. London, I've never left it, is a ziggurat maze of random possibilities, the contactless mixing of eyeballs, the lubricated immersion in the millions.

I returned to Hop Gardens, back of the slab of St. Martin's Hotel that looks cheaply constructed as a generic sixties façade, only it's a reconstructed copy without the faux American impulse to go underfunded modern. The pink light keeps showing me things I haven't seen before like holo ghosts stepped out of the walls. You can produce a 360-degree immersive video of the interior of a plane so potential flyers can experience business and first class, but you can't account for who thumbed the seatback with a sticky finger from crisps. London's the same. The more you look, the more you find in a meta-reality what others don't see. It's been happening in me for so long, collecting the capital's fingerprint, with all its complex emergent behaviours. Looking is like visual mafia, a raid on the apparent together with an extortion of the contents of reality.

So I sit there behind GymBox and Jones & Payne, dumped where real people hang out on the edges of reality. Most significant info comes out of alleys as the leak in the system. The mind's like a granulated piece of chewing gum left underfoot in this passage to pick up bits. If entanglement does exist, as a provable phenomenon it must travel at least 10,000 times faster than light in flagrant defiance of special relativity. But I'm quantum intelligence. It's 1594 and as a futures tourist 2084.

Hop Gardens is Google geography—you can scroll the place, but not me, and get your street map location. Bedfordbury, Covent Garden, back of it, and this guy in a black pixie hat and black sunglasses unpeeling a raspberry wad of fifties. He flattens the creases in counting out maybe 2K in notes. Gotta be drug money, I can sniff it; a re-sewn interior in a herringbone 3-button wool jacket, probably pulled from T.K. Maxx. That's my snapshot assessment, as he skins cash like a banana.

I'll be back to Howard as a time-faded tourist in thirty minutes, and I won't stick. He's a convenience only. He doesn't know there's a transcript of four centuries in my arteries, like a customised longevity messenger. If I took an 80-day mission to Mars with the pioneering Space X, as part of the new interstellar ethnicity of space vitamins, I'd arrive with the mixed reality of a five-centuries timeline in my brain's neuronal memory slots.

It's always the same burn-out procedure when Howard comes in still wired from the floor, squeezed by stress and cortisol as drenched steroid hormone, his blue and white striped Westwood shirt sticky with sweat. His job's immersive and only booze takes him out. I do a martini cocktail like a fuel-injected race car. I rinse the glass with French vermouth first, gin, vodka, botanical-rich vermouth, cava, tonic with slice, and a single olive. Howard drinks the first with the mule kick of a courier starting a motorbike, and throws his head back from the punch. He'll drink four straight off to get

real, and talk work, then, to interest me, novels we're reading—William Gibson as cyber stylist, Michel Houellebecq
as polemical maraca, Jake Arnott as investigative underworld
chronicler and J.G. Ballard as exhaust plume from the future.
At a point after dinner, at home or in a Mayfair restaurant,
he invariably fades into the grey zone. It's day and it's night;
and in the layer between like jam in a Victoria sponge, I
lie awake, and by switching on time travel as my resource,
it's early 1590s, and I'm part of the writing hooligan Will
Shakespeare's life, living in muddy, verminous Shoreditch.

5

MISTER W.S.

He wouldn't ever tell me his exact age, but when we got together he was probably early twenties, his celebrity just starting to add highlights to his eyes. I was telling Howard this last week at the Forest on the Roof at Selfridges, as he liked me to make up improbable stories that were in fact true, as part of the street-lore of rent. The view out over London was a diamond skyline of brutally confrontational towers, and through its imposing corridors I could see history as an object—a specific place Shoreditch, in which I'd hung out with W.S. in the 1590s as prototypical bohemians. The place was still there, incorporating the sub-districts of Hoxton and Haggerston, as a hub for east London-based hipster web technology companies, as inner-city cool, but to me it was also encrypted in a time reversal to which I alone had access. Howard in his Ralph Lauren navy blue v-neck was too occupied picking at a blackberry and cassis cupcake to even notice the build of rapidly emergent indigo storm clouds stacking over the capital.

Back then, Kit Marlowe and Thom Watson were on Hollywell Street, now the Shoreditch High Street, and us around the corner, living on red wine, smoked eel, oysters, bread and cheese and psychoactive smoke. W.S. was reclusive and just worked, socialising in pubs only in East Cheap, with other actors. He'd talk to me and write at the same time, and never correct; he just had the line right and kept the first take. He'd say that revision demanded the sort of leisure he didn't have. He was writing primarily to get pops on stage, the poetry was something given him that came with the package. It also came with the smoke. We were both atypical junkies.

Howard is venting his frustration that his flight back from Dubai was delayed due to a radioactive leak from a consignment of cancer drugs that shut down his terminal while a disaster management team cleaned up the leak. He still hadn't got back on top of his curve, feeling foggily jet-lagged and displaced. There's a man looking me over all the time while we're talking and drinking, and I decide on impulse to slip out with him simultaneously, and in the black marble slap of the toilet we exchange numbers. American, biomed research-er, 40s, we'll connect over money at a later date. It's all part of my incurable mission to find the perfect stranger.

Back to W.S.: there was this alien spook Henry Maunder living at Bishopsgate—messenger of the chamber—a creepy operative who could get into you like killer flu. Maunder, what sort of name is that, other than sounding mean and slippery like a dead end alley? A man with vodka-coloured eyes you couldn't properly focus, and a twist in his speech of duplicitous lies. His motive hid behind words, and he wanted for some reason to get in with W.S., presumably for info on Kit Marlowe. He bought us rounds, strong hoppy beer or wine, and I got under his radar, while W.S. used him as a psychological type in one of his plays and was clearly up for peeling Maunder for money. We'd meet him in and around Norton Folgate, and the third or fourth time we met him in a closed room where cash was offered on the table. He'd clearly stopped speaking to me and his muffled conversation was directed fast and on the underside to W.S., who was sort of middle-distance drunk but still on top of his spin.

From what I only partly understood Southampton, a.k.a. Henry Wriothesley, wanted Kit taken out or looked over—he was subverting moral propriety by openly advocating gay sex and pushing it as a lawless amoral alternative to convention, as well as writing too far above himself on continuous over-reach. It was a breach that threatened Shakespeare's living, was how Maunder phrased it. Maunder, like all his type, including store detectives, (i.e. Selfridges), was clearly one criminal trying to apprehend another. Strip any SD of his simulated identity and what you get is a shoplifter who does it synthetically through others. Maunder's no-colour eyes slid under your skin like keyless car theft. His steals were DNA strands, bits of personality with their coded data, neural storage, cellular anomalies, biology worked to the surface without any legal sanction.

I'd seen him at odd times on the river bus wrapped in an oversized black coat and greedy for his own company. You didn't look at him because he was already looking at you. You had to go bank and acknowledge the choppy transitioning green water. There was some sort of correlation between the river's reflective snapshots of the city and his focus on whatever you had to hide in the corners of your eyes. A sort of toplogy espionage meets human.

Maybe my drink was spiked. I remembered only the radio hum of voices floating as background to my being there, as third party. W.S. helped me out into the rainy street and walked me back home as I sobered in the drench. When we got back he had sex with me, while I lay there wasted, like Howard has done sometimes, fucking over my sensibility in the quarantined Mayfair quarter. And it's not me they're exploiting, it's some fantasy imposed on my body as frontierless object.

W.S. didn't have real friends in London, only acquaintances, who he used on his chopping board for shredded psychology. He grated human characteristics like parmesan, disinterested in anything but his ability to use language as a substitute for lack of emotional feelings. Like all writers of predatory ambition he stole what he could use. Doesn't everyone? I've stolen resources from so many of my clients in that dangerous exchange, rent, in which love is replaced by money and power annihilated by desire.

He wasn't any different from the rest. He was starting out but earning both as an actor and playwright and thought he could buy me. You can only buy beauty through poetry and not money; and that's what the sonnits are about. He attempted to appropriate my body through elevated diction I couldn't really understand, and even less so now that language has changed into text. There's a new version of the sonnits by Jeremy Reed, called *Shakespeare in Soho*, a subversive attempt to radically modernise language, place and theme, situating the action in Soho between W.S., me as a male escort and Lucy Negro as a black whore. I like my re-make, the triangulated sex tangle, and the fact he's put me in the present, rather than the historically documented past. I want to meet him somehow in the places where he regularly writes and drinks in Soho, as someone ambiguous, edgy, arrogantly outside mainstream literature, and right in the moment.

W.S. rarely spoke of his wife and children; it was like they existed as obligatory facts in a life given over to work and predominantly male company. He was invariably awkward with women, even with Lucy, who was hijacked into our complex relations, more by her extreme jealousy of me, than her feelings for him as a common punter.

What's in the perfect face? Didn't he keep putting a subjective spin on body beautiful in the sonnits? In them I'm the closest physical ideal to the unattainable. And of course, who am I to argue?

In the time I've been living with Howard, David Bowie died. Or in my terms of quantum re-posting, did he? What about his imported rebirth in the lightning bolt-shaped constellation named after him by Belgian Radio Studio Brussels and the MIRA public observatory. Seven stars as his star fortress, a glam palatial studio full of astronaut deserters turned psychotic by immersion in deep space. Sigma Librae, Spica, Alpha Virginis, Zeta Sartoris, SAA204132 and Beta sigma Octantis Trianguli Australis.

I talked Bowie to Howard drenching my metaphors in hair dye, and not letting on my secret of meeting him in Bateman's buildings in Soho in 1970, with the almost emergent Ziggy separating from the Beckenam Arts Lab folkie as a pop wannabe who was going nowhere special. He was still managed by Ken Pitt at the time and living on/off at Manchester Square, and not yet the poppy-red urban spaceboy he was to become on the back of 'Starman' as androgynously engineered alien. You can find the beginnings of the pretty boy look in my circle, back in 1591, in the portrait thought to be the only likeness of Kit Marlowe, a red-haired starman who came back from the future as David Bowie.

Like everyone, Howard knew the standout music, but really only through the pop-friendly Hunky Dory and the faggoty persona Ziggy Stardust, as epochal alien humanoid personifying glam rock. The sort of PTD pandemic caused by Bowie's unexpected death from metastatised liver cancer unconsciously touched Howard, like a transient dip into his own subjective death fantasies about how and where he would end in the big scope of things. Bowie's death had thrown a switch in him and he'd increased his drinking, fought with his mother over her financial portfolio, lost money on the market, and clearly got nervously roughed up. He'd even gone onto the Google Sky initiative dubbed Stardust allowing fans to create personal tributes within the constellation's borders, each of the tributes combining to brighten the interior of the constellation, making it easy to pinpoint in the simulated sky galaxy.

Howard didn't really take in Black Star, with its lengthy, scorched-earth, saxy feel generated by a searching NY jazz outfit as accompaniment to one unsettling scenario after another, like a bacterial smear across melody. Urgent, contemporary, elliptical as a skyline of mirror towers, Bowie's musical architecture failed Howard for lack of pop. To him it was as though Bowie had descended into a thirty-light-year well and was singing down in the bottom. Sad Grass, Clockwork Orange's Nadsat, gay palare, an amalgam of buried cancer references, the whole thing dragged to the edge of the edge; but it wasn't for Howard who liked pop as pop in upbeat flavours.

Howard of course, wanted to eat somewhere else, not that I cared in my minimal food repertoire. With the help of a taxi we slummed it at Mercate Metropolitana at Newington Causeway, where you never want for overloaded Korean-accented burgers stuffed with kimchi and ganjang in a food concept located in 45,000 sq. ft. of battered industrial space close to Elephant and Castle. Pinewood benches, a sort of pizzeria wall for robo-foodies, Howard focused on a brimming foccacia stuffed with stracchino as a squeezy ooze, while I disinterestedly searched for vegan.

I remember thinking how W.S. like all writers who shop for inspiration found Falstaff and his entourage drinking in East Cheap bars and got majorly into their lugubrious conversation, as he always did, as the plagiarist listener. When he moved to St. Helen's Bishopsgate and then south of the river to the Liberty of the Clink in Southwark, he did the same, listened to pub politics and played the part of impartial spy to the bohemian demimonde. I'd join him sometimes, so he didn't get a reputation as an incurable loner, and it was nearly always raining off the grey river, big aqueous thumbprints that stuck on the window, or outside in the corners of the eyes. He drank hard and didn't show it, and wanted sex that really didn't involve his mind, only the raw skin of his body, like someone I didn't always know in his determination. Drunk, he'd piss poetry so coldly, you'd never know he cared; it was just writing. And it was money. The next morning he'd smoke, dry visions rather than wet ones, and seem to know he was in the process of creating Shakespeare, like building a one-man rocket and a star simultaneously.

Using me was the starting point of the sonnits he idealised what in reality he felt guilty over abusing. Mostly he denied his homosexuality. What I didn't know at the time was that he had something going with Kit, or it was rumoured; and the implications were serious, like a slippery tangle of spaghetti in the complex machinations of espionage. Sometimes he'd disappear to Warwickshire for family reasons that he kept secret, like sublingually dissolving a pill. Writing historically, as he often did, gave him a sort of transpersonal empathy with extreme psychologies, mad kings, village shamen, mushroomy folklore, deviated tricksters, lubricated ministers, stuff he didn't otherwise have, but discovered in himself in the process of writing. He ruined people by sticking them in the juicer of his brain processes and leaving them pulped, like the fucking sonnits wiped me out. I've got no way out of history until the end of time—I'm inexorably Mr. W.H. rent to Mr. W.S. What does that make me; a glam escort converted into sticky unreliable history: a piece of chewing gum stuck with precious stones picked up off the street?

I'll tell you a secret. W.S., Kit and I made it in a river warehouse with black smoke choking the air, and sailors giving us head at 3 a.m. in a city so dark it was like light resistant Vantablack. We had toughs on the door, sodden with rum and hemp, and the one constable who came knocking was walked off into an adjoining builder's yard. Kit took the can for it, when Southampton got word of our involvement with rough trade on the docks. There was no coming back on it for Kit; he lost patronage and the plot thickened like London weather. For Kit it was like being pulled by his brain cells and not his hair into an interrogation room beneath Whitehall. Walsingham, Southampton, Burleigh and Cecil, they moved in on him like a tornado's build.

Today, I can look up Burleigh Mansions on Wiki. That's how the novel's changed radically: pre-Google it was under-researched, factually erroneous in its data, more like a redshift brain beating in the heart of the universe. It's not that people go forward, it's more that tech redesigns the brain: neural networks, backpropagation, random forests, Bayesian networks, quadratic classifiers, that sort of remake.

I told you Howard's a dedicated foodie; it's his picky reward for rigging Libor or whatever he does. The fetish object of an absinthe/pistachio ice cream from Badiana of Florence excites him like synaesthetic sex for its particular green, like Venice on an autumn day. Or to him it's the taste-bud side of money, edible cash. I'd rather live on nutri food pills if I could, or injectable food.

At a certain point in writing a novel you start to make a word count as quantitative progress. To W.S. it was a job like engineered pop. You fed the audience with words that switched on a resource they didn't know they possessed. They only discovered afterwards what he'd done and couldn't of course repeat it for themselves. That's why before the death of pop kids used to buy records.

It's always autumn in the narrow passage of Hop Gardens squeezed between two slabs of architecture. My genes are worth billions for their longevity. If I made myself known I'd be gene-hijacked for the secret of my anomalous telemeres. I mean, it's already happening to people who carry sixties and seventies genes as mythic epochs that are still arriving from the future, their neurons downloaded cryogenically into a replicable brain. And my generational import is apparently unbreakable in its continuity. I look at the RSC programme at the Barbican and the Theatre Royal Haymarket, and the works are still there: *The Alchemist*, Ben Jonson, *Doctor Faustus*, Christopher Marlowe, *Cymbeline*, William Shakespeare, *King Lear* and *Love's Labour Lost*, William Shakespeare all frozen into reverse time-travel. Unaffected by time, they're all still there in lurid LEDs and neon, swimming gold, red, orange and blue across the Haymarket or St. Martin's Lane. It's the same language, same names, just updated production and a modified ball of manipulative context to validate their contemporaneity. It's like I can't ever abandon living in his shadow, like I'm a nomad on the far side of the moon. Writers use people like car insurance; there's no compensation for me or anyone for being exploitatively fictionalised. When he wrote the sonnit snapshots in the 1590s he wasn't yet the magnanimously celebrated celeb he's morphed into, firing up millions of superfluous doctoral theses. I'm the durable enigma, the cerise bubblegum string you stretch across investigative assaults on the Bodleian, without ever claiming my true identity. I exist in history's shadow, like I once did hiding in a doorway outside Burger King at Piccadilly Circus, knowing my wait for the right person would convert raindrops into hard currency.

I'll tell you more than you'll ever know: W.S., Henry fucking Maunder, Southampton, all with a sticky fingerprint on cutting Kit Marlowe back and sticking his genius with a knife—it was cold-blooded murder, cold as a plane stowaway hunched into the landing tackle's casing. The motives were shame, guilt, jealousy and class: the need to cut someone down who'd outgrown them. Kit had discovered tomorrow exists before today, that the future is complete and that time runs both ways, and it didn't fit with the scheme of things. W.S. was more grounded; a root crop in comparison to Kit who placed himself in the frontline of raw eloquent punk. Why is it I think of Kit when a robot probe touches down on Mars to collect planetary samples in the search for microbial life.

They'd leave London, get out of town to thicken their talk on Kit in some country manor, like a meat maestro at Hawksmoor bruising carcinogenic rump. W.S. claimed it had to do with company rivalry, which it never did, patronage, whatever he made up to account for his debased absence. When I saw Kit in and around his Norton Folgate quarter I didn't say nothing, just smoked with him and bit into gossip. I couldn't tell him I'd still be reading him in five hundred years, and that we'd relocate in Leicester Square as tourists from the future, coincidentally listening to buskers and habituated to benzos.

I could tell you so much of the visceral metaphysic of the dodgy quango that murdered Kit. And of my world of transitioning between clients, from the rainy street to a bespoke interior, rooms painted in gradations of grey mixed from several pigments, floorboards in shades of charcoal tinted with purple. What do I add? In the kitchen, the geometric angles of Cole & Sons Curio, piling on zing; the man who brought me there collapsed into the louche luxury of a juniper green throw on a master bed? You have to sell to know the pattern of in and out; you don't belong, but you see the best London interiors for a fee. It's called being on the game.

And with W.S. I couldn't get it out of him why he had it in for Kit; and of course he pretended ignorance. Of course he knew I knew what he was doing and that threw rows at the wall like dirty plates. Drunk, he'd accuse me of being too dumb to understand his work, of being locked out of the sonnits in which he'd idealised me, of ruining his name through my selling sex, the whole vituperative retribution he wished for me lowering my esteem to the quarter-inch coffee dregs in a chunky white cup. After pulling me apart, he'd turn on himself, claiming he was a debased monster, that nobody should associate with writers as they were the result of personality disorders; and then he'd break things, smash up the room and storm out into the ubiquitous rain, shouting he was going to jump into the river and the world would be glad of it.

The hours after he'd gone were the lowest I'd experienced. By blaming himself he'd reinforced my lack of worth, my low self-esteem, the periodic demoralisation I felt at living off my looks without any other call in life. Our relationship at these times was as heavy as the river, as cumbersome as a Saturn V moon rocket abandoned on its base, and untreatable. I threw him out and he came back carrying the Thames on his shoulder like a grey alligator.

I tell you, (gossip) Howard's got to know India's reputed richest man (A.T.) who lives in his own tower in Mumbai, a sort of customised Shard, surrounded by badlands and debilitating poverty. Howard polarises those types who generate black-box dollars, rupees, pounds, yen, ruble, renminbi, etc., through algorithmic trading as the market dominant. He's also my dietary opposite and soaks in game cobbler, slow-cooked in red wine with roasted quail eggs. Partner him with Jamie Oliver and they'd both cannibalise each other in peeled slices to a soundtrack by Morrissey.

Fuck for vegan, that's my credo, green cum for asparagus-green people. (The editor of this novel will say erase this line, the Booker's mainstream clean.)

Let's move on. W.S. always said that the best writers are little known in their lifetime, as they subvert systems. He managed the curve, but was innately sceptical of celebrity, too drunk, too rural, too lacking in culture: he hung out with criminals more than dukes; it was easier like that to share common causes. And weed was his visionary psychoactive; we all smoked it on the docks in a trancy, stoned glow. India, China, Africa, he took in those continents through a pipe. I remember sitting on a wharf watching a serpent swallow the rainbow and spit it out into a drizzled contrail. I watched it happen while a beefy docker loped by towards a decanting tank. He saw me, but not what I was seeing; he was outside the skin like a condom's latex walls. W.S. hoisted his bulk into a play; fatties are invariably peeled into comic, like stripping an artichoke.

And there was this dude Gabriel Spencer, an actor in the Admiral's company, who hung out with us for a time. A volatile star in the making, he fed a vicious and ungovernable temper with drink. He'd sometimes join us in pubs, although he was part of Ben Jonson's gang. He'd spent time in Marshalsea prison with Jonson over various anarchic ideas expressed in the play *Isle of Dogs*. Maybe he was subterfuge for Ben, scouting for work in progress, but he induced in me the same sort of cautious curiosity you get when you make accidental eye contact with an animal. Although he'd been acquitted on grounds of self-defence he'd killed James Freake, a goldsmith's son, at a barber's shop in St. Leonard's Shoreditch on 3 December 1596, after the boy had attacked him with a heavy copper candlestick in a fight. Gabriel had driven his sword six inches deep into the boy's right temple, and he'd died three days later of the wound. Gabriel was like Syd Vicious, a yobby dyslexic psycho with a killer underside. He once slammed a butcher's knife into a bar room mirror, thinking his reflection was coming to get him. He was a red crophead punk who played himself on stage as an offensive twat who worked out with steroids as muscle enhancer. W.S. was afraid of him for good reason, as his homophobia threw violent shapes around the bar, looking to trip a suspect. But he was always in demand by several companies—his stage appeal coming from his natural contempt for the arts, and his rude boy attitude quickly winning over the crowds.

And it had to happen as the future completing the past, back of the Curtain theatre in Hoxton Fields; the two men focusing there with swords on a cold gold September afternoon, each determined to see the other dead. They'd been at each other for weeks over money. Gabriel claimed he was owed and drank himself psychotic, while Jonson was preoccupied with the staging of *Every Man In His Humour* in which W.S. had a part and was equally about to trip a fuse. W.S. witnessed the brawl. The two men stripped to white shirts walking out side by side into common ground bushed up by purple loosestrife. Murder was in the balance, and both men squared and bellowed at each other before engaging. Gabriel was armed with the better weapon and was ten years younger, on top of things in his steaming rage and quickly drew blood, stabbing Jonson in the right arm. Righting his backfoot balance after inflicting the wound, the momentary lapse of focus cost him his life, as Jonson drove a blade deep into his chest, killing him outright, and kicking the body backwards into a ditch.

People tend to despise poets. What did the gossipy theatre entrepreneur Philip Henslowe call Jonson, a common bricklayer. I can pull it up on my phone. 'I have lost one of my company and it hurts me greatly; that is Gabriel, for he is slain in Hoxton Fields by the hands of Benjamin Jonson bricklayer.'

Molecular bricks build poems, and Ben if he had raw hands shape-shifted his material with the facility to morph lead fillings into diamond, like Russian mafia in their blacked-out, bulky, Russian-built Volgas.

Murder, happening every day in contemporary London, was also the talk hitched to our historic gossip. Ben, Kit, Thom Kyd, Thom Watson, they all got into street fights, like poetry was being carved viscerally into the skin, as a body art that involved marshals and being dumped in Newgate or Marshalsea. W.S. kept out of street brawls. Self-preservation was optimal with him, he was aware of the special gift he carried and the need to do it right. He never fully integrated into any social class, he felt intimidated by aristos, out of place with other writers, had little in common with ordinary people, and avoided street toughs. Even drunk he manifested an invincible sense of self-control, like nothing could ever really get at him. It was only his rages that were disproportionate to his indomitable sense of self-assurance. He was so entirely self-motivated that he probably didn't feel much for anybody except how they fitted into a schematic that benefited his work. Bowie once said he was like a robot offstage, and that performing was the only time he felt emotion, being Ziggy rather than David; and acting did the same for W.S., bounced him out of self-preoccupation into character.

Ben Jonson pleaded guilty to manslaughter at the Old Bailey and it looked like he was for the Tyburn tree where they strung them up like plaited flesh to roll, tongue protruding on a rope. He got off by benefit of clergy, in that he was able to recite passages from the scriptures, but was branded on the base of his left thumb with a T, as a sign that if he reoffended he would be executed without appeal.

W.S. and Ben could both drink five maybe six man-size glasses of Castalian wine in rapid succession to torch-up their psychological realities. W.S. tolerated Ben because they were never wholly in competition, and Ben wasn't like him same-sex attracted. You wanna know more, read Thom Gunn's Introduction to Ben Jonson *Selected Poems*, 1974. Gunn carved the raw pigment out of the Elizabethans and reinvented it thematically to write about biker boys and the nineties pandemic—AIDS.

Who is Mr. W.H., a Wikipaedia entry? I'm writing this and you can't see me or experience me, I'm just language. I'm pushing alphabet down the road and it reads like a substitute for facial recognition, factoids, conspiracy theories—who killed Christopher Marlowe ? I'll tell you later.

You can't sanitise Elizabethan culture. The plague soaked into our cells like a nerve agent. The only precaution was rudimentary hygiene, boiling drinking water and keeping clear of the infected like toxic waste. The black plague was like malware, a botnet wiping a company by a rogue clued-up hacker. Some people's luck remains up and not down, and I stayed up. You read Thom Gunn's *The Man With Night Sweats*, his elegies for dead friends nuked by HIV as untreatable retroviral assassin at the time, and you have a revamped Thomas Wyatt, retrofitting form to his contemporary gay lifestyle in California, the epicentre of the plague. Black t-shirt, skinny jeans, black buckled biker boots, Gunn has one foot on Cole Street, and the other five centuries back in Shoreditch, where we hung out in a bunker existence attempting to resist Yersinia pestis bacterium, and the symptomatic apple-sized swollen lymph glands in the groin and armpits, chills and solid headaches. W.S. was pathologically afraid of contamination and kept dodging in and out of the capital to his country pals. Human physical decay, it's the prime biological mover in the sonnits, it's the principle of entropy words can attempt to alter, but never stop. And that was his ultimate despair. He'd slap the walls with his hands, telling me never to age, 'NEVER FUCKING LOSE YOUR LOOKS. IF YOU DO I'LL DIE. HEAR ME?'

I did, and I've never lost my reinvented looks. I've remained the archetypal Johnny, the alias for most escorts, the ageless boy who collects eyes in the crowd. The one who provokes curiosity even in straight men alerted to the B-side of their sexuality, and wanting to spend time with me. In the eighties (history) you could rent rooms by the hour at the now demolished Regent Palace Hotel at Piccadilly Circus, like a monolithic brothel drenched by the lurid neon advertising signs, now replaced by an ultra-high definition 4K resolution screen futureproofing the space, while retaining the familiar patchwork aesthetic. It was the rent boy epicentre, the randomised pick-up zone for a monetised subculture. Those were different times, waiting out in the colour-tinted rain for the right voice tone, the right shade of what's it—Farrow & Ball black? Only lonely outlaws cut it there, people who collected rain in their hearts and drank it nightly, like I did. We had our style, licks of black eyeliner, skinny jeans and enough projected attitude to stop a tank. Who'd I meet there: half the world on Friday, the other half on Saturday. Would W.S. have stopped for me? He did, only he was someone else, trying to reconnect with the reality of a person who was once my lover. If he got a synchronistic flashback recognising me, it wasn't sustained and I refused his offer, and watched him cross over to the other side and watched him proposition a skinny boy with nothing to lose. That was a close one. Four centuries divided us and we missed the intersection by seconds. I was invariably staring into myself rather than face spotting, mixing up my past with the present, like paints. I let others look and find me, I never approached a stranger; it's demeaning. You've got to be the one in demand; you don't pick up a punter, he does that to you.

The boy who went off with the person I assumed was W.S.; I spoke to him later in the day. Black wool knit pixie hat, fake leather jacket, brutally skinny jeans, Doc Martens, the usual streetwise, damaged type. He'd been on the Dilly two years he told me, didn't really have a home, but a cute winning smile, a scattering of acne pits, a grey irised twinkle. The look of the dispossessed, disenfranchised, hunted, and the guilt and defensive chip that comes with it—watcha gonna do about it. I squeezed him some cash and got him to talk as much as happened.

'Guy was a bit distant,' he said. 'Icy, like some of them are, and in a very controlled way. Wanted me back at his place in Shoreditch, three floors, books, a lot of theatre posters and stuff. We took a taxi over and I didn't say a word. He poured himself a drink as soon as we arrived. I don't drink on a job, only drugs.'

'Did you let him fuck you?' I asked, still uneasy about the man's possible historic identity.

'I don't do that,' the boy said. 'I told him it was oral only with a rubber, or I was leaving. I've learnt how to fuck with key cards, so I can get out if there's problems with a punter, and he can't get back in.'

The boy sneered in that avenging grammar that gives rent one over the punter for being used. Selling sex never meets with equality; the punter resents paying and the boy feels degraded in the process. And that's how life works out as an amoral conundrum in which winning or losing is the same.

'Let slip he had a wife though, and two kids somewhere in the countryside, Stratford I think it was. Wouldn't do him again, though.'

I watched the boy dissolve back into the crowd, his alienation acute under the red, blue and green neons. There was something in his story reached a deep space in me, although I still couldn't quite connect with the possibility of the stranger being W.S. And for weeks after that I hung out there looking for this man, one in the churning anonymous millions drawn to this place as the hub of sexual gravity. Hanging out there with always one hundred people in your view is like listening to the capital's heartbeat right under you in the subterranean navel of the Piccadilly line, as the dialectic of alienation.

What I remember of life with W.S. was episodic and always interrupted by his busy work schedule. There was time for work, but not for me, and after a time I gave up caring. Our rows when they occurred were invariably triggered by me touching on anything personal it wasn't permissible to peel. Any mention of his wife and he'd flare. Any reference to other women in his life, Jane Davenant, Marie Mountjoy or Lucy Negro, and it was the same, as though his gated privacy had been breached. I'd got an ear on him at the Red Bull at Clerkenwell, the Boar's Head in East Cheap, where punks, hipsters and hussies regarded him as sinister, because he was always alone in the sense of lonely. I heard from them about his regular visits to the west London suburb of Brentford, a brothel quarter where you bought candy—girls or boys—and that he didn't do white. It's what I heard, that's all. Brentford was a notorious locus for the criminal underworld as Hastings is today, a hideout for criminal gangs wanted in London. Doubtless he in part wanted to pinch up material for his plays, but his motives were always dodgy in living on the edges of society. His mind reminds me of the complexity of the tube map in which physical distance was shrunk to relativistic in the attempt to downsize enormity.

It wasn't like we broke up or anything, it was in part his workload that took him off, and his obsession with age and idealising me to a point whereby he felt old and ugly by comparison. The thing is, he was never young. Some people are born middle-aged, think William Burroughs or Lou Reed, you can't imagine them young, and he was like that too. It was like he'd lived to be forty before he was born. And he knew it. He had a phobia about mirrors and wouldn't look himself in the face. It made him a bad lover, as though he had something to prove because he lacked personal identity. It was a bit like having sex with someone not right with his body.

Of course I owe my historic identity to Thom Thorpe's ambiguously phrased title page, designed typographically to resemble an inscription on a Roman funerary monument, the W.H. being decoded sometimes, and erroneously, as a memorial tribute to William Holme, who died in 1607, two years before the sonnits. I leave it to you. It takes two baby. For what it's worth, Will Holme like Thom Thorpe was a publishing apprentice in the 1580s, and hung out with the playwrights Ben Jonson and George Chapman, as a sort of social networker. I remember him, rather like Thom, head full of type, the way printers always appear to be assembling words in their head when you talk to them. A small man, serious, fundamentally myopic, he got on my nerves by his obsessions. If you believe he's the recipient of the cryptic dedication, then you have to believe Thorpe dedicated Shakespeare's book to a friend, without consulting W.S. As I still have the original manuscript, I of course have a different story, the one I'm writing.

The chances that you'll believe me are the same as you picking up a sex worker. It's an accidental intention, some sort of intuitive response that doesn't so much pull you out of character as place you in a window where you belong. In a room full of mirrors you recognise the aspect of yourself that was always going to fuck this random person.

The future is arguably what will happen in time after the present, or it's already complete, and I've always travelled its curve towards what I call the big light cone. Astrophysicists will tell you that while a person can move backwards or forwards in the three spatial dimensions, you are only able to move forwards in time, as the fourth dimension. But in my experience of reality it's possible also to physically pinch up time so that it flows both ways, and that contravening the laws of physics the dead might return to life and live backwards to birth, as part of quantum weirdness. I'm living evidence of subverting time into personal continuity. And with us it's a pattern. The big players in this unresolved game, me, Kit Marlowe, W.S. and his henchmen are all to my awareness in different stages of partially retrieving historic identity.

Take Howard. He tells me he remembers nothing of his past other than what intermittently scratches his memory like fretwork. He lives quite happily with the misconception of linear time, as though he's in-flight between London and Zurich. He'll grab three miniatures of Bombay Sapphire enroute, and assume on arrival he's the same person as the one who boarded in London.

What will he try to tell me? Not that a cloud at takeoff was shaped like a luminous artichoke, but Outhink turbulence. It affects operations and costs airlines over 100m dollars a year. But now, working with IBM Watson, carriers are developing an intelligent detection system, combining IoT sensor data, billions of data points from The Weather Company and real-time updates from nearby pilots. It's all about the cognitive cockpit. It's big bucks.

One of Howard's perverse kicks is sometimes to take me as obvious to meet a morally ambiguous client, when he knows the arrangement will turn a financial trick, despite breaches of either criminal, civil or professional codes. Take the chairman of X, who I'm told got rich from the metallurgical businesses of a collusive Russian investment arm. I can spot it straight away Farrow & Ball's Black Blue in Stuart's palatial Park Square east apartment, column-like juniper curtains, minimalist lamps, glitzy chandeliers, a desk I'm told is made from Habitat metal bases with an MDF top—it's money physicalised into drenched aesthetic. And straightway on a bookshelf curved like a brainstem I notice a gilded rebound copy of the Sonnits, only it reads Sonnets, probably unread, the tooling looking like gold liquid mascara, the convoluted syntax as unmalleable as Frank Cooper's chunky thick cut Oxford Marmalade. The dedication follows me everywhere. Imagine reading the sell by date on a product in your fridge as 1609; but books are permitted this time-slipped privilege.

I can see Stuart is a bit sniffy at first about my relations with Howard, but he starts to warm. I surprise him by asking him if he's ever read the Sonnits, and he takes on a glow in telling me what I didn't want to hear, that it's the puzzle of identities that fascinates him. Who for instance was the young man as sexual object, and likewise the elusive identitiless dark lady.

He's distracted from talking property portfolios and seems inwardly absorbed by the ripple I've created in mentioning a work I've come to think of as mine by default. The Sonnits.

Stuart refilled my glass like he was giving the pour a haircut in weak gravity, and suddenly looked at me as though he recognised me implicitly from some different reality we'd both forgotten and were alerted to now as a simultaneously shared secret.

'I don't know why, but I'm sure we've met somewhere before,' he said searchingly. And after a delay: 'Piccadilly Circus of course. Do you remember?'

I was marginally thrown, but instantly came back at him. 'When you're hanging out there, facial recognition blurs. You don't really personalise faces unless you go off with someone.'

'I remember your stunning looks,' Stuart said, 'and you haven't changed. That's why in my own way I associate your looks with an imaginary Mr. W.H. In my own reading of the sonnits he remains, I don't know why, the blond boy, a sort of ageless fiction who is also a reality.'

Howard laughed and reviewed the maroon fist of wine in his glass, while I framed a mental snapshot of a man nervously stepping out under the arches in the late 6pm sunshine, dark suit, trying to act invisible, like he wasn't there physically, but was risking it, like street food. He was doubtless stored somewhere in my memory data, amongst all the degradables, the oxidised images irretrievably sunk into the brain's grey hamburger. But he was in me, and he knew it. He was maybe the sort who wouldn't take their shirt or Harrods tie off at the Regent Palace Hotel, and who paid you extra to classify the memory and pretend sex never happened, and it was really somebody else. I'd known that type, circumspect, undecodable, taking a one-off punt, and screwed up on guilt to the point of dissociation. All contact collapsed into a dodgy verbal contract of misdirected sex and money as dialect on a rudimentary bed. And that's what I was in part to W.S.; the bad end of the affair, the one left abandoned on the bed, like the last man on earth, while my impassive, disconnected lover went off as though it'd never happened, or was already experience formulated into language, the poem he was going to write if he did, substituting it for indifferent sex. He was mostly like that, cold and not cooked.

I snapped out of distraction, looked Stuart over, and said, 'I remember now,' (of course I was lying). 'We met outside Burger King, wasn't it, and you took me for a drink in St. James' before going back to yours in Knightsbridge?'

He smiled. 'You're close,' he said, as though he was important in my stereotypical casting.

You know the rest. Terms and cash payment before getting into fake character for sex, the split silver condom foil like a hologram on the bedside table, the bespoke suit neatly folded, the hum of a lift in the building's navel, the peremptory secrecy clause, the pine tang of soap, the traceable hint of Dior cologne on pigment.

You know the rest. The candid attempt to fit incompatible bodies; the alienation you try to make good; the embarrassed silence afterwards; the slight tug of guilt that it happened in this way, as a sordidly cold transaction for pristine notes from an ATM. That's it condensed: the track bounced down.

You know the rest.

6

STICKING A DUDE

I've got ten strips of Indian non-generic 10mg Valium for Kit, and insist by text the pickup's Leicester Square. It's not only that I like drawing a spy into a pedestrianised public space, like skinning a snake, but also I feed on the exhaust of public spaces and their contactless streaming of faces, maybe one hundred in view all the time.

I've insisted it's him personally, as I don't do drug couriers, it's too dodgy. It's not that I need the money; it's more that he's my clandestinely historic link to the equally time-slipped W.S. as a living USB stick of his original chromosomes with a few missing that process genius. Or that's my intuitive take on it. I know on my pulses there's another murder in the making, however it happens, a fisted knife, a drone, telepathic zapp, nerve agent, a drive-by marksman. Whatever the virtual schematic driving the whole thing forward, I'm a part of it, an integrant into the unresolved sprawl of the centuries that have me still here sitting out in the middle of London listening to a busker manage 'Here Comes The Sun.'

Of course I know, note the present tense, the strategy of events leading to Kit's supposed murder at Deptford Strand on Wednesday 30 May 1593, a blade being driven through the right eye's orbital fissure, after an apparent altercation in a back room involving three men, one of which, Ingram Frizer, was acquitted of manslaughter. According to records Kit—and he's already late—didn't even have identity enough for a name; he's called Christopher Morley by William Danby, Coroner, and dumped into the black sack of conspiracy theories at the bottom of the sink.

'And so it befell in that affray the same Ingram (sounds like a car salesman) in defence of his life, with the dagger aforesaid of the value of 12d gave the said Christopher then and there a mortal wound over his right eye of the depth of two inches and of the width of one inch; of which mortal wound the aforesaid Christopher Morley instantly died.'

You believe that? It's like squashing Aristotle's definition of tragedy into a ketchup-dribbled burger. It's all part of the uncanny valley where robot serial killers hang out waiting for commands.

My morbid fascination with the eerie and the almost human derives from having been rent. It found its apogee at Piccadilly Circus as a neon hub where facial ambiguity crept up my spine in the puffs of toxic traffic haze diffused over Regent Street. In Leicester Square today there's a parade of killer clowns, a mad rampage of pathological burlesque that substitutes murder for fun. It's like bad acid, you confuse hallucinated for real, only to find out the real is the hallucination. Do you think Kit Marlowe died like that as an extra-judicial MI6 hit? Who was Christopher Morley, the right man or the wrong one? Or Christopher Marlie, Marlor, Marley, as he was variably named in the coroner's inquisition, who were these cloned aliases? And is there a tissue of multiple lives so that we can go on killing someone over and over as a tourist from tomorrow?

I sit and wait on the granite ledge outside the public toilets in the square, and watch peoples' immersion in mixed reality, their virtual devices and their real-time perception of the environment. I still get a thrill from being stationary in a West End crowd, as though I'm suspect by sitting still, when other people are transitioning towards a chosen destination. If you sit or stand still, people look at you to ascertain why you're there. Your motives are infected with suspicion simply for hanging out. You're thought to be creepy. The uncanny valley says make your peripheral more humanoid in appearance and it becomes marginally appealing, but go too far and our reaction is one of unease. Imagine a biker formation of white plastic peripherals holding the central reservation on the Marylebone Road.

Got all this weird stuff in my head, as Kit's late for his pickup. But I try best as I can to feel for an affair that happened 500 years ago in a London islanded by black bad-land marshes. Today the dialect's shanking by hoodies, as well as a capital that's a cybercriminal focus, its critical national infrastructure at risk, so too its industrial control systems. I got it in my phone what Kit leaked about espionage: today the main five nerve agents manufactured in dedicated labs are tabun, sarin, soman, GF and VX, as colourless organphosphorous liquids.

When Kit shows at last, he's different molecules, like rain beading a camera lens, and looks exhausted, as though the nature of cyberdefence has pushed him out a light-year or two. He's gated by green Ray-Bans, wears a pewter-buttoned jean jacket over a black shirt and cuffed Levi's with tan desert boots. He's what you expect an agent to be, unidentifiable.

He comes and sits down next to me without acknowledgement. I note the different shapes of his eyes, glasses lowered, and how the left one turned on me is flecked with green in the upper quadrant. He's cold; we're both a type.

He addresses middle-distance as he says to me, 'I suppose you've felt it too, he's around. W.S. is tracking me, and I'm sure he'll come looking for you too.'

I hand him his dependency in a sealed envelope. Ten bubble pack strips that he transfers to his pocket. He looks at me hard and I know he means it, when he says, 'Thanks, you've saved me.'

I should know, I can't get this stuff out of my blood, it's in there like a pharmaceutical dirty bomb. It's a habit I can't break, it's blue granules bind to my receptor sites like moon grit.

'This is as good as anywhere to talk,' he says, scoping the precinct to downsize the potential for risk. There's a breeze slices through the gold sunshine, and a garrulous troop of French school kids crossing in the direction of the Empire.

'You realise I could crash this whole square,' he says, 'with an app. There's someone at loose in this city who can finger end time with the impact of WW10.'

I leave off speculation, as he knows I know the person intended. He breaks a pill in two and replaces the other half in its perforated slot, like a dusty crescent moon.

'He's not Shoreditch High Street anymore, he's Charles Street, Mayfair, the same block as you.' He threw me a look like a spook freezing my blood.

'What do you mean?' I asked. 'The same block as me,' at the same time going into instant denial.

'I'm not in the habit of getting things wrong,' Kit said. 'My mistake was of course my murder, if you believe the fact of me being sliced in a small room in Deptford and being jumped by three men, as history tells you.'

To my knowledge I'd never told him I lived with Howard in Charles Street, so he must have done his work as intelligence.

'You're trying to scare me, aren't you?' I said, knowing it was for real. I sensed intuitively he was working towards the exchange of concealed knowledge, mine on who really killed him, and his on the key player in both our lives, who was back in the game.

I looked off into a group of four auburn-haired Asian girls, probably Korean, dressed in skinnies and boots, all busy filming a torchy girl busker, wearing a fake three-quarters length leopard print coat, and singing over a backing track to Amy Winehouse's 'Back to Black' with a fusion of Hackney inflection and Dutch hip-hop. She wasn't going anywhere, but trying, and that's what it was about, pulling people into a circle for fifteen minutes with the rain building in wall-to-wall clouds over the Mall.

'What I know of tech,' I said, 'I've largely picked up from my financial analyst friend.'

'A lot of my job is routine,' he said. 'You know, just more attempted DDOS. The attackers are recruiting very specific devices like CCTV cameras, digital video recorders, home routers and other embedded computers attached to the internet as part of the internet of things. You don't need to understand, but it differs from your usual botnet attack using traditional computers by randomness.'

'It's not my interest,' I said, 'but Howard keeps talking about IOTS, is it, and how they don't really protect from malware.'

'He's right,' Kit said, academically. 'They're mostly ineffectual and built by small Chinese and Taiwanese companies, lacking expertise, and at a tiny profit margin. Most of those devices are not only faulty, but they can't be patched.'

Most of what Kit related skimmed me. It was the notion that W.S. was possibly living in the same Mayfair block as me that scared up history. I tried to make a catalogue of the few occupants of the building I remembered seeing coming and going at various times; but there was no clear mental snapshot stood out as a possibility. In fact, I realised that I'd never really accounted for other people, even on our floor, as being other than anonymous, impersonal, and packaged into secure privacy. Most of the transitioning occupants were according to Howard, either hedge funders fraudulently selling tomorrow as today, the children of super-rich bankers attending Eaton Square upper school, honey-trapped diplomats, stepped down ambassadors, etc.

'Does anyone fit his recreation?' Kit asked. 'Think on it, he's there, and you should know.'

'You wouldn't know anyone lived there, most of the time,' I said. 'It's like that, mostly anonymous.'

'Think clearly,' Kit said. 'You do that by a process of elimination to find the one face you want. I'm not asking you to be a face-recogniser, but your past should have cultivated that facility.'

I watched a bright opal raindrop roll over the back of my hand as a premonitory sign of rain to come, building over the square in densely packed nimbostratus. I raided whatever I could of visual recall and partially retrieved the memory of a tall man; thirties at a guess, disguised more by his own sense of secrecy than wraparounds as a defensive accessory. I remembered sharing a lift with him, and as usual avoiding my own mirrored reflection, but having the intuitive feeling, or was I processing this for Kit that we'd met somewhere before in a different reality. In a flashback I saw him leave the building in the opposite direction to me that is towards Park Lane, while I went Piccadilly. So I told Kit about this accidental association in my building and how it didn't really mean anything at the time, but could be significant.

'You're right; it could be anyone,' he said, 'but it could also be him. He never really adapted to London life, he remained provincially rural, whereas I got streetwise and into trouble with the law. Let's go walk for a bit, I don't want to be on cameras here. Believe me, surveillance will be inside your head soon. The Japanese have already created an algorithm that could result in computers knowing what you are thinking and dreaming. It's all part of an AI takeover.'

The rain suddenly came on in a torrential surge as he spoke, having the crowds run for temporary shelter from its blinding flash. They looked like people running at the end of time, looking for their particular terminal to be processed into their next design for the future. At least it seemed like that to me in the pounding downpour as we made it to Coventry Street to shelter in a doorway.

We stood there facing down the rain and Kit said out of the blue, 'Maunder. You remember Henry Maunder, a creepy operative in Burleigh's pay, the one who walked like gel, he did for me too, and you at the time were fully aware of it.'

There was a guy crumpled into a doorway, psychotically free-associating and clearly on spice, the cheap, ratty drug turning the homeless mad. Suddenly there was the loud reverberant bang of what sounded like gunshots, and two moped riders segued into view, upping throttle into the roar of skidding getaway. People were suddenly scattering in different directions across the drenched square, while a dense mob surrounded what I knew intuitively was a gang killing. Rogue gun hipsters were now an integral part of the capital, raiding Apple stores or snatching phones or watches off unsuspecting pedestrians.

Like me, Kit didn't react to the incident, and the downpour abruptly stopped, he steered me away from the crime-site as a convoy of blue lights streamed towards what I suspected was a revenge killing. 'You know very well I got off manslaughter charges,' he said, 'and I'll never know if it was me or Thom Watson stuck the dude in Hog Lane. Two moped riders, probably armed with acid, neither will know the other's responsibility. It's like that. It's the law decides. As you know, I was acquitted.'

Kit headed towards Panton Street, and without saying a word depressed the buzzer on a white painted door of a building under scaffolding that appeared deserted. Getting no reply he used a command app on his phone to get in. We entered a grey walled hall that led directly into a large kitchen space, the walls painted Jaffa orange, and a man wearing a black wool pixie hat and grey denim shirt was sitting at a table, his mind in his phone, like he was scrolling through his thought shapes as they came up.

'So it's you Kit,' the man said, eliciting no surprise, not even looking at him, the voice mechanical like an in-flight update on turbulence.

'Too tired to come to the door,' Kit responded, 'or working on counter-terrorism? This is Will, by the way. He's connected.'

'I know all about him,' the man said diffidently. 'I'm Henry.' He got up, thin in a way that was propulsively energised, the facial scar on his left cheek coming on like neon. He pulled three lemon mugs from a metallic rack and filled them from a coffee maker, the opaque liquid giving off an acrid Turkish tang. 'You know,' he said, 'you can warp time, not for rapid journeys around the galaxy, but only if you consider the future is complete. It's part of my job to know time runs both ways, and that's why you're here.'

'Stick to reality,' Kit said. 'W.S. is my case and yours, and he's right on our backs in this hub.'

I stared into the black pit of my coffee like obsidian gunk. The introduction was superfluous, it could only be Henry Maunder as geeky espionage re-entered my life as another tourist from the future implicated in the plot.

Kit remained standing angularly against one of the Jaffa orange walls, as though better making his presence felt. 'Know anything about the shooting in the square?' Kit asked. 'The two moped riders in balaclavas who took off, while we were under cover from the rain.'

Henry dug into a pack of M&S Dark Chocolate Digestives, extracting one and making an initial bite. 'Look, I'm not part of the Super-Recognizer Unit, you know—it's probably another drug-related gang murder. Why are you here?'

'You should know,' Kit said, cold. 'Let me tell you in code. You go out for six months and you turn around and you come back for six months, and while you are transitioning you go fast, while your clock continues slow. Something like that: get me? Time-travellers are undetectable by choice, it's all part of living parallel.'

Henry didn't respond, but went back into his phone as prosthetic cortex, like he was roaming his brain. Kit stood there implacably closed, back to a luridly orange wall, facing down Henry's different reality. So this was undercover I realised, a numberless, outwardly deserted house in the West End, stripped of all fixtures like an industrial bunker, except for an anomalous psychedelic orange workspace in which whatever happened, including wet jobs, was classified. You'd clearly no more squeeze anything out of Henry than you would the refreshed walls.

'Whatever you've got for me, send,' Kit said. Henry didn't respond, just kept on immersed in mixed reality as his encrypted resource.

We went back out into an air charged with menace. You could tell something bad had happened, it rushed at you like a tube. It didn't seem to bother Kit, who despite his street-alertness was clearly somewhere else. 'It keeps coming back to me,' he said, 'big chunks of memory. It was west down Watling Street and right for St. Augustine's Gate into Paul's Churchyard and Andrew Wise's bookshop at the Angel Paul's Yard. That's where I stole books or sold manuscripts in exchange for them. I had this lawyer, Richard Kitchen, he got me off so many exchanges in return for you know what. I realise I was stoned a lot of the time and saw life through mismatched eyes. It was at times, no matter the squalor like travelling downriver towards a luminous portal that turned out only to be a headlight in the fog.'

We headed towards the Mall and its columns of giant peeled plane trees to escape the sirens in a retrofuture capital coated in end time. 'Let's have a drink at the ICA,' Kit said, 'I could do with it,' and for a disquieting moment I viewed us as two people in an altered state quite literally walking out of one century into another.

We sat in a corner of the modernist simplicity of the Rochelle Canteen, and almost spontaneously Kit sliced through the prelims to tell me that only quite recently he'd discovered a Blue Blazer. 'It sounds very Fleming, but it isn't. It's two jiggers of Scotch, a sugar lump and very hot water. You set the liquid on fire and pour from one glass to the other adding a twist of lemon peel on top. Simple, and hammers you if you do four or five.'

I remembered Kit delusionally drunk in Shoreditch, and an escaped black bear nosing the dockside, its propulsive muscle barrelling at a sailor out of the fog. And now this, our attempt over gin slings to patch disparate times together like a modular phone, in an arts lab featuring Tacita Dean.

The ICA generated its usual feel of neutrality, as though it was a space tourism port, rather than a white stucco Nash House complex with a bloodstain on the wall of the administrative offices preserved under glass, as Norman Rosenthal's, from an assault made on him as arts director in the seventies by a group of anarchists.

Kit looked at his drink as clearly disproportionate to his needs. 'You know,' he said, 'and my historic murder is naturally my obsession, Ingram Frizer was just another lowlife snoop like me, counterintelligence paid on both sides. Today we process quantum intelligence in our nervous systems, back then it was shanking with a knife. Spies are like guys queuing for Raman noodles at KANADA and trying to decode the slippery entanglement.'

It was coming on rain outside, swishy dollops slung against the Mall-side windows, the volume increasing to a surround-sound pelting roar. Rain was the one constant in London's history, a light polluted downpour substituting for the atomised dazzle of sixteenth-century drench.

'I only know my side of it got from W.S.,' I said. 'He was screwed up by the plot and wanted to talk, lubricated of course by drink. Maunder was a name came up all the time, so too Danby, Watson, Chapman, Skeres, Baines, Poley, Frizer, Burleigh, Walsingham, one identity concealed by another.'

'Don't I know it,' Kit said. 'Fuckers. I was the rogue gene, the punk who got into the wrong place at the right time, or something like that. I was the big mouth who exposed their lies by talking truth.'

'I wasn't part of the inside track, remember,' I made clear. 'I got his lies to cover for another tissue of deception. He was greased with corruption, like bankers are today.'

'In order to move on,' Kit said, 'I need to know who killed me and if I really died like history tells me. There's real and there's virtual, and that's another tool of deception, because you can't be both simultaneously in real-time.'

I tried to run time backwards, but you can never properly retrieve the past without reinventing it. Kit was looking at me full on like he could sit inside my brain and look out at me; it was that weird. It came to me he was treating the mind like piecing together a jumbo jet's nests of internal wiring without accessing the fault.

'Snoops are really urban nomads,' Kit said out of his drink. 'I can tell you, your man was at Eleanor Bull's house, invited to lunch there, and just like today it was raining hard in the creek. It's a big thing killing somebody, and you don't just walk away clean. Where did he go to clean up his guilt?'

'I don't know,' I said, 'he used me and came and went; I

could never keep track of him. Or do I tell you?'

'Go on,' Kit said, as though he had it all complete, and needed me to catch up.

'He came to my place in the middle of the night banging on the door. I thought it was a marshall doing a house search, and when I went down and opened up he fell forward into me and I had to help him up the stairs. He was shaking all over and his clothes were drenched in mud. He wouldn't tell me what had happened, so I lit the remains of a joint and it relaxed him down a bit. I thought maybe he'd been mugged or roughed up in the streets.'

'You know he did it,' Kit said accusingly, 'the rest were duped into his service and paid by intelligence.'

I threw a look at the bar to help endorse why we were here in another time, as a group of square-fringed Asian girls polarised to their phones took up the table next to ours. What I knew belonged to a timeline as warped as killing your parents before you were born so as not to be convicted of murder. I didn't have answers for Kit, only the realisation that being gay as an urban subculture invited the same trouble then as it did now.

When Kit went back to the bar for refills I could feel the start of a migraine tightening in my frontal lobes like silver dazzle paint. The rain must have given over as a wet lemony light filtered back in through the windows in long ellipses.

Kit placed our glasses on the table, and remarked, 'cyber spying is like the dissolve between gin and tonic; you appropriate classified information with no traceable fingerprint.'

I was right on the edge of the edge, anticipating how I'd feel if I came out with it and told him he was right in thinking it was W.S. filled his mouth with blood, like tomato soup.

'What if I told you it was him,' I said, feeling the words thicken in the admission.

'Was who?' Kit asked, sinking his second gin.

'The man who made and broke me,' I replied, allusively.

Kit put the rest of his gin away and went back to the bar for another double. I could feel the past coming back like a plane from some forgotten war, a damaged Spitfire landing invisibly parallel with a Boeing on a Heathrow runway.

'The reason we're here,' Kit said, 'is the past sticks to us. To get free we have to unravel its entanglement. I can only do that by finding out the truth. Who killed me?'

'You already know,' I said, 'history's complete and we drag along behind. Isn't that right? And even if he's back in town and living in my mansion block, it doesn't mean I'll find him. His reality is different to mine and that's what's so spooky. It's like being mugged by the dark instead of a person.'

'You don't need me to tell you,' Kit said, 'the sonnets aren't about love; they're about projecting his own feelings on to you. They're quite obviously not felt, they're empty windows in which rhetoric substitutes for feeling. They're all about him, not you.'

'The reader doesn't see it, but it's the typical rent/punter combo. When they tell you they love you its like cappuccino froth. And if they really did it's stuck in them hard as a diamond and never comes out. They usually hate themselves for feeling it. '

'He's all of those things,' Kit said. 'He was so singularly concentrated on his work that people were objects in his life: skin reduced to a worktop.'

I threw my mind back on his untreatable coldness. I'd pretend to be asleep and watch him writing a sonnit, working incorrigibly fast while drinking or smoking a joint. He'd only stop to catch up with his thoughts, like he was either too far ahead or too far behind the train he was trying to catch. He didn't sweat; he wrote with an easy facility to match thought with language in a fluent dissolve.

'I could take him out now by a viral or nerve agent,' Kit

said, 'but the issue's too personal for that. We have to meet, and he's still not quite there yet; he's almost turned the corner into knowing me again.'

'And me too, presumably,' I said, feeling the freeze travel up my spine at the prospect of re-encountering the man who had fucked me into historic repute/disrepute.

Kit eyed the drowned lime in his iced glass, and looked up with eerie weird. 'Dodgy people don't change,' he said 'he'll be trawling the darknet or exercising the muscle in his brain to subjugate others.'

I realised looking at him that he probably couldn't get drunk, and that drinking probably only reset the need, rather than changed his reality. He was doubtless I thought, as lonely as me, two reconstructed evacuees tipped to the edge of an incurable alienation that grew deeper with time like the ache in the heart of the universe.

There was another subterranean rumble of sound energies shook the walls, as we spoke, like the reverb of a bomb in the underground.

'Another one,' Kit said dispassionately, as though the common occurrence diminished the effects of terrorism. 'Bombs are so old world, and describe their limitations and not their strength. In cyber counter-intelligence we consider them cumbersome physicals.'

Just looking at Kit increased my own sense of terrifying isolation. Nobody alive would ever believe my sad identity as Mr. W.H.; it just wasn't on, and the loneliness of my state was like being classified as an alien, dropped in on the exhaust of a time-slip.

Kit diced the ice cubes in his glass like maracas, as a sign it was time to split. We got outside into the drizzled light and walked back up the leafy Mall together, like traversing a corridor from one century into another, five times, to get back into the momentous West End, where he went under for a tube, leaving me to go back to Hop Gardens on foot to continue writing this like an urban nomad disinherited from identifiable time.

I took up my place in the shadow of the hotel, feeling my plot big as a skyscraper downsized into my brain. Sitting there in the alley I wondered about the impossible accident of W.S. filing through and recognising me as his historic fuck. Not that I've ever been cheap; I've demanded what women usually get, money, patronage, security, a roof over my head. Nobody has ever bought me; W.S. had me on loan, as Howard does now, and the bond's never cemented; it could break up any day in a crashing possessive row. That's me and I couldn't care. I've hung out on streets with raindrops for eyeliner, unpossessably elusive on a Westminster pavement tracked by millions and been looked over and turned down the lot as unprepossessing to my taste. In Hop Gardens I rehabilitate my real identity in a world rapidly approaching end time. I have this crazy feeling that the world will end sooner than I could walk across the Sahara with my earbuds in to exclude the roar of the red sky falling.

Today, Leonard Cohen died into song—You Want It Darker taking him out on black cabalistic exhaust. I sat and thought of how mysticism was his sustaining vitamin, like there was a gold sublingual pill he sucked on and that diffused its ingredients into his song. His voice was so low down it seemed to come out of his foot rather than his throat, it's the cooked tone of a cigarette smoked down to the last glowing pinch. Leonard as I imagined him was now in the newly arrived death queue, guitar case in hand shuffling through creepy Arrivals. All his global fan-base was free to imagine his afterlife differently, now that there was no longer a physical geography in which to locate him. To me he was a transitioning light cone, a blue raincoat slung over his bony shoulders, following in the desultory line to the guards at the gate. There's no ham sandwich to stop for, no burger stall, he can't like me bite into a veggie wrap, designed for the urban busy from Eat.

Howard's text prompts me to read of a flash crash on Wall Street by an independent trader whose spoof trades deliberately tried to drive down prices. It's a tool used to destabilise the market by spoof traders designed to lower prices and lead to the placing of genuine orders to take advantage of the deficit. The manipulable logic of causing U.S. stock markets to plunge, like a plane hitting turbulence, was lost on me, but as instinctual as breath to Howard's meta-mathematics. I knew I'd get an evening of rant on my return and that the martini cocktails would escalate to a boozed apogee as Howard drank his way into tomorrow with a rattling castanet of ice in his glass.

My more immediate concerns though, were with the possibility of the enigmatic time-traveller W.S. living in my Charles Street block. In my subliminal history I had the vague notion of meeting someone on the way out, three-quarters profile, who'd exchanged eyes more out of surprise than recognition, almost like catching in the street. I didn't read anything into it at the time, other than mutual curiosity, two sympathetic strangers leaving a scratch on each other's awareness in passing: nothing more than that. I was so used to being looked over that he was just another.

I walked back home through the rush hour crowds, the stomping configuration of tribal march coming up as a phe-romonal boost in the big city crowds all headed for the underground from 5-7 p.m. soaking into West End ambience. Walking for me always refreshed the present, like light is inspiration and motion its rhythm. I was in no hurry to outstrip the crowds, and headed towards my old hangout patch at a now pedestrianised Piccadilly Circus. The usual tourist snap-shotters congregated around Eros outside the Athenaeum. It was another time, another place; a generational takeover by a new youth. I sort of kept away from my old hub of illicit activities where lurid neon billboards were replaced by an 11 million pixellated a new recognition technology screen influenced by the people and things around it. I stopped off momentarily out of nostalgia, no longer a hustler reading faces for the right one to make contact, but simply another face in the anonymously streaming crowd. The sky was gentian blue over the Haymarket, the whole quarter policed by black cabs with their yellow welcome lights standing out solicitously in the chasing dusk.

I crossed over to the main Piccadilly highway and headed in the direction of Green Park, my old inquisitiveness and stand-out looks having eyes thrown at me in passing. It was always that thrill of transient eye contact excited knowing we'd never meet again. Looking at the crowds, it's like tomorrow will continue forever, the silent majority pushing forward to the underground and disappearing into the sink in their deadening conformity.

I got back to Green Park, a big green and orange light washed into blue atmosphere over the park's quadrant and two leather-skinned bikers were sharing tips at the lights, like helmeted aliens, the biker's intelligence, one Triumph, one Yamaha, issuing directly from their heartbeat rather than the rev counter. They both came off the lights into a commandeering, loopy roar for spearheading dominance on the highway. I watched them intuitively target and molest one on either side an embassy limo's sedate luxury, opaqued windows and imperial crawl. One of the bikers took out a spray can and squirted an acid green aerosol over the rear window before flying off into the layered dark. It was like pissing on privilege, squirting green acrylic at endorsed politico status.

A short walk and I was into Belgravia where the super-rich purchase investment homes with criminally laundered money. There was no real difference between Coutts and the drain in my experience of knowing both.

When I got to the corner of Charles Street I could see this man arguing with a black girl outside my block. I got into a doorway clustered with cameras and watched. The more I looked the more I entertained the suspicion it could be him; the man who had nailed me to history. Short of taking atoms apart and rebuilding them, I couldn't of course be sure, but I had the intuitive notion this was the man I couldn't describe to Kit, who'd lit through me on our residential floor, tall, dark suited, oval-faced, and curious in a way that wasn't so much analytical as cognitive, as though he was remembering now what was already there. I was convinced, without proof it was the remade W.S. facing down a blonde-rinsed black girl, curvily bottled into jeans worn like masking tape. They were arguing over something and clearly only restrained by the fact they were in public. I could hear the girl shout at him, 'You owe me mister; it's another two hundred. Shut up and pay, you bastard.'

They stood there; folded into argument, the vicious altercation staying level, with the girl rising above it periodically to repeat, 'fuck off,' like a dirty mantra. He'd lowered his voice, so I couldn't properly hear his part of the angry run-in, only hers, 'you're a fucking cheat. I won't go with you again, motherfucker.'

It suddenly occurred to me, against all reason, that this was possibly Lucy Negro, the black Shoreditch honeytrap, the slumming hottie he'd visited when he was bored with me, and trying to prove straight. This was the sex worker he'd told me did A, O, and O with O, and who was presumably still doing the same for higher-income Belgravia punters. It seemed a long shot but was this Lucy Negro, Lucy Diamond, Black Luce, whatever he called her—Lucy on the second floor of a shabbily lit walk-up.

86

I waited my time in the unaccountably quiet street, as the two lit into each other with renewed antagonism. Lucy, if it really was her, kept jabbing a finger at him accusingly, forcing him back on the defensive. 'You've always used people, you shit,' she screamed. 'What do you do to earn a living?'

The argument went silent as an Yves-Klein-blue Lexus entered the street and parked with volatility. I saw him go into his black coat and attempt to settle the issue with cash. She stood back inspecting what he'd given her, and without lowering her voice, launched, 'you're always so fucking mean, not even a tip.'

At that, she took off in the direction of Park Lane: a lurid neon orange sunset coming on like an interplanetary traffic light. She turned round a last time and volubly shouted 'wanker.'

I stayed put in my doorway, not really believing it was the historically ambiguous W.S. emerged as a destabilised time-traveller to somehow relive the unresolved past. From my viewpoint I watched Howard slip into the building, almost simultaneously with the stranger, just as it started to rain, big beady drops in direct descent, twinkling like the blue carats in a De Biers diamond.

7

LUCY NEGRO'S ASS

Margot, of course it was Howard's sort of place to stuff on Great Queen Street, the waiters looking anomalously stuffy in black dinner jackets and Tom Ford white cotton shirts, redolent of La Dolce Vita revisited in a postmodern slip. The place characteristically repulsed me for its stacks of skinned meat. Try getting a cow out of its hide, and clean up the mess like a gargantuan miscarriage.

It's spendy; Howard starts with a butch platter of salami spoilt with top notes of fennel seed and an aged prosciutto that's like visceral tissue. It goes like that with him, the protein build, like a construction site, a robust dish of rare game that's sleazy pink, eaten with glazed chestnuts and braised Savoy cabbage with bacon. I wonder at the mix of dead life in his gut culture—the dictionary of bacteria colonising there microbially. I keep to a simply tailored green tagliatelle, and think lemongrass, juniper and bitter dandelion as antidote to stripped flesh. And it doesn't stop for the syrupy protraction of two hours, in which he concludes with rum baba soaked louchely in tangerine douse. Howard treats food like money markets; each course is an investment in foodie pathologies.

Lucy Negro or Black Luce. Kit moved in on her as a creepy pattern of espionage materialising amongst the apparently deathless milieu to which we inextricably belonged. He'd traced her to Lewisham with its moody sky full of red and yellow cranes, like Lego floating in micro-gravity, having picked up sensitive tips at the sweaty Fox & Firkin pub where he bounced down his identity to normal. Lucy was to all accounts living in a dusted down Victorian semi-detached, north of the railway, where properties commanded seven-figure sums, a one-time squat repurposed into 2 bed floors, one of which was Lucy's hideaway from selling sex in prime London. She'd been sighted not only in the pub but also accidentally at Model Market with its mixed street kitchen. Kit's nose had found her. He'd got into her phone that lacked end-to-end encryption across all platforms and accessed text. 'Will, to say everything and nothing to you to say what I could not say last night too drunk + lest my forced poise of distance was shattered + I came tumbling down to say I'll kill you if I can't have you, to say everything and nothing to you +

Nothing really made sense in the coded text? And why of all people Lucy Negro? It could have been any Lucy, like 'Lucy in the Sky with Diamonds.' If this really was Lucy come wormholing out of my past into the altered present, and given London accelerated accidental finds, I was sure she would come at me one day, out and about, as I do, west ending. Lewisham's strong growth didn't do anything for my postcode aesthetic in living on the hub of the capital's heartbeat.

I could feel the bleaching of my relationship with Howard starting to grow. The fade was like the rub on jeans, the chafing to white threads in euphoric blue. Soon there would be kneeholes and the irreparable falling apart. Howard drank to counter the demoralising realisation that he was in effect buying me to compensate for his lack of looks. His lifestyle was one of brutally self-punitive hedonism, inflated salaries linked to disproportionate bonuses, snug business class long haul, pills for hypertension, the stomach bump indicative of middle-age, sweaty moral degradation, a lick of Vetiver filming the thin veneer of corruption. For him money is a social lubricant, it's his immersive status, and if I told him who I believe I am, he'd most likely send me into rehab at the Priory to try to straighten out.

But Lucy, or Black Luce, I remember contemporary readers of the sonnits knew her identity as a sort of sexual voodoo. She wore diamond rings for favours given in a room looking out over the syrupy green river. She was the black curve who walked like liquid sex and loved bling. You could have her, but at the risk of being hexed.

I couldn't resist the time-slip game of looking for her now, as part of the distorted schematic that had brought Kit back into my life as historic update. Even sitting under the store rooftop at John Lewis, with Howard, drinking mulled negronis, I could smell my past, the damp redolence of W.S.' crotch as olfactory memory, rather than plane fuel emissions choking the airways. And there's always a spottable homophobe sitting out on every terrace, like this one, a facial copy of a discredited East European autocrat throwing looks at me like he'd kill.

I was already evolving the fantasy of catching Lucy out by visiting her as a punter before revealing my true identity to provoke the admission of hers. It's not that I can't do girls, and in this case it's a means of unlocking history through her body and discovering sonnits I haven't read in the folds of her skin. Maybe her motive is like mine; it's the need to be wanted takes me back to what I do, exploit my looks for money, while keeping my inner life exclusively mine and impermeable. Like W.S., Howard hasn't got one millimetre below my skin into knowing me as a real person. Instead it's accepted I'm a categorised function, rent as the lowest denominator on the social scale. To know why I sold sex I needed a correlative story and I hoped to find it in Lucy Negro.

There's no fixed boundaries to this city: London changes out of all recognition through the greed of its developers, while still retaining its big red heart muscle under Piccadilly Circus, where you hear it beat loudest. Bombs on the tube, honour killings, gangs conducting turf wars, moped raiders using acid as a chemical weapon, radicalised cells, knives pulled like a prosthetic finger for a wrong glance into an eye quadrant, or a taunt on social media. In fact crime was so commonplace it appeared normal and went almost unnoticed as part of the new lawless, desensitised consensus. Life was like a Burroughs novel launched into reality, *Naked Lunch* as raw ethics on the street. Only yesterday, two masked gunmen had kidnapped a Whitehall minister and driven him shackled to Connaught Square and executed him outside the heavily guarded Blair fortress, and driven off at high speed into the London warren of getaways. It was even harder to apprehend criminals now than it was in lawless Tudor times, when street marshals ran blind against murder, clueless in the sticky dark.

According to Kit who I was now seeing on a regular basis he had track of Lucy's diagram of the city. She'd address hopped to Canning Town, and while retaining a Knightsbridge flat for work, wasn't otherwise in the gold cake-filler of Belgravia. According to Kit she'd recently been sighted at The Berkeley Health Club and Spa at Wilton place with a city trader sipping champagne fingers in a black leather pencil skirt like masking tape. Lucy and money, no one ever consensually fucked her, only the illusion money buys like a virtual body in a robot brothel. It was only Shakespeare who'd waded into her like he'd done the Thames shallows looking for bacterial gold.

Out of Luce curiosity—I could have been stalking a fake copy—I went east to Canning Town and to London City Island, a 12-acre mini-Manhattan on the Leamouth Peninsula, just a lipstick-red pedestrian bridge from Canning Town with its residential and mixed-use developments, its period juxtaposition of Victorian gas holders and Brutalist architecture like a psychotic build. I'd already got eye-massaged on the way over, count three or four stereotypical city loners consumed by the weird math of buying flesh like real estate. I exchanged numbers with two of them, a pensive fog-eyed barrister, cash-rich with a twinkle, and an obvious ex-public school type, syrupy voice, rehearsed manners, punctiliously conventional, pink and white dot socks with oxblood brogues. They'll both do for a top up on a rainy day.

Peeling off the shadow thrown by Balfron Tower separating Lady Dock from Canary Wharf, I got a sniff of place as I always do, facing up to a new strain of London's organism—the tribal dialect of what was crumbling wasteland reconstructed as money built into the sky. The place smelled of river traffic, and the dank riverine damp that soaks into every pore of the city's skin, and is the crotch odour of the rammed metropolis.

I hung out, doubting why I was there, and because I'm a cloud-spotter, noted grey building into white stacks of alto-cumulus, the huge silence of cloud abstracts always filling me with a sense of spatial awe at their continuously soundless collisions. There were black girls everywhere, all I assumed indistinguishable from a gene-edited Lucy, and I went into a Costa to take stock of my thoughts and refocus on my being there. Almost immediately I got an intuitive whiff of someone putting sensors on me, as I settled to my double espresso and ginger snaps. The lugubrious leak of a man dressed retro in a velvet-trimmed Crombie was trying to lift me into eye contact to get a hold, and I instinctively resisted. And it wasn't like the propositioning to which I was accustomed; it was more like someone hacking into me to have me remember. I was distracted momentarily in my quest by two black girls at a nearby table sharing phone-snaps, and in the process reminding myself that Lucy would have died in the seventeenth century, most likely of an STD.

Without warning the guy who'd been quizzing me sliced over, threw me a look, and coolly said, 'We know each other, don't we?' And I didn't.

'I think you've got the wrong person,' I said, annoyed by the invasion of my privacy. 'I'm not local, if that's what you're thinking.'

'Neither am I,' he said, sitting down opposite, as though I was expecting him. There were creepy brainwaves surging through me, as I looked him over, wondering if he was another one-time punter, and immediately smelling fake in his twisting my attention.

'It's been a long time,' he said, as though we shared history. 'You do remember me, don't you?' he said, pushing up his look. 'You're rent, aren't you, only you don't age, but I know your backstory, and it dates back centuries. It began at the Mermaid, the Boar's Head, Tudor dives; you were there, remember those big spitting wood fires, the booze so strong we collapsed. Everyone knew you were his boy, you know who I mean. This country's built out of his language.'

'I don't get you,' I said. 'How can you possibly remember me from centuries ago, or me, you, it's crazy.'

I knew there was far more to this than a casual brush-off. It was obvious the man was some sort of intelligence in the way you knew security in stores, dressed like the customers, as a smart dodge. The man in the dark blue jumper with no prominent stand-out features was the one who pulled out ID when he'd got hold of your elbow in John Lewis.

'It's not the first time I've tracked you,' he said, and I noticed the red arabesques in the corners of his eyes like mashed sunset. 'I've been in and out of your business all the time as a snoop. Didn't introduce myself, I'm Henry. Surname's a bit of a slouch, Maunder.'

The idea of the key players in my past all reappearing like entangled particles put me into a mental sweat, as though none of them had ever really died.

'Look,' I said, 'I came in here to have a bit of time to my-self on my phone, not to be interrogated by a stranger. Could you leave me alone?'

'But you know who I am, don't you,' he said, insidiously. 'I got Kit done once, and you're back seeing him, and his killers are around again too. You always turned me down sexually. We'll see about that,'

I looked away to refocus the world, but Henry, or whoever he was, sat there looking unconscionably nasty, like there was no softening point in his nature. Every time he looked at me it felt like someone had pinched a nerve with frozen fingers. He was a sort of mix of old school gangster on grainy film-stock and cyber geek harvesting data from social media. At some point he stood up and said, 'I'll be seeing you. Nobody throws me off; I'm right in your works. Better believe me. You don't ya?'

I ignored him as he made for the exit, wondering if I hadn't imagined it all as a sort of parallel processing, only he was somehow too real. I finished my espresso and feeling flaky from the encounter headed out into a tangy river breeze to pick up the Docklands railway, beaten this time, but determined to see it through. I transitioned back to the West End like physical time-travel, Lucy on my mind, and conscious how you couldn't put clothes on her; she always walked nude with a taut wobble. The sky was down lower, a greenish cloudbase with dirty floaters stacking into sculptural figures. I took a benzo and headed immediately for Hop Gardens where I was getting to know people who used the alley, just for a casual word, particularly the homeless who used it as a refuge in which to drink in public. It was coming on 5 p.m. in the river of faces headed for the underground; and I sat and imagined Lucy as one of 14 million options in the capital's hub of lives forwarded into the possibilities of tomorrow. I wondered too what would happen in this game of random chance if I didn't go home to Charles Street, but took up with a stranger and re-invented my life accordingly. But scheme as I did, I knew the redoubtable sonnit man would find me out wherever I went in this weirdly extended configuration of lives, all shuttled on a time-loop like the Circle Line. It was drones scared me, weaponised hobby drones launched by pilots to take someone out autonomously by facial recognition. Illegal drone footage from airborne vehicles was the new efficient espionage over central London, the violation of air space limitations leading to rogue drones being zapped on a daily basis. Drones had added still another weapon to the mechanistics of killing by manless software, pioneering still another extension of human expendability in the end time war with AI that would scramble the planet. If Orwell got 1984 right as the alien mind virus surveillance of the human species adopted by their genes then I felt sure the present was closing in on the complete future. And I'm nobody you'd want to meet except inside a sonnit.

Howard's theme of the day is high-end property being used as a reserve currency by global kleptocrats, and his own endorsement of crypto-currencies by the city's pro-corporate oligarchs—his type by default. With property prices being driven up by overseas criminals wanting to sequester their assets in the U.K., Howard's pockets were lined. It was the good life for some that I live off. It was also alpha male greed as I saw it preparing the design for post-apocalypse and the big crash. Howard said I read too much Ballard, but I could feel the hot red exhaust plume coming.

Howard—he's bought an orange Ralph Lauren crewneck for weekends, obsessionally refers to criminally facilitated tax evasion, and little else. I've been with so many rich punters who never explained their financial infrastructure. It's tedious with him but includes a bit of rough sparkle. According to Howard diamond and mineral wealth is usually extracted by political elites, funnelled via London to old empire stock in the overseas territories, then repatriated back to the U.K. It's a bit like recycling your own blood from a bank.

I fired a text to Kit with just two words. Henry Maunder. It felt like hijacking history to be on this distorted time loop where spooks came out of hiding to stand in corners of the present.

I've got reason to worry. There was a girl came running into Hop Gardens today, crying her eyes out and calling for help, blood streaming down one arm. 'Help me, somebody help me,' she screamed. 'He's injected me with Ebola, help me.' She collapsed in the middle of the alley, and before we could do anything as shocked spectators, this lowering hoodie still holding a hypodermic appeared, wa shouting abuse at her and threatening to spike her again. Someone must have phoned police, because the guy took off on the instant back into St. Martin's Lane, loping urgently, and unopposed in his getaway. A street marshall gave chase, leaving his colleague to attend to the girl before emergency services arrived to take her away.

I stood in the shock of it all, dazed by trauma and utterly powerless to act. My only distraction was in noticing a strawberry band of sky unfolding over Burleigh Mansions in the process of weather. I'm a romantic and the sky doses me with something transcendent, despite myself. It wasn't like that with W.S.; he needed to hack through folded emotions to get there. He was rural before urban and weather had its command in the cycle of seasons first, before it became adjectival. I used to think I was more the poet in a fixed relationship in which he wrote physically and I did it in my head. Whatever it was it happened like that in cheap rooms in Shoreditch with rain slamming the window. And what would I find now if I time-slipped back there instead of forward, other than a grey chilly space vacated forever.

I've got a friend of Howard's I go to as a shadow, called Mike. Mike runs a wholesale drugs distribution network selling batches of crystal meth dyed aqua, green, orange, to distinguish it on the market. Dye sachets litter his improvised home-lab, his kitchen table where he cooks meth, often the blue of the narcotic created by fictional drug baron Walter White in *Breaking Bad*. He does pink for his queer friends, orange for clubbers, pure white for serious users who inject, and has a courier transport packages to users around London, referring to the deliveries as T-bags. He's got millions of pounds of assets including a hotel in Dubai, and intends to colour-code every primary and secondary colour as part of his crystal artistry in pushing meth into greedy addictive cells.

Mike's got a single bedroom flat in Burleigh Mansions, a block of red brick buildings where you can live anonymously as being off world. I drop by sometimes to get a wakey for Howard's recreational use at weekends. Mike's all the time tweaking molecules to up the quotient, and maintains a simple lifestyle to avoid the scrutiny attached to big spender. He spends in Dubai or Thailand under a fake identity and retrenches to austerity on his return to the U.K. Howard has of course advised on math, how to bury money in the network of treasure islands.

'I wouldn't be alive if I was trackable,' he tells me in his wired way, buying tea—Earl Grey and chocolate digestives from Tesco. 'People really get damaged on this stuff. Strokes, cardiac arrest, aneurisms, you know, it's all part of recreation; but tell Howard to go easy on it. He's always demanding more each time and that's a bad sign. It puts your blood pressure right up.'

'I never touch it,' I say. 'I really don't like speed, it messes up my head.'

'I only do it sometimes,' Mike says, sipping from a dark blue mug, 'just to get rock hard if I need. I've got this Malaysian hottie at present comes over, married to a cold accountant, and she's in her panties before I've even shut the door. Doesn't know what I do, or care—the lab's off-limits—it's like a mini-arsenal: chemicals are soluble weapons. All she wants is sex.'

I look at Mike and wonder if he too isn't a visitor from tomorrow come back as part of the insolubly intricate game in which I'm a player. People said W.S. was a cabalist, a Rosicrucian, a punky Freemason, certainly to my mind something of his legacy was buried at a crossroads in the rainbow.

Mike takes out his phone and shows me Yuki as a nude artifact, her body posted in naturally complex angles, undressing mostly, or self-consciously throwing her arms up at Mike's phone video. I could see he wanted me to stay a bit, cooking drugs is a lonely thing in central London, he sometimes calls it moonwalking to live so concealed on the hub of things. I can see Mike doesn't have friends, only clients for crystal. Apart from casual sex he doesn't seem to have any quality time, his only escapism is into wealth he can't openly spend.

'Have another cup,' he says, pouring into my chipped blue mug. Help yourself with biscuits.' It's sad downtime.

I can smell his bathtub chemicals and his loneliness and distinguish one strain from another as parts of himself he doesn't like, but can't disown without dismantling his identity. I'm sure he's got plastic bags of cash concealed in the flat, but he's sort of fidgety nervous today, and I wonder if it's through passively inhaling the drug he mixes.

'I'm kinda bi,' he tells me, and I'd sensed it coming. 'I go with guys, then I drink coz I think I shouldn't, ya know. It's like that. I can't help myself, it just happens.' He looks at me as though the sadness in him is going to well into tears, his nut-brown eyes full of reflective introspection and chews on another chocolate digestive, exacting a crescent bite.

'By the way Will, and don't get alarmed, there was somebody in my pub looking for you. Don't know how he connected us, and it's not like I'd give anything away, you know what I mean. It kind of scared me though. Tall man, dressed in black, didn't have a London accent, sort of home-counties type. Looks like a loner. Could hold his drink.'

'How do you know it was me he was looking for?'

'I just knew it. He described you close enough and said you were an old friend, Will or W.H. I said I don't know who you're talking about, everyone knows a Will.' After that he shut up, and moved deeper into the bar and he stayed a while before leaving. But I noticed as he went out how everyone looked at him, sort of followed him with their eyes. I didn't like it. The man's creepy.'

'It can't be me he's looking for,' I said, in the attempt to block the conversation. 'It's obviously just some weirdo; I mean they're everywhere. There's millions of Wills in this city.'

'But he described you like I'm looking at you. I knew it was you, but I didn't let on. The guy doesn't mean nothing to me.'

I paid Mike for the crystal wrap and left feeling a column of fear climb up my spine. I flipped a benzo before going out to the street, a gritty blue granular chemical edge-remover and waited for the drug come up. For the first time I speculated imaginatively what it would be like to be W.S.' twink again, the escort come in from the cold to reconfigure the inequality in relations. He'd set my name up to be used like a car brand through the centuries, and I still didn't know why. The closeness he implied was on his part, not mine. I never loved him, I was just too curious to let go, and he built epic loss out of it.

I had time to kill before meeting with Howard at the Piccadilly Meridian, and crossed over in the direction of the National Portrait Gallery and slotted into the trancy autonomy of the crowds headed that way. The benzo was starting to brighten me, alter space in my head and around me. I was going with the idea of my book, the one you're reading, when someone tapped me on the shoulder and I swung around to confront Kit's wraparound Ray-Bans. 'It's the benzo man,' he said. 'Does Mike do these as well as crystal?'

'Are you stalking me?' I asked, feeling the walls of my cortex removed from inside.

'Don't need to,' he replied, 'but recommend you do a course at London App Brewery that'll teach you how to code using Swift and Java as basics. I can swipe into your mind, but I don't.'

I sort of instinctively headed us back into Bear Street, and the reek of junk food as reconstituted beef paste. 'You've got a lot to learn,' Kit said, 'as essence rather than basic. It's like everyday physics. Take the foam floating on top of a cappuccino. If you put a spoon on top of the froth it will fall through. Whip them both up into froth and the spoon will rest on top. The physics is in the bubbles and W.S. is like that to us.'

'If I'm right, he's on my tail,' I said. 'Mike told me he was snooping at the Salisbury, listing me for what he could find.'

'He came to the Mews,' Kit said. 'My security cameras sprayed him with synthetic DNA and dye like ATM security. I've relocated temporarily, not out of fear, but to get a better overview of his movements, if he really is what we think.'

I could feel my throat close on the sticky ramifications of espionage, and at the same time was conscious of another explosion deep underground.

'There are algorithms which, when given a brain scan of someone looking at a picture can reconstruct the original image. I can do it faster. I can pinpoint a specific thought shape if I want and appropriate it for data analysis. I can slice right into him without him ever knowing it happened.'

'Everything's coded in this fucking city,' I said. 'I preferred it real. '

'The thing is to be blunt,' Kit said. 'W.S. is probably an unkillable entity. He always channelled knowledge, dangerous stuff he couldn't handle, in his writing, and this is the price. It wasn't just that I wrote about Faust, we were really touching evil in those theatre pits, like rolling an escaped bear in the mud.'

Looking around me, I tried to remember that real life in all its mutant variants was going on around me in the square. There was a beefy policeman dressed in a yellow vest keeping watch on the crowds by the corner of Leicester Court, and the ubiquitous sharing of delayed visual recognition in tourists seeing London perhaps for the first time in putting it onto their phones. I was aware in the big curve of things, nothing ever came real; we simply imagined what we knew, stretching reality in that way without any empirical backup. 1590 or now, it didn't matter in the transitioning, nothing stayed, and like Kit I wanted more than anything to escape the loop that dragged me back to a particular time and place.

Kit looked at me hard. 'All that pointlessness in attempting to decode the sonnits, crunch them into numbers—you know I was reading how 97, 98 and 99 apparently allude to my death and the guilt or separation W.S. experienced over my assumed murder. Do you really know what murder means?'

'Not in the sense of having experienced it,' I said, noting in my peripheral vision a black girl dressed in a white tee and skinnies that could have been Lucy or any randomised stranger I'll never know.

'It's more appalling than you can imagine,' Kit said. 'I'll yell you, it's like a bomb exploding inside your brain, a big hallucinated fireball. Every cell in your body screams with protest that it's being extinguished. Want to hear more?'

'Go on,' I said, just as a busker struck into a gritty version of Dylan's 'Wheels of Fire.'

'I'll tell you, you're sucked into one dark vault after another, through a tunnel blacker than the tube, and there's what looks like guards on either side, holographic marshals, then you explode like a supernova into whatever is your temporary remake . . .'

'Look,' I said, suddenly alarmed. 'That black girl in the vinyl jeans, that's Lucy isn't it, or am I going mad? It's got to be her.'

Kit did something on a device and said, 'Yes, it's her, Lucy. I've got a match in historic update.'

Lucy stood there loitering in the white daze of dirty urban sunlight. I watched as she sat down on a ledge, legs crossed, and coolly scoped in the transitioning foot traffic. When she threw a look our way I was conscious of her neon red lipstick, and that she was as aware of us as we were of her.

'Take this,' Kit said, handing me the black on black casing of an unbranded obsidian phone. 'Nobody can ghost, snoop or hack you with this device, not in cyberspace or meatspace. It's totally secure. Use it to contact me, understand.'

He left abruptly in the way that he had of appearing to dematerialise. I watched him slice through the crowds, if the person I was watching was still really him or an illusion, his blended universe having the affordances of both superior intelligence and the international vulnerability that travelled with it.

Instinctively I refocused Lucy, perhaps pressing refresh to retrieve a new tweet, aware from my own experiences of selling sex that she would appear available to the predatory, simply by sitting out solo. I got back of her and quizzed her body statistics and sensual morphology, still convinced it was Lucy as an unexplained visitor from the future. Oversized gold hoop earrings, black hair streaked radially blonde, a black moulded vest providing a midriff band, black vinyl jeans looking like they were nail gloss polished on her bum, the usual. She looked expensively pickupable, like I had at Piccadilly Circus, but similarly removed from commonplace; and also potential aggro, as she'd always been, chippy about her skin colour, and as likely to prove truculent, as please. I'd seen her, five centuries back or forward boot W.S. out into the rain with his clothes thrown down the stairs as a derisory postscript.

What I wanted from Black Luce wasn't sex, but to decode the thumbprints on her soul. Like ghostery in a browser I wanted to snoop on her tangled fuck past, and access the names of the big and small who'd traded cash for cum. I felt some direct correlation with her in our deviated lives. Luce clearly cooked money, like Mike bathtub crystal, and Howard I'd discovered had hacked my offshore accounts to exploit what could be salvaged. With this in my mind I got up closer as she roamed through her phone. And for some reason, as I got nearer, I remembered what W.S. had said about her, that her curves was like the rotation of a spoon pulling honey from a jar. Black honey: and someone like me whose wants exceeded their needs.

I wedged in close to her and tried my luck. 'I know you from somewhere,' I said, quizzically, trying at the same time to sound disengaged. At first she ignored me, like strangers do, as instinctual defence. When I tried again, she threw me a cold look, and said bluntly, 'Do you?'

'I know it's rude to approach strangers,' I tried, 'but I thought you'd understand.'

'Understand what?' she said incredulously, increasingly annoyed, went stone-cold on me, crossed her arms and pre-tended indifference. I stared off self-consciously abashed, reading in her reflex mechanisms my own strategies used to effect against propositioning strangers.

'You looking to buy sex?' she asked, coldly out of the blue.

I risked it, and moved fractionally closer to her on the public ledge, seeing in her responses the sort of intuitive char-acter assessment I would be making in her place, and if you knew the pattern it mostly worked.

'No,' I said, 'I was certain for some reason we'd met before. I mean a long time ago.'

She looked at me harder, and said, 'You sure you're interested in girls? I am.'

That threw me for a moment; then I tried it on. 'I'm Will,' I said, or you might remember me as Mr. W.H. does that mean anything to you?'

She seemed momentarily to go into an abstracted fugue, before returning to me. 'You can't be serious,' she said. 'I know that name from somewhere, but it's too far back to remember. Who are you and what do you want?'

'You.' I said. 'It's impossible to explain, but you'll understand as we go along.'

'You're weird,' she said. 'Why should I trust you? You don't even know if I'm an escort, and you're telling me we need to get together. Actually, I've got a place in Knightsbridge, but it'll cost, luv. My skin ain't cheap.'

It didn't seem real. One moment we were talking in the square and the next taxiing through densely streaming traffic, trailing a red 14 bus to Knightsbridge with the monolithic Qatar owned Harrods barracks looking like an Art Nouveau sarcophagus in reflective sunlight. Lucy didn't speak, she'd gone into professional mode, no secrets given, just cool dissociative awareness of our obvious disconnect. I knew the whole protocol so well, the switch-off and reset process of selling sex without apparent emotion, like something collected from the fridge without ownership.

Lucy's studio had a mirrored ceiling, lipstick-red painted walls, tacky gilt finish, the room dominated by a king-size bed with a maroon throw, an obligatory bottle of lubricant and tissues on a bedside table, the unlived-in, cold mechanistics of the place speaking for itself as a sex-worker's apartment.

'It's five hundred cash,' she said, 'for straight sex, or a card.' I'd done my research and had the money in ATM sharp blush-pink fifties, twice the amount in case, in a green snakeskin wallet given me by a punter. Lucy counted the cash like dealing cards and deposited it in her bag as of no consequence.

Mechanically lifting her top off, she sat in her black push-up D-cups, the straps collapsed off her shoulders and tugged off her jeans. This is what W.S. used to get, I kept thinking, as she went nude and positioned herself on the bed. And I realised I was doing this to try and experience what he had in a different time and place that was still now.

'What do you want?' she asked. 'O, A, O with O, submissive,' listing her menu. She snicked open a Durex Invisible foil, saying, 'Tthere's no bareback honey; it's a rubber, only. It's thirty minutes; you pay double if you want to extend, right.'

As I began uncharacteristically fucking Lucy Negro, Black Luce, Diamond Lucy, if this really was her imported from the future, I was trying to imagine how it felt for W.S., was it better than me, and if the sensation I was feeling, the intense pre-glow tingle of friction building to a light bulb moment that was always shattering. Lucy had her legs folded round my back, as I grew more persistently urgent in my focus. And all the time I could see flashback flicks of W.S. with her, glowering for the cash bargained reward and totally removed by his own separation from the act. And as I neared orgasm I could see clearly through a focused space-time into what I recognised as 1590ish—W.S.'s brown topcoat and leather knee boots were tangled on the floor, his hat crumpled under his right knee being used for positional leverage, the two of them looped together like a twisty mandala. It was like we'd exchanged identities in a time reversal, this snapshot of a timeframe that had resisted oxidisation and was recreated in my conscious now, luminous as halogen. It was like he was the dominant I could never remove from my thoughts, the rogue warden who'd hijacked my identity. I came in a big coronal flash of energies, rolled off Lucy and faced the mutant image of W.S., standing there like a halo viewing the crumpled disorder of the bed.

8

QUANTUM STIR FRY

I'm sitting with Howard drinking on Soho's Broadwick Street, a whisky cocktail of blended Jim Beam and Laphroaig with Earl Grey and floral orange to accent the smoky mix. We're in a drinks lab—and the shots smoulder rather than burn in their pathway to the gut. I keep behind Howard's momentum knowing if I got drunk he'd exploit my vulnerability with his predatory trader instinct as a type who redeems my sort. He forgets of course it's the punter who shops and blames rent for being available at a price.

What would he say if I told him my real name, my historic identity as the most speculatively famous rent boy in history, the subject of futile scholarly decoding of numbers, the excavation of mismatched names, thesis espionage, like looking for someone who may never have existed. He'd call me delusional, psychotic, and ready for another stay at the Priory's sweetshop. He's like all those banker-cyclists slumming it on hipster bikes to mask their plutocratic impulse to roll society.

Howard's on about a lunch he had with the chief executive of Bellevue Cloud about opening four new data facilities outside China, namely in Dubai, Germany, Japan and Australia. Beijing's strategic emphasis on building homegrown cloud technology and its stringent licensing restrictions meant the unit had flourished domestically and was now expanding with a 1bn infrastructure investment which was where Howard's analysis came in, and my hearing it all as a serious breach of confidentiality.

Howard drank like most financiers to try and get real and invariably only grew more scrambled around his fractured identity. He tried out personalities searching for the right morphic resonance to qualify creativity, and grew more progressively confused in his search for an imaginary identity. In his recreationally deconstructed Paul Smith he soaked up the atmosphere of what money could buy and liquefy—expensive booze. When I went off to the toilet he looked transparently insecure, as though I was going to pick up and disappear. I pushed a black door open on an anodyne marble unit smelling of blue deodorant cubes, and Kit was facing me back to the wall in his green reflective Ray-Bans. 'You can't get out now,' he said. 'My phone's sealed the door—instant biometrics.'

I came off the shock of it, and out of nowhere, said, 'those Ray-Bans, is it because you were stabbed through the eye? Is that why you never take them off? Who are you?' Kit lowered the green lens framing his right eye and I caught a brief flash of the eye reputedly punctured and slit open by Ingram Frizer. I could see clearly his eyes were mismatched, in the way that David Bowie's aniscoria was characterised by a left pupil that was permanently dilated, and in Kit's case clearly the right, as genetic deposit.

Kit popped the buttons on his jeans and told me to go down on him, and it was over within minutes, his excitement peaking prematurely, the fade in his look appearing like the exhaustion of centuries eating into his nervous system. It was all over so fast it appeared never to have happened, as I exited back to Howard, who was looking pickily at the menu.

'You were gone a bit,' he said quizzically, 'everything all right? I fancy the butter-garnished brisket buns with pickled red chillies and punchy ketchup,' he went on; 'I've had them before. The meat's succulently macho and even comes served in butchers' paper. I know it's not you.'

I suppressed my dietary revulsion, reasoning that most men in the financial infrastructure adopted a blood diet. It was part of the systemised belief in standard masculinity and feral protein.

'Would you like a week in Dubai?' Howard asked. 'I've got important business there and I'm sure we could find some interesting nightlife.'

'Not for me,' I said. 'I'm too attached to London as the basis for the book I'm writing. But thank you all the same.'

'Thought you'd say that,' he said, 'you're always writing and never show me a line. I suppose that's because I'm in it.'

'I'll show you when it's finished,' I lied, knowing I'd leave him before that, and that my subjective overview on our relationship wouldn't match with his. I knew intuitively he wouldn't believe a word of the schematic, not only his own involvement in my life, but the fact I was an authentic drop-in from the future reliving aspects of my past. Anyhow, I knew the fact I'd used him as a real character in the novel would infuriate, and that I'd unsparingly stitched him up as unethical space-boy on the dealing floor, and that he'd never forgive me. That was part of the thrill of writing it—the destabilising danger.

'You really should show me something, one day,' he continued. 'I mean, I tell you what I can about my work, at least the more shareable aspects of finance. You're so secretive with your book it's unnerving.'

And of course I was; the book was my blood in the way of fuel being a car. The two couldn't be separated, and I didn't know which was which, and certainly Howard couldn't help in deciding the differential.

And you, whoever you are reading this, do you think I'm mad, delusional with multiple personality disorders?—I'm asking you this, and not Howard, jammed into a bun doused with pickled chillis and crunching numbers as gastronomy. My singular claim on the sonnits and the fact I own the original manuscript isn't conclusive evidence of me being the illimitably elusive Mr. W.H. car-chased across the centuries by historic analysts. If they met me they'd be thrown by my looks and my readily offensive attitude, sitting on a ledge back of St. Martin's Lane Hotel, writing this organically before the rain comes on in streaky monochrome.

Howard chews and orders more drinks, always two, so that he can drink mine for me. Inveterately non-scene, he chooses Soho as his recreational hub because it's not exclusively gay, and the crossover with celebrity and digital media doesn't single him out as being identified by his sexuality. That's life. There's a couple sitting next to us talking Russian, she's platinum, high-sculpted cheekbones, jade eyes and a black leather mini that's slunk to her crotch under the table. He's vodka-shot-cold, cropped silverish grizzle, ruthlessly focused on some laundered incentive, his indomitable macho in denial of the statistical blonde he's facing. They visibly don't complement each other—his facial forensics allows no compromise for her exploitative femininity. She knows it, and her revenge is to float her eyes at whoever makes random contact, as though she's really available for options. They both look like they belong to the rich stateless nomads who own ghost properties in London without belonging to the capital's cultural infrastructure, but more to a dentist tourism pursued in unmarked armour-plated BMWs.

Howard's too concentrated into mastication of his stacked bun to notice their stand-out features; her looks radiating like the three-dimensional effects of a diamond, and his cold emotional lock-in. They're a temporary distraction to my core worry of the impossibility of W.S. living as silent occupant on our floor, like an off-world time-traveller not fully realised as human. And come to think of it, I've never heard domestic noises of any kind issuing from his apartment. He's to my mind like the spy in the bag, questionably counterintelligence, a sharpened operative living on the edges of reality. One thought leads inevitably to another and I speculate on the black spine of London's geography, and if the city isn't somehow the beginning and the end time as an attractor to importing apocalypse, and how Kit and W.S. are in some way inextricably linked to its final destiny. I've heard it often enough over the years, the insanity stored in its underground passages as the amplified bass of unimaginable deep future. It's what the homeless sometimes hear with their ear to the pavement—a periodic roar like the hydrogen burn of a rocket launch rumbling the stratosphere. It's in the ionised detergent smell of London, its ozone and altered carbon, its remorseless archetypal indifference to every human atrocity.

I watch Howard sopping up intense gastro juices while I'm imagining quantum eschatology—the universal brain gone into collapsed entropy, black holes evaporating, the big crunch in which the sun diminishes to the size of a red traffic light before going out conclusively. And to me it's London's concrete brain that will majorly initialise the inexorable destruction of traces of human presence, our only identifiable signature perhaps being the chemical remnant of our pollution.

Howard finishes up pre-dessert. He's having he informs me a cheese cake flavoured with Turkish Delight to finish, the floral ingredients he reads off unembarrassed by their cheesy antecedents.

'You look a bit concerned,' he says to me, 'anything wrong?'

'I was thinking,' I say, 'about our neighbour, I mean the one who's never there. What do you think he does for a living?'

'You mean the tall guy with thinning hair, always dressed in black, who looks a bit like a snoop? Our invisible occupant, as you call him. Are you planning to be his twink? You might be out of luck, I sometimes see him with a black girl, quite clearly an escort. A bit classy though.'

'Has nobody ever mentioned him to you, I mean spread a rumour?'

'Why are you so curious?' Howard asked, spooning. 'There's probably fifteen million people in London you'll never know, so why him?'

'But you know something,' I said, 'that's why you won't tell me.'

'All right,' Howard said, picking at the syrupy overlap of his dessert. 'Look, if you really want to know, and don't quote me on it, I've heard he's part of Bletchley Park, as top cyber security. Bletchley, if you don't know, was home to Britain's expert code breakers in WW2.'

'How do you know that?' I asked, suspicious of whatever osmosis he'd performed on the man I was convinced was my antagonist, W.S.

'Because he told me himself,' Howard said, defensively, as though wanting closure.

'Why, and when?' I asked, trying as best I could to suppress curiosity.

Howard looked up from his dessert, and it was somebody I didn't know framed in his expression, and perhaps the real Howard who I didn't really allow to show very often but who was always there. I could see the red bits in his corneas, like a snail's foot collects grit, and had that creepy feeling he was unknowably separated simply by the alienation of being human. I mean, language was all I had to open gateways into the organic fluids in which he lived.

'So you do see him sometimes?' I asked, not pressing it, but firm.

'He's a client,' Howard said, 'so I've sort of got to know things about him. In fact, I took him to lunch last month, to the Ivy.'

I could feel the plot thicken like detritus in my blood, knowing that even if I could download my consciousness onto my phone and spend a year reviewing it, I'd never unravel the physics of why I felt myself to be at the core of a historic black hole steeped in radiation.

'Client profiles are confidential,' Howard said, 'but I can tell you he's rich. If writing ever earns for you what it does for him, you'll be very lucky.'

'What does he write?' I asked, my interest concealed in my apparently disinterested tone.

'I'm not sure,' Howard said, again flipping facial recognition, as though I'd taken his looks for granted for so long as a misconception I'd forgotten how he really looked in close up. 'He's got a lot of money tied up in theatre, but that's probably a front for laundering or intelligence operations. Fake identity is all part of the exploitation of commercial entities, you see it all the time in my job.'

'Go on,' I said, winning a smile from an adjoining table.

'Anyhow, that's all I know really,' Howard said, 'other than that he's away most of the time, and not anywhere exciting. For some reason he's got a house in Warwickshire and hangs out there from time to time.'

I looked away into a gateway of personal history that seemed to exist further than the black replicable wall-to-wall galaxies and their ultimate ends in cold cosmic indifference. Time was infected, that much I knew, not only by bioterrorism and the index of manufactured airborne viruses, but our insoluble memory traces coded into its loop.

Howard fusses over ordering a speciality cocktail called Penicillin—a smoky lab infused tequila, peat smoke, lime and ginger, he informs me, like reading out the contraindications of a drug. He settles for his blended medicine, as though he needs this final build of toxins to liberate him into a more conducive reality.

'Do you think he's a fantasist?' I ask, still resolved on the irrational certainty that Shakespeare was back in my life for some reason and on my tail.

'Who knows,' Howard said, 'but we'll investigate him for possible fraud. We do an international search on all potential clients.'

'There's something about him,' I said, 'that seems paranormal, if you know what I mean, spooky in the way of being in the wrong time, like he doesn't belong to the present, and is just trying it out to see if he fits. At least that's how he seems to me, like some sort of bad adaption to human.'

'I wouldn't go that far,' Howard said. 'He's normal dodgy, we meet them all the time.'

Finished up, Howard suggested an obligatory black cab to take us back to St. James'. London to me always appeared a series of arbitrarily linked war zones from the relative safety of a power-locked taxi blasting its way with hybrid tech through the rough and the privileged, gangsta estates and the comparative wealth of status postcodes. This, too, was like another form of time-travel, crossing oxidised bridges like transitioning between life and death.

When we got outside, there was an ambush. I saw this hoodie in a white top run directly towards two guys getting into a silver Audi, and shoot the man entering the driver's door right through the head from point-blank range. The explosion was solid as death, as the man crumpled and convulsed from the direct hit. This was Soho on a Sunday afternoon, as a shocked crowd converged on the body in a noisy rush.

'Let's get out of here,' Howard said, as we retreated down a side street right into the oncoming yellow welcome light of a taxi, and threw ourselves inside.

'Looks like there's been another stabbing,' the cabbie said, segueing for space and picking off a dozy colleague at the lights. We neither of us spoke, glad of a secure mobile space that shipped us away from the murder we'd partially witnessed, but both of us totally shook up by the cold-blooded street ambush we'd witnessed.

Most London councils kept street lighting down so low the city seemed in many postcodes to have reverted to fifties lighting with a dull pineapple glow. I imagined fifties Soho would have been like this as we slalomed down Greek Street as a cut-through to Shaftesbury Avenue.

Howard wasn't talking his way out of shock, but sat collapsed back into his seat. London was London, you left one crisis zone for another, and it was like exchanging countries, the demographic was so different. We got back to the comparative safety of St. James' with its obtrusive cameras, biometrics and video surveillance protecting implacable mansion blocks. It was a sort of gold film of money hung over the quarter, gold particles like you get in an injection for prohibitive arthritic pain, only dusted into a cloud.

We got inside and went up in the mirrored lift, and arriving at our floor, I immediately noticed the door to W.S.' apartment was open, and that the desk security officer who I knew as Jim, was coming out of the flat and securely locking the door.

Howard threw a quizzical look, clearly alarmed, and said, 'I hope there hasn't been a robbery next door. That's the last thing we need.'

Hoping the problem was just maintenance I was still more worried than I cared to show. Anything to do with W.S. was the stuff of my metaphysical pit; the ontological insecurity by which I lived. When we got inside and Howard slumped on the sofa, I checked the end-to-end encryption phone I'd received from Kit. There was a coded text that I opened. I read RHM Z CT. I knew the interpretation. Richard Henry Maunder murdered Canning Town. For some reason I immediately associated the security breach next door with W.S., as though the two incidents were in some way related, and that the man I conceived of as my adversary was in some way linked to the murder of this notorious undercover creep, who I suspected was directly implicated in Kit's murder on that muddy foggy day at Deptford Creek, when an eye as big as the sun had gone out.

In the living room Howard was at last de-tied and jacketless, measuring the ratio of his digestion against the spiralling restaurant bill with evident satisfaction. Z in Kit's code meant liquid or taken out, and I could feel no least squeeze of sympathy for the insidiously menacing Maunder and my last scrape with him on a visit to Canning town. Maunder was so hidden from himself, I doubted any amount of peeling back the layers of identity would reveal the man, and anyhow with secret service involved there could be no trial or inquest. The body would be vacuumed and rained into the Thames like incinerated piss. Life was cheap in the capital where knifing was commonplace as a takeaway.

Howard sat boozily scrolling his inbox for emails that popped in 24/7 with global time differentiation, having poured himself a fat Bombay Sapphire with the glow of tonic. Marketing and gin nurtured each other in his world, the bubbles of one molecularly colliding with the other. I could see he was still shaken a bit by the reality of randomised street murder, while I'd bounced off that into a darker espionage killing, involving doubtless GCHQ intelligence at the prompting of MI6. What I feared was I too was on someone's hit list, tracked by my phone or physically watched by someone pretending to be someone else, and too normal to be observed: the man on the opposite yellow scaffolding, the driver parked up stationary in a black Addison Lee executive Mercedes Benz.

Howard was still rumbling about money markets, wanting me to listen before his brain went out like tripping a fuse.

'People think we're in exodus,' he said, 'but just look at the skyline. There's the 73-storey Trellis at 1 Undershaft, the £1 billion tower at 22 Bishopsgate, that's 59 storeys high. What else? The Scalpel, the Cheesegrater and all of Canary Wharf as blue sky thinking. We're in the process of consolidating fifty new towers, not dispersing, honey. Just look at the location of all the new skyscrapers near the Bank of England, not in some fucking East End fringe area. That's no accident. The real core of the action is near to One Lombard Street, the Coq D'Argent and crucially the City.'

I listened to him going down his own throat. 'You know, any big foreign institution would rather the Bank and the Prudential Regulation Authority handled the risk policy they won't. At the high end, for fuck's sake, financial services are a people business. Where you keep an office is up to you, but most prefer to be up in the London sky. That's where it all happens, off-world.'

Howard hadn't crashed yet, he was still radio noisy and his brain thudded. 'We're still sexy,' he said. 'Just look at the construction work being laid for the future, eventually we'll have towers on the moon. We're not baling out...'

I watched him hit a pocket of couch sleep; it was a predictable pattern, with partial attempts to awake, before a slurry exit to bed and dead sleep until the alarm. I checked my phone, but there was nothing back from Kit. The building appeared silent in the way you get the feeling you're on long haul in the middle of London in a mansion block. There was no sound of further action in W.S.' apartment, and again I obsessed over the fear the whole thing was of my own making, a paranoid bubble that had more to do with my own alarmingly anomalous identity than anything else. I was by my very existence a spy from the future trying to write a book that would help liberate me from my past. Howard had flaked now, and the capital maintained its white noise cone like a psychotic algorithm producing outcomes that its programmes could never have predicted.

I started writing again as a means of evaluating the latent terror I felt over W.S.' renewed existence in my life, like an irrepressible time-traveller who kept navigating psychic highways back. I resisted drinking more, as a seriously wasted Howard dragged himself off the couch in a trancy daze and made for the bedroom and tomorrow, when he'd shower and adroitly redress for work c/o Turnbull & Asser and Paul Smith from a 30-suit plus bespoke wardrobe. Howard was simply a convenience to me, until I found Mister Right, that elusively inaccessible illusion who if he showed up was always on the other side of the track. I'd seen him once under the street at Piccadilly, foggy grey eyes, blond hair in a retro fifties pile-up, sage green tweed jacket cut for a 28-inch killer waist, designer aura, gone with a smile posted backwards running for a tube, like I'd seen Bowie at 30, and lost him. It was that absolute, that final. And sometimes, hoping by some sort of magical time reversal to retrieve him, I'd return to the exact spot where I'd seen him, and wait there for a rerun to happen. And I realised so much of life was like that, living with things that had happened rather than those still to come. If philosophy's actual fuck, except for Plato; then I get in on intuitive surges. If you're able mentally to take someone apart in thirty seconds on the street, when picking up, as an investigative snapshot, then you're capable of doing most anything.

I sat there listening to the capital's unstoppable organism, suddenly alerted to a coded text. I puzzled at the cryptic contents then got it. W.S./L.N. + D.M. 19/9 11 a.m. 144. From that I inferred that W.S. and Lucy Negro were now aware of each other, and that I should be at Devonshire Mews tomorrow at 11 a.m. The 144 I took to be a reference to sonnit 144, as the distillation of W.S.' bisexuality—'The better angel is a man right fair/The worser spirit a woman coloured ill.'

On impulse, and with Howard now crashed, I decided to go over to Knightsbridge and hopefully confront Lucy about W.S.' whereabouts. I wanted to know how advanced he was in his strategy to take out Kit, presumably me, and Lucy. I decided to walk the short distance over, the lit up shells of department stores bulked there like urban cenotaphs at the end of time. This much I knew, they'd all rotted into history—Southampton, Burghley, Walsingham, Johnson, Chapman, Kyd, Bacon, queer and straight detritus downsized into ash or bone, and no longer identifiable in the bleed into temporal oblivion. They'd gone like all the rent boys I knew at Piccadilly Circus, monetising their skinny drugged bodies with flat-eyed punters come out of the crowd dripping in red neons.

A fuzzy drizzle hung in arcs over Mayfair, loopy yellow smudges smeared on the atmosphere and Park Lane was a racetrack of determined thundering taxis. (To me, interrupted narrative here, it's the descriptive drives narrative in the way colour does film, rather than artificial plot as infrastructure, haven't I told you this before, the death of mainstream fiction manufactured like Korean cars).

Harrods was lit up like a Star-trek movie-set, window-shoppers thumbing their faces on to eye-candy, as though encountering the last rites in commodities before the big crash. There were the usual female and male prostitutes hanging outside on the taxi rank, hoping to pick up black gold or a late night sex tourist accidentally happening by. Both looked interesting, a middle-eastern girl in killer heels and a leather Joanna skirt and a boy with a greased down retro look, leather zippered jacket, chinos and cool loafers. I threw looks at both of them and took a corner to Lucy's block where prostitutes shelled out £1K a week for a squeezed studio facility.

I didn't really know what I wanted of Lucy, other than that I had to see her, but arrived I was starting to lose my fired-up impetus, and walked down the street debating whether to go on or turn back. I felt I'd lost my peak to strip her of facts, and hung around feeling self-conscious, as though passersby were somehow aware of my dilemma.

I walked past her block three times, the unnamed sticker on her video door entry system remembered as 3 from my one time there, and kept on delaying depressing the buzzer. I moved a few doors up and instinctively startled as a man came hurriedly out of her block, that I immediately took for W.S., characteristically dressed in black, and take off fast, bringing a taxi down almost immediately and folding into its interior. Although we'd made no immediate eye contact I sensed he'd picked up on me peripherally, as I had on him. It was like some sort of parallel-processing, he most probably returning to the building I'd just left, and me on the way up to see the woman he'd most likely just fucked. I waited at least five minutes so that Lucy wouldn't think it was her last client returned, fingered her buzzer and waited for her voice to pop on the video-entry. There was a hesitation before she familiarised herself with my voice, saying, 'it's the third floor, come up, luv,' unsealing the door to admit me into a chequered hall. Although she had me on camera she unlocked the door tentatively, and was still in her bra and panties, with a large royal blue bruise under her left eye that made her appear unfocused, one eye on me, the other looking like a blue poached egg cooked in gel.

'The fucker hit me,' she said, pointing to her inflammatory bruise, 'landed one on me. He's mad, said he was beating me for something I'd done in the past. The only reason I let you in was in case he comes back.'

Lucy sat down pressing an icepack to her pulped eye, and I could see the tears rolling down her face, big liquid drops that tumbled on to her chin and off. She was shaking and too angry to attempt to comfort. 'He's fucking mean and evil, he wants things for which he won't pay. Tells me each time he comes here I should recognise him from another life, or some such rubbish, and beats me because I can't. '

I suppressed the impulse to say, 'he's my neighbour,' and poured Lucy a drink from a sticky bottle of sambuca that stood on the bedside table.

'Now I can't work with this eye,' she said, 'this is going to cost me the rent. I didn't have a maid tonight, and anyhow you can't stop someone smacking you.'

'What made him do it?' I asked, feeling I shouldn't be here, and yet compelled to stay as part of my own questionable involvement in a plot stretched across time like the underground network built into the city and linking arbitrary destinations. And all the time it was growing stronger in me this sense of a pathway to an alternative state existing behind all of material reality and somehow inescapably a part too of London's oxidative history sunk into track.

'It's not the first time,' Lucy said, reapplying her icepack. 'He's been here before, says he's married but wants me to move in with his wife, for fuck's sake. He wants A, and when I refuse, he slaps me. He's crazy. He says we've both got too much on each other from our earlier involvement. I don't know what he means. You told me something similar when you picked me up in Leicester Square, like I should know you from another time?'

Lucy looked me over with hostile body language, like she suspected I was somehow in on this scam. My offer to take her to A&E was rejected outright, as she settled to a second drink. I sat there unobtrusively and listened her out. 'He's gay,' she said, 'like you. His only way into women is like men. I meet it all the time in my game. It's you he's looking for and he turns on me.'

'What do you mean?' I asked. 'You told me, didn't you, you were Will or W.H., and that's who he goes on about all the time he's here. It's all on video, there's cameras in this room, but for obvious reasons I don't want the police involved, do I?'

I looked at the Mayfair sordidness of it all, the violent tack of a prostitute being assaulted in a high-end block back of Harrods, the commonality of Britain's most acknowledged playwright mashing her eye to blackcurrant jelly, and me sitting there helplessly alienated, trying to fit the bits of Lego together that won't. Try as I so often do in the re-assemblage, there's always something missing in the pattern; the package won't come right, and the answer's perhaps somewhere in the sonnits I can't locate, or maybe don't want to find.'

'Look Lucy,' I said, 'I've got nothing to do with this assault, only that to me it's like we're all pulled into a world where it's Sunday, when it's Friday in the real. This is hard to understand, but we're possibly sort of remakes from a period of time when we all knew each other. And some of us like myself, are more conscious of it than others.'

Lucy studied her glass, her red talons running its sides. 'God it hurts,' she said, readdressing her eye, 'the bastard, he'll pay for this, you see.'

'Try and remember what he really came here for, and what he told you, it wasn't just sex. It's important. If he isn't stopped, he could turn serial. He's someone come in through the back door of time.'

'What do you mean?' Lucy asked, stopping still in her thoughts, as though in an act of retrieval.

'There's a group of people in this city, and let's say we're all historically connected through things we've dragged forward with us that should have been settled long ago, and I'm afraid you're part of this. It's hard to believe but we're in a way leftovers or returnees from Shakespeare's period and the huge influence he's asserted. I don't know why, anymore than you.'

Lucy who'd stopped shaking and covered up, looked like she was reflectively sorting. I wondered too if something in her was unaccountably attracted to this man who beat her up, as though pain was a perverse way of deepening the bond by bringing him so fully into awareness,

'He's been here quite often,' she said. 'Sometimes he just wants to sit and talk about things I don't really get, like the properties he owns, and his own plays he says he goes and sees. He keeps wanting to take me to the theatre, but I'd lose earnings.'

She sat there looking confused and broken, kneading her eye and inwardly reliving whatever violence had happened in this room—'a great reckoning in a little room' came to my mind, like Kit had received, or so the story went.

'What plays did he want you to see?' I asked, sounding incredulous.

'Always bloody Shakespeare,' she said. 'It's of no interest to me, I'm not that sort of person. A club maybe, but not a theatre.'

'Will you be all right?' I asked, not wanting to overstay, and feeling rinsed by the electrics in the room.

'I've got some painkillers,' she said, 'and he's not likely to be back tonight. If he turns up again, I'll call the police.'

I noticed a foil of Norco pills by the bed that I knew were the killer drug Fentanyl, an opioid probably originating from labs in China, where the ingredients were legal, and then moved between multiple freight handlers so their origins are hard to trace. I'd heard there were Chinese pressing Fentanyl pills in London, thousands a day, an exact science, in which a few grams too much can kill. 'Don't take these,' I said, 'they're a hundred times stronger than heroin and you could overdose. Where did you get them?'

'I didn't know they were there,' Lucy said. 'A client must have left them, maybe they fell out of a pocket.'

'Could he have left them?' I asked. 'I mean W.S., the man who beat you up earlier. Think about that,' I said, as I pocketed the foil for safekeeping.

'Look, don't go just yet,' she said, and I could see she was frightened and wanted to talk. 'It's not as simple as I've just told you,' she said, returning to her glass and starting to relax down. I noticed her toes were painted neon red as glossed points of fascination.

'It's complicated,' Lucy said. 'I know I shouldn't, but I've got feelings for him. I both like him and hate him and right now I'd kill him if I could, but something stops me. You know what I mean?'

I was partly expecting this, the emotional ramifications of long-term attraction, as much fed by the need to hate as love, with neither emotion supplying a healthy basis to a paid relationship.

'Basically, we hate each other,' she said, 'but somehow we can't be without it, sometimes I make him slap me, provoke him like as a black bitch, but tonight he could have killed me.'

'Did you ask to get hit tonight?'

'No, she said, biting the underside of her nether lip, and looking so hard at me it was like she was smashing her way into my consciousness. 'It came out of nowhere, a mountain of anger. He just lost it and started shouting boys were better, and he'd go off and get one online. That's when your name came up, and I remembered it. He said his best sex had been with you and the thrill had travelled down the centuries.'

This was the exact news I didn't want to hear, that my apparent co-returnee from the future existed parallel to my own reconstruction now, and that we were both aware we were reliving history through some unexplained time-slip in our personal destinies. And as I was his exact neighbour, I reasoned it had to be that he didn't fully recognise me yet, but that the awareness was growing.

'He's looking for you,' Lucy said. 'I don't know how long this has been going on, or what he wants, but he's dangerous.'

'It's more to do with the fact he's unable to die,' I said; 'none of us are. He's overdosed on time, like we have, by what's it, five centuries, or something.'

'You're right,' she said, visibly scrolling through the autonomous streaming of her thought processes, before turning on me. 'We're all according to you in some weird what's it, relationship, with all these chance meet-ups, none of it makes sense.'

Lucy was starting to give in her professional mode, she was doing what I do with punters, offer a compromise that can't be taken up, but which appears to humanise the transaction, while keeping emotions off-limits.

'I wish I'd never met him,' she said. 'There's some people you just can't get rid of in life, and he's that sort of baggage. I get the feeling that even dead he'd be pursuing me, it's that sticky. What can I do, he's inside my head?'

There wasn't any answer to Lucy's desperate question in the quantum jungle. It was like W.S. could ship his brain across the galaxy, but it was more than that, and had to do with the whole complex algorithm of historically unresolved issues that couldn't be absorbed into death, but remained individuated and returned.

'There's no easy solution to this,' I said. 'What I'm hoping is that we can all come together at some stage and talk. If we're infected by time, in the sense of carrying some sort of mind virus, then we need to know. I'm not sure if any of this makes sense.'

'Some of it,' Lucy said, 'but stay just a little longer, a few minutes if you can.' She took out a vape, and I knew immediately the e-liquid was drug-based, rather than nicotine. You could buy e-liquids on the dark web loaded with synthetic cannabinoids, as well as heroin and methamphetamine. Delivery via the lungs was generally a more effectively dangerous route than most other pathways, but I couldn't tell her that now. I could smell something synthetically recreational in her discharge, and kept away.

'I mean I know about the two of you,' she said, 'as you know about me, but that's in the past, but somehow it's returned, as though we're living it all again now.' She sipped at a slowly savoured release, after keeping it way down in her lungs, and looked hammered.

Seeing her more relaxed, I got up cautiously and told her I needed to go, despite her persistent efforts to detain me. I took the precipitous stairs down and exited the building into arcs of purplish light caused by the fuzzy rain, and walked past the usual contingency of black cabs curating the block. Mostly geeked to ear-buds the drivers sat inside lit cabins like long haul pilots facing into the future as London geography in which old and new melded somehow into modular postmodern. London, I knew, was always the ideated memory of London, and never real. It was a city in which everyone inhabited a different reality encrypted into individual consciousness and essentially un-shareable. But of one thing I was increasingly sure, and that was that W.S.' heartbeat was at the black core of the metropolis, as its oxidative drive, and I would set about finding its exact physical location and if necessary meet him there, like two strangers in a whiffy tunnel after the tube shuts down.

I started to walk back across a rained-on quadrant pastiched into a mini-Manhattan, the high-end girl escorts still hanging outside Harrods as a monumental consumer sarcophagus offering the fake sex I too administered to losers, all those rushed, lubricated fantasies ending in a condom teat like a space helmet. The rain was starting to push people in, and I shoved my hands in my jeans pockets and felt consoled by the thickening rinse. Rain was lyrical; it drew atomised Chinese characters on the air and altered my mood by its hissy ambience. Wanna sing the blues, then walk through the streaming rain deep in a city or across a field with the night coming down like a luminous river. It's something like poetry, the sort that ends up in anthologies that don't really do edge, but more conciliatory comfort. I walked on in the drench, and sometimes just that's a sufficient reason to live, the luxurious rhythm of walking that throws up ideas and momentum in the process. After Lucy, it was the simplicity I needed, this feel-good easy lick all the way back through shimmying deserted streets, back home to Charles Street, St. James.'

9

STICKY FINGERS

Howard's at it again, I mean the infrastructure of financial software. There's a Singapore trader in his company who refuses to surrender stolen software worth tens of millions of algorithmic codes used to trade the market. As a quantitative analyst writing trading strategies for financial institutions including Goldman Sachs, the creep's a biomaths threat to the city. They're looking to unlawfully scan his brain signals by a process of neuroimaging to access the codes stored in his synaptic memory. It doesn't take much logic to perceive that given the chance Howard might well do the same and scoot to the Cayman Islands with his pirated data. He's wearing a black and white candy-striped Ralph Lauren button-down under a charcoal fleck blazer, about as smartly casual as they allow admin, and he knows it.

According to Howard's material enzymes, the Bermudan insurance giant Axis Capital has taken up residence on levels two and three at 52 Lime Street, otherwise known as The Scalpel, an angular commercial skyscraper with 37,564 square metres of office floor on 38 storeys, built for the insurance company W.R. Berkley. To Howard numbers are simply crunched data, the £500m construction has already earned, in that the future is always the investment destination, and never the present. He's got a friend who is part of the design team for Kohn Penderson Fox, and like Howard a palate for barrel-aged East London gin, and the other juniper goodies like Stepsmith, Half Hitch and Portobello Road. Howard picks his brands from Mayfair's Hedonism or gets slipped them by clients for greased favours.

I've got my book and a questionable morality that arguably contests his dodgy business ethic for lapsed propriety. Ultimately, nobody cares in his game, unless the fraud commands media attention, or gets personal with friends. I write in interrupted surges, the way of all big city writing, and wish everything could be condensed into one unforgettable book like Elizabeth Smart's By Grand Central Station I Sat Down And Wept, as an epic storm of lyrically insightful emotion that continues to grow in time, and to be stretched into each new generation's awareness of what it means now. Instead, I drive on in the urban shattering of splintered consciousness, doing what I can to link the bits I've got. Books now are like the carbon smog hung over the city, a contaminant residue no one really wants to address. Nobody attempts to read the global piles stacked into book-mountains as tall and severe as the Himalayas. Once you start on the foot-slopes you give up from boredom and exhaustive effort in trying to find the good from the bad. Howard, like most brainers doesn't see their purpose, he says life itself is a story and we don't need to invent alternatives, as the plot changes all the time in everyday life.

I keep my book secret from him; in fact, I mostly leave the handwritten text with a friend who lives in the new apartment block on Bedfordbury, back of the cut-through, Hop Gardens, where I write. I buy my notebooks at Paperchase and work it along from there, A4-size Wiro Kraft and a green Pentel sign pen. These are my tools for an imaginative travelogue, but one that is also crucially real, a pursuit in charged language as sensual as cannabis-sensitised footsie.

I leave Howard's breakfast imperatives, the berried gel storeyed on his toast, the coffee black as car grease, and go off to my West End hub soaked in toxic fumes, diesel emissions, including tiny PM2.5 particulates that damage the immune system, as part of an unchecked smoking gun to the respiratory health of Londoners. But naturally, the thrill of it is that my book and the events it relates, run concurrently, so that one forces the issue of the other as a process of entanglement. And you know it before I tell you I buy a falafel and hummus wrap at Eat on St. Martin's Lane as part of the muscle of my work. In an hour's time I'll meet Kit in the Lemon Tree at the foot of Bedfordbury, that's as off world as you can get in this grid of pelting, hostile foot traffic.

Anyhow, I don't care for literature, anymore than W.S. or Kit ever did; they were too busy writing to ever bother about its classification. You're only free to create if you don't acknowledge maps: hitch yourself to the past and you drag a burnt-out shell of a tank with you salvaged from the ruins of Aleppo.

There's terrorist bombs taking out part of the city, big dentistry gaps in commuter track and in the right places, the ministerial warrens of Whitehall and Westminster, right in the meaty gut of the acquisitive quango. The cells responsible were the more dangerous for not being affiliated to any of the radicalised religio-political factions known to anti-terrorist police, but striking at random across the bashed capital like robo-bombers. And at Bank, explosive experts had dismantled a white bot packed with sufficient homemade explosives to blow the station apart. And for Howard even the tube has its own rich map—the Bakerloo line having the highest average annual turnover and growth rate, with the Jubilee line in second place, followed by the Victoria and Central lines, as a sort of financial vectoring, with him monitoring companies with a reported annual turnover in excess of £5m, and a registered trading address in central London.

As an extension of this book I've started rewriting W.S.' Sonnits, fucking them into a reinvented update, my own London geography mapped on my own preferred compass, but keeping the triangulated focus of the original, and doing it recreationally as a form of revenge for being so brutally exposed in the often sterile originals. Think of all the people who have read about Lucy and I over the centuries, passively dominated by W.S.' irrefutable terms, and with no voice of our own to correct the story or brand it lies. So this little game is my way of redressing the issue, getting my own back on his self-interested use of me as subject. I've been re-imagined as a sexual object by everyone inquisitive. I mean, was I blond, chinchilla, jet black, brick-red—he was so self-consumed he never even mentioned my hair colour, or if my eyes were blue, grey, green, brown, two-tone, or whatever. Nobody ever re-marks on W.S.' lack of perceived detail, and how his focus in the sonnits is nearly always inward to psychological character-istics and observed personality. Where is the aesthetic of my look in the sonnits, how do you imagine my figure, my cock, when you come out of reading them? I'm just an abstract, a romantic ideal on which to project his fears of age, loss and death. The reader lacks the knowledge that if he was sexually motivated, I wasn't. I squeezed him for cash and got caught up in the undercurrent of a relationship I'd never invited. Sex with him was like a ferry commute from Greenwich, interpret that in your own salacious way.

There's a Polish girl from a café I use, sitting next to me on the ledge, who keeps throwing eyes at my handwriting, green eyes like jades, and I'm sort of self-consciously protective of what I'm writing, and when she asks me what it is, I say, as I always do, 'oh it's sort of time-travel,' and that describing the contents would be like trying to reconstruct the wrap I've just eaten. She tells me she's Anya from Krakow, and her voice goes unexpectedly downstairs with sadness, and up again when she tells me she's in a girl band called Venom who do garage because Lou Reed changed her mind over, whatever that means. She thinks it weird I write by hand—it's a bit like unravelling miles of DNA each day, and wants to know if she can find any of my books at a store; and I have to disappoint her by telling her this is my first attempt, and that I have no agent, and may end up torching my efforts. 'It could be a movie,' she says, as though that's the singular objective in writing, and I say, 'Stranger things have happened,' and look away with disinterest. She wants to swap numbers, and we do, and goes off phone in hand like a backup brain, navigating her own private pathway into a city that's always consecutively generational. At thirty you're in the present, at forty you're in the past, with no omissions.

I immerse myself in writing before the secret meet at the Lemon Tree, knowing that Kit will arrive Ray-Bans incognito, as though he's a year out of time with you and his brain perhaps not even his own property. Hop Gardens leaks social inequality, a huddle of homeless drinkers sat on the wall with bulky holdalls at their feet, and the ubiquitous hotel workers on cigarette breaks, the whole conduit informed by an overlap of cultures on the edges of society. I hang there because of the dichotomy, the raw mix of those stuck somewhere they can't shift and probably won't ever. And if you went under this alley through chalk and clay, the lesion would reveal a subterranea circa 1500, blackness, rats, ammoniac stench; a coagulated artery into the underworld. The layered centuries above don't alter the raw rudimentary fundamentals below in the sink.

When the rain comes on I disappear round the corner into the Lemon Tree, intimate but roomy, and the sort of reticent milieu who won't pick up on us. I go into the bar and it's off-peak with a few guys roaming their phones and settle for a glass of house white. Kit arrives almost simultaneously, Ray-Bans, black blazer, washed jeans, casual that's right without noticeable effort. He's closed off as usual, his preoccupations masked by the equivalent of 32 layers of car lacquer, if you tried to get to them. It's always like his genes are old film stock digitised into upgrade, and resistant, like he'll live another hundred years, and you won't notice the difference.

We sat upstairs in the room overlooking the street, the rainy sunshine giving the glow of reflective orange spex. 'How's your neighbour?' Kit asked, disinterested, because he already had the story. 'He's beaten up Lucy, I'm told, and as you were there that night, you'll know.'

He'd got me again, by telling me what I was intending to tell him. 'I don't know,' I said, 'I haven't seen him, ever since I saw a security guard coming out of his apartment. That got me worried, because I still don't know why the man went in there. What if there are bodies in the fridge?'

'He's not into cannibalism,' Kit said, 'bathtub feed. There was this guy ate someone at Vauxhall last year, over a period of three weeks. Person he ate was a member of MI6, so he couldn't arrest him. His filleted skeleton was found in the bath. It takes all types.'

'You would have made a play of that at one time,' I said, not telling him I was writing him up but assuming he knew because he was probably inside my brain like a camera watching me write. Brain hacking was undoubtedly one of his paranormal facilities, and for some reason I had this unnerving sense he could see the molecular construction of atoms in my cells, and if necessary, take them apart.

'There's to be a meeting,' Kit said, peremptorily. 'The three of us: place and time have still to be decided.' He fizzed a zipper of bubbles in his Kendrick's . 'There's no danger; I have him covered. What we don't know yet is his particular specifics of humanity, how much of W.S.' memory capacity is still classified, and how much loosened into an awareness of his true identity. I get the feeling, and it's only that, he's retrieved most of his historic memory.'

I listened to dampened city noise, and tried to believe all this was really happening—the insertion of the unmediated past into the present—and the unshakeable feeling that it all had to do with end time and that London was the capital designated to roll in whatever form it took, into the giant red nuclear sun.

'By the way, I've moved out of the Mews,' Kit said. 'I'll code you the new address. I made a mistake with the boy you met. I can't afford that—a habit isn't part of my job.'

He looked somewhere, not out of the window, but at some phylum of thought taking shape in his mind. Two Indian girls, quite clearly work colleagues by their engaged gossipy rapport, came into the room, and the conversational hit was office politics, as the glue that stuck them together in a science of pulling rivals apart. I was relieved they seemed to take as little notice of us as we of them.

'I can't tell you yet why W.S. is so dangerous,' Kit said. 'It would scare you out; but it will become apparent. You're safe for now. More than that I can't promise.'

'The other day,' I said, re-routing, 'I went to an exhibition called Preserved Memories. The photographer had shot rural landscape that reminded him of growing up, and using double-exposure without digital manipulation, had fitted the locations into sealed jars, as kind of unageing snapshots. I feel like we're all stuck in similar memory jars. You, me, W.S., Lucy, and whoever else is still around, like the trio at Eleanor Bull's.'

'Frizer, Poley, Skeres,' Kit said, like a mantra, as though dissolving five centuries on his tongue in an instantaneous flashback. 'Yes, they're around too, like dirt under the fingernails, psychic gunk. We're all returnees, who can't properly live, because we never really died.'

Again, I felt the acute loneliness of the time-traveller stretched across an inexorable slip. Howard was a superfluous fact on this journey, another stop-off point on a future that was already complete. So too were the faceless millions out there in the city, their alienated lives downsized by the daily commute. Kit's forensic personality didn't help either, despite its venous networks having channelled poetry that once had the muscle of giants. I could hear the strangulated wail of horns in traffic locked on the Strand, a metallic freeze of irascible energies wanting to shift.

Kit was totally focused on reading a message with a studied concentration that excluded me entirely. I knew intuitively he'd up and go soon, disappearing into the back of the city on a trace evanescent as a thought. His blond hair framing his good looks appeared naturally windswept, as though effortlessly created without his care. On the contrary, I was the pretty boy who self-consciously worked at it, skincare, hair care: the whole preoccupying obsession with self-appearance as expensively maintained eye-candy.

Kit had gone deeper into decoding text, like he'd got ahead of humans into the next move. Watching him I was flipped back into my past and into the adventurism of having done it all in surrendering to a stranger for a lucrative reward. I'd cherry picked them off the concourse at Piccadilly Circus underground, had husbands want to leave their wives for me, remained unbuyably elusive, as the one needed all the more for never having been owned. I was the sonnits kid, the one people wrote poems about on bathroom mirrors and I couldn't care.

Kit looked up at me like I'd been away, still streaming raw data internally and said, 'I'm onto something and it's got to do with our man, W.S. He momentarily looked into his phone mirror, made a tiny hair revision, and said, 'I'll be in touch.' Then he was gone, as though he was never really there and I was talking to a copy. I stayed on, finished my drink, and was immediately aware of a guy with black punk jeans out at the knee who sat down opposite. I looked him over searchingly, with a strange feeling we'd met before, but in my life I'd seen and been seen by so many strangers that I live with the apprehension all the time that I'm known for what I do. He'd got black hair cropped short and looked introspectively dubious, as though scheming something that wasn't yet resolved or sorted. Casually dressed in jeans and a charcoal jumper, he sipped at his beer cuff, and for some reason I grew curious without knowing why. My interest was heightened by the fact he'd placed a marked paperback copy of William Gibson's Spook Country, next to his glass, one of my favourite futurology novels, that was almost weird enough to account for my anomalous afterlife.

He threw me ambiguous looks from the corners of his eyes, as though we might have known each other, but didn't. To avoid recurrent eye contact I looked out of the window at light coming in as a free commodity from the universe, as it turned the hairs on the back of my hand gold. He must have noticed my glass was dead, and shot at me, 'Can I get you a drink; mind if I join you?'

I took him up on his offer and he went downstairs and came back up with our drinks, sat down angularly, his legs blocking me from getting up, and said, 'I'm Ingram by the way, I know your partner Howard,' catching me out as double-shock, the name associated in my mind with one of Kit's killers, and of course with my lugubrious partner.

'I'm Will,' I said, 'and I don't know why, but I have the feeling you already know who I am.'

'Why do you think that Mr. W.H.' he laughed, 'you could be anyone, we've only just met after all.

'So what's Howard up to at present?' he asked, as though he had one up on me and wasn't going to tell.

'In Singapore at present,' I said, 'if you don't already know, then on to Dubai, I suppose.'

He pulled on his lippy beer froth, and said, 'I'm sure we've met before, and by the way I'm at Burberry,' as the sort of rehearsed tag punters try on as a fake intro, only I sensed his slippery tone carried a different underlying message.

'I don't think so,' I said, determined not to give him the advantage.

'Memory's a funny thing,' he said. 'People forget miles of it, at least what they want to, or rather I do. When you're in finance you falsify everything and construct your own math.'

I felt instinctively I didn't like the man, or his obvious benchmark duplicity. I also objected to him invading my private space in this way, when all I really wanted was to con-figure the next moves in my book like a bendy narrative.

'You and Howard are an item, aren't you?' he said, with an incisive twist. 'Guess you're well suited.'

'What do you mean by that?' I asked.

'Well, you know,' he said, 'things aren't always what they seem, are they?'

I thought of just getting up and walking out, leaving him in mid-sentence, but something stopped me, maybe the sus-picion he was seeing Howard and had something on me.

'So what's happening at Burberry?' I threw at him. 'You did say you worked there.'

'It wouldn't make technical sense if I told you,' he said. 'Hong Kong and the US.. are good, terrorist attacks in Europe though deter the usual influx of the wealthy, so we wobble a bit, but overall, it's good.'

It was the usual sales pitch, only unfocused, general, and could have been applied to any luxury brand. I could feel my antipathy to the man starting to creep up my spine, like a luridly injectable dye.

'I need to go soon,' I said cursorily, trying to suppress my impulsive need to get away from his sticky company.

'Some people never change,' he said, obliquely implying me, in the muffled way that punters sometimes use so that the phrase appears general rather than directed personally.

"What do you mean by that?' I asked, feeling increasingly uncomfortable in his presence.

'I've seen you around, in the past,' he said. 'I guess a lot of people have. You've got the look.'

I could almost detect a drop in the quality of light flooding the window, as though we'd time-slipped back to a zone where things were grainier, murkier in the strange math of history, and the viscerally transcendent times to which I'd belonged.

'What do you want?' I asked, turning on him coldly, with increased force.

'You met someone I'm looking for, while I was in the downstairs bar,' he said. 'Kit Marlowe, or whatever name he goes under now. We've got some unfinished business, I'm sure as a friend, he'll tell you what. I remember when the two of you had something going,' he said, demolishing a third of his beer in a single lift of his glass.

'Look, I don't know who you are or what you are trying to prove,' I said, 'and as for Howard he's never mentioned you in any capacity.'

'That's not surprising,' the man said, 'given he's cheating on you.'

I laughed impulsively, wanting in part to believe him so that Howard would in turn have no redress for the number of times I had betrayed him.

'And what's that got to do with me?' I asked, blaming myself internally that I hadn't already left before he started digging.

'We'll see,' he said cryptically, moving another third of his glass down to an amber meniscus on the grungy tabletop.

'I'm going,' I said, wanting to maintain my cool in the face of his vicious jabs at undermining me, and took the precipitous stairs down to the street, and sneaked back into Hop Gardens where police were body-searching an immigrant up against the peeled door of a building, his defiantly uncompromising attitude doing him no favours as an act of resistance. Forcefully handcuffed, he was summarily marched down the alley, dragging his heels, and out to St. Martin's Lane and the sirens announcing a blue lights' arrival. I sat down in my familiar spot on the wall and let things with Ingram filter through. The name, Ingram Frizer, Marlowe's reputed historic killer kept coming up as an association I didn't want to make, a one-time rogue operative in State pay, or whoever he was in his malevolent role in espionage. If this really was the same man, as I suspected, then it was as though time was being reverse engineered and the future brought into post-apocalyptic review through reformatting the past. Howard's dealings with this lugubrious individual, if they really existed, I put down to his liberal use of recreational drugs at the weeks and his attraction to chemsex with the druggy anonymous. As for me, I was like a colour that could never be singularly absorbed it seems, but was always diffused into another tissue of identity as Mr. W.H. The mobile workforce around me with its ThinkPad connectivity and cloud-based policies linked to centralised portals was simply the digital counterpart of my gateway into personal data stored in history. And always I came back to the Sonnits as my password, those word-solids that were specific to my continued identity. It was their architecture that formed the building blocks of my DNA and amino acids, the mind-cloud in which I lived as two initials, the H being the insoluble enigma resistantly imported into Shakespearean studies as the ultimately elusive jackpot. I'd converted that H into so many aliases, the deception only went deeper on my part, and with Howard and all my previous sugar daddies, they knew me only as Will H. and were simply told not to push it further. Most rent boys or escorts used invented names to the point they'd feel they were actually lying if they told you their real name.

I got back to my writing effort, involving real words carved by my hand while immersed in the city's invasive white noise. A helicopter most likely launched from the heliport at Battersea and tracking up between Barnes and Canary Wharf at 1,000 feet went over as churning reverberation in the centralised air. A Chinese girl, I knew as Sumin, who worked at the local Starbucks on St. Martin's Lane, came through the passage where I was sitting, recognised me and stopped. I knew her only with her hair tied-up at work, but off-duty she wore it long, tan streaks worked into indigenous black, the effect lifting her cheekbones and narrowing her face. She came and sat down next to me on the wall, her sunny personality momentarily polarised to my distinctive handwriting with its consistently even spacing. For a moment, her very different life had me forget Ingram Frizer and the whole Kit Marlowe network of crypto-identities, and my chief antagonist W.S. as the spook in my brain. In answer to my conversational questions she spoke briefly about her job, her family, the China she had left to free up her life by working and studying here. She looked in the window of each question and seemed happy to answer. There was a cadmium-orange smudge of sky back of us and I finger-pointed the colour as a shared momentary focus, something to remember, when this was gone, like an orange fingerprint on a memory cell.

Sumin liked, she said, being part of the Starbucks demographic, the hard, but rewarding teamwork, the fluent, routinal discipline of the job, that wasn't so much about coffee as social exchange in an environment that promoted a mobile officespace within café life. I told her on my part I was attracted to the sea-green logo with its Moby Dick connotations, and that the chain to my mind was like islands in the urban ocean to which we all belonged. I told her a little of the Melville association, and how the logo looked like someone learning to swim in a mint green oval, or something like that, remembering how Starbuck, like so many seamen on long haul, in Melville's experience had taken to hallucinating women thought to inhabit imaginary islands.

Sumin stayed on in her quiet glow, her apparent calm seeming outwardly to accept life at its own gradient. There was a regular footfall in the passage of people cutting through north south into wherever the city took them from there in their random dispersal. I told Sumin to her surprise that I often wrote in this alley, as a pathway that seemed instructive to what I was doing in my book, that was a novel in the making, and very much a day to day fictionalised account of what I was living. She checked her phone, telling me she needed to go on to language school, and agreeing to meet up when she was less busy, turning to wave affirmatively as she exited the passage for the tube. I sat on with my disturbance and writing sharing the same resonance. What was tweaking me internally was that this stranger calling himself Ingram was somehow in collusion with Howard in matters that affected me, as well as Kit, and indirectly Lucy. And in my paranoid susceptibility I debated the possibility that Howard was in some way conspiring with our neighbour, knew his true identity, and correspondingly mine in relation to W.S. Even if, as I knew, this was pushing it, I couldn't help entertain the suspicion I was being squeezed by a rogue mechanics independent of my control. If I trusted anyone in this reassemblage of past identities, it was probably Lucy in part, as the least motivated by malevolence. And wouldn't it be possible, I tried on myself, for Howard to be the ideal financial analyst for the lugubrious W.S. with his likely portfolio of properties. That Howard was dodgier than his clients was logical, in the way police are arguably the best criminals, his acuity as a financier growing more refined through acquaintance with the illicit machinations

140

of the clients he represented. Recently he was on about the yellow stuff falling to a 10-month low. He was obsessed by the drop in the market, with spot gold prices going down more than one per cent, after the US Federal Reserve raised US interest rates from 0.5 to 0.75 per cent. They'd all suffered; Fresnillo, Randgold resources and the Russian gold producer Polymetal, and he'd thrown it at me as though I was a share-holder needing a breakdown on resources. The only gold I cared about was in my veins and fed into the brain chemistry of my writing.

Everyone was currently on terror alert. They'd built a ring of steel to protect some of the Square Mile's highest skyscrap-ers from renewed terrorist attack, incorporating manned checkpoints, rising street bollards, restricted roads and crash-proof barricades to enhance the City's defences by controlling the flow of traffic into the heart of the financial district. It was naturally Howard who'd informed that the eastern cluster of towers built around Bishopsgate were highly sensitive to the threat of a hostile vehicle-borne attack. Lorry bomb attacks were the chief focus of counter-terrorism, and a secure cordon now sealed off key routes to Undershaft, St. Mary Axe and Leadenhall Street, with limited access to a wider zone without pre-booking and/or security vetting. All of these strictures were integrated into Howard's working life, together with the fact that trading was hardwired to a concrete and bolts shell that could be annihilated by guerrilla lorries at anytime in a collapsed cone of red fire.

Suddenly, I saw him again; the man who'd confronted me in the pub, as Ingram, slip into the alley and sit further up on the wall, phone in hand, and throwing a long look in my direction. It was the same person all right, the instant freeze communicating fear throughout my nervous system. At a time of cyberespionage and malware codes, it was scary to see the man's physicals little changed since I'd last known him back in the stinking pit of Elizabethan London. He was at the time in on W.S.' affairs, and the one who reputedly sliced Kit Marlowe's internal carotid artery by punching a blade just above his right eyeball. Frizer was an extortionist back then, a loan-shark who together with his partner Nicholas Skeres were adept, slippery accomplices who'd greased a pathway to W.S. as well as to Thom Walsingham, Kit's patron, and a young cousin of the great spymaster Sir Francis Walsingham. All this retrievable backstory came up in sight of the man, as though history was in part accidentally recreated by attracting neural junctions colliding in available time zones, like Hop Gardens. Frizer stank: he'd always had disposable capital and had purchased the Angel Inn, where as a commodity-broker he'd harnessed his interests to the equally acquisitive W.S. They were greased together, as I recalled, with Frizer upwardly mobile, a fixer, and worse a deviated homophobe, using male-to-male hatred to work up defence.

What exactly drew Frizer and Kit together I didn't know, but it smelled of a lowlife racket. The attraction to W.S. was obvious; both were financial predators who wrapped people up like supermarket chickens. And sitting here now, five centuries ahead, he kept trying to attract my attention by throwing his eyes at me, like he'd done before, whenever I'd seen him with W.S. at the Crown at Bishopsgate, the Maidenhead by the Town Ditch, the Bear, the Ragged Staff at Charing Cross, you name it, dives where criminals gathered, and so too secret intelligence.

I had the feeling too that he was sighting me in wearable camera sunglasses that can take HD photos and videos, and upload the content straight to the app via a smartphone. I debated my move for fear of being followed on foot or into the tube's warren of underground corridors. In this world of assumed quantum casualties I had every reason to believe that if this person was Ingram Frizer, then his one-time accomplices Nicholas Skeres and Robert Poley could similarly be reconstructed wakeys pulled into the unresolved plot. To me we were all returnees into a modern day rewrite, like I could as easily slip back to lowering Cripplegate, 1590, as I could physically push time forward into deep future, and a starless sky burnt up by protein decay, the only residue being a thin exhaust of neutrinos drifting out at lightspeed. In my wildest imagination we were a conflux of bandits, capable by our dual-time status of throwing a switch on apocalypse, the very thing W.S. had attempted to achieve through his plays.

I sat there immobilised and cracked a benzo 10mg and slipped the half under my tongue. The acrid taste of addiction came up, the metallic tang that lived in my juices as chronic dependency. There were hotel workers taking cigarette breaks in the alley, the usual exchange of chat and phone, and the orange cloud moment I'd shared with Sumin had nosed off to be replaced by other vaporous nomads.

When I looked up again Ingram had been joined by two guys of a similar sort of age, all casually dressed, but somehow, I sensed, determined in their grouping to execute whatever plan brought them together. One of the men sat down next to Ingram, while the other remained standing and telling them something that kept them totally attentive. The one who remained standing lit up a pre-rolled joint and the dope smell shunted botanicals down the alley. I sniffed the residue greedily, remembering so many nights of getting stoned with W.S. sprawled across my bed, muddied knee-boots kicked off, the lines he was writing carved into his face. And nights with Kit too, the real dopehead who used weed like George Michael as an opioid layer on everything he did. The three were locked into conversation, insidious thugs who if I'd got it right had chewed tobacco inside Marshalsea prison, their Southwark careers oiled by cheating, fucking and extortion. Interrogation rooms, cells, they'd known the whole forensics of the system and come out bleached, crooked and twisted as a Suzuki bike smashed into a wall. They were simply criminals paid by higher criminals, who as code-breakers extracted sensitive data, operated as entangled double-agents, and as terrorists and counterterrorist's inhabiting the same body, most likely with a suicide belt concealed at the waist. These were in my paranoia cyber-operatives who turned up inside your brain, while relegating you to theirs, so you didn't any longer know who you are or who had borrowed your brain. You couldn't win in their game; it was like trying to sort strand by strand a cauldron of spaghetti.

I sat there totally confused, aware in the past I'd been brain-hacked by this lot, and it was a bit like eight tube carriages leave a station and only seven arrive in the transition from Westminster to St. James' Park, and there's no accountability, no footage recording the tampering. All I know is this book's everything to me, even if the sky falls in the process of writing it. And how big a weight would that be, zero-mass collapsing on my head—what would the entire sky weigh if I caught it on a drug spoon?

I need to tell you a bit of history. I've lived to be able to sniff the sinister that always enter by the back door into your life, like these men. Scheming, impulsive squabbling, these three if I was right in my crazy hunch had stitched up Kit Marlowe, with Ingram Frizer duped into being the fall guy for W.S. There were other schemers like the playwright, Thomas Kyd, another conman who'd told the authorities under duress that Kit Marlowe was gay and that dope and boys were all part of his underworld lifestyle. I got it up impulsive on my phone the Privy Council's warrant for Marlowe's arrest through the offices of the greaseball Henry Maunder. Maunder it seems was ordered 'to repair to the house of Mr. Tho Walsingham in Kent, or to any other place where he shall understand Christofer Marlow to be remaining, and by virtue hereof to apprehend and bring him to the court in his company. And in case of need to require aid.'

And I'll tell you something else now I'm into reversing time. There was Richard Baines, another agent who'd got into Kit's life, like waking up to find a stranger in bed who has all your passwords. It was Baines I remember who accused Kit of propagating the belief that Jesus and his trainee John, were lovers, something that went down with the authorities like a Boeing crashed into the graphite-coloured Thames. This was in part the backstory to Marlowe's murder, the conspiracy stratum or subplot to the Deptford killing where I believe W.S. stepped into a shabby room with a broken light bulb and within minutes a red viscous pool of blood coagulated on Eleanor Bull's wooden floor. Not three witnesses to the murder as recorded in the coroner's report, but four, inclusive of W.S., in the violent reckoning that came out of their meeting. No homicide charges were ever brought at an inquest held at the site of the crime, the perpetrator who of course wasn't present, was acquitted on the grounds of self-defence, and this jerk up the alley, Frizer, was formally taken into custody, before being issued with an immediate formal pardon. His substitution for W.S. was to my mind all part of the governmental whitewash, the scam initialised by a corrupt hierarchy who endorsed W.S. as the capital's best investment for State propaganda through his crowd-pleasing plays.

At least that's how I read it, as the principal focus of the Sonnits—this continuously mass-market pointer to everything I'd prefer to forget. And why can't the dedication be expunged, I mean Mr. W.H. that sounds like the question-able title of a Lou Reed song. Why publishers persisted with the dedication, like it was hardwired to the text, I didn't understand, but wanted it wiped like spray-bandit graffiti from the carriage door of a tube. I've searched through every paperback reprint emergent on the market over the years, always to find my initials harnessed to the contents, as though somehow I am the pathway to the design. It's like W.S. is still exploiting me by a cryptic word-game all these centuries later. If I told you my age when it all started you'd blame him and have the dedication removed by authorisation of the courts.

All of this stuff comes up as I try to avoid anything more than peripheral eye contact with the three. That they've singled me out in their awareness naturally unnerves me. I instinctually convert them into an abstract, a sort of sepia blur that I don't want to bring into definition. I feel as worn down in parts as a Boeing flown 300 times round the world and broken down into metal for cans. This endless attachment to time, to five centuries of it looped into episodic recall bleaches me into brainfade. I can hear the city's rumbling bass grunt, or it's my panicked heartbeat transmitting ectopic beats. For a moment I'm not sure whether to chance my luck by loping towards the Bedfordbury exit, right in their faces to confuse them, or to slip ahead of a group passing through as cover back into St. Martin's Lane.

I sat on, momentarily distracted by a young Japanese couple dressed as idiosyncratically improvised post-punk manga, an amalgam of retro-future looking to make a fashion moment now in a capital in which trending could rarely free itself of the influence of the near past. I was temporarily absorbed by their post-human styles, and looked up to find Kit standing there gated by reflectives. He looked at me hard, or was it the smart glasses, and said, 'Get out of here, real cool; I'll walk with you, and these guys know I'm armed, and even my diamond filling is intelligent.

I stood up with him shielding me, in the pretence I'd been waiting for him all along. 'Left at the entrance and fast,' Kit said. 'It's an unmarked black Mercedes, armour-plated, rocket-propelled grenades, a litre of blood on board . . . now, just go...' Kit automated the deep muscle car, as we both jumped into its blackout cabin, into what felt like leather lounge seats, before the twin-turbo kicked in. 'They won't follow this,' Kit said, coasting into Whitehall, it's not the sort of car you'd associate with a poet.' For once, he smiled, at the same time picking off a silver Audi like it belonged to the last century.

'We're clear,' he said diffidently. 'I suppose you've an idea who those guys were in the alley?'

'One of them's called Ingram,' I said. 'He got into conversation with me at the Lemon Tree after you'd gone, then got nasty in ways that I couldn't get back at.'

'Ingram Frizer,' Kit said, emphatically, 'with two of the cell, Nick Skeres and presumably Robert Poley, all sort of loosely affiliated to espionage. Frizer's still borderline personality and schizoid.'

I kept thinking this wasn't happening on a millennial London afternoon choking with diesel fumes as Kit drove through Westminster towards Vauxhall, and the shimmying dazzle of light coming off the back of the river. The river carried with it the same disorientating motion I associated with air-pocketing time-slips, a morph between jet-lag and space-sickness, only you never let go time in the process of being rushed through a transit-portal into an interzone.

Kit parked his benchmark Merc behind a security gate at Millbank. 'Want to see cool tech?' he asked, and pressed a dash button and the car's high gloss spray changed from black to metallic silver, as an immediate remake skin. 'Can't tell you how this is done,' he said, cryptically, 'but it makes the car unreadable to pursuers.'

We got out from a vehicle that seemed different from the one in which we'd arrived, rather like 16th century players walking towards the river five-hundred years later. 'We've come this far,' Kit said, as we crossed over into Victoria Gardens and looked at the river sliding muddily like combat dress towards Nine Elms and its gargantuan metallised towers turned gold by refracted sunlight. The tidal smell of London came up in conflicting currents scrolling through swampish history into the day we breathed. Someone on the pebbled shore was using a digital metal detector to interrogate river effluvium. He kept hoovering the shingle like a gold prospector. There were boats moored on the tide, and a police tug arguing its way downriver on the choppy wake of a barge freighted with cargo. A standard, opportune Thames snapshot, only we didn't belong and knew it, we were half in time and half out, like time-slippers only visible to each other. The concrete ledge over the drop was our only physical boundary to hang onto, the ochre beach getting progressively overwritten by a translucent incoming tide. All Kit said, eyeballing me, was 'let's fuck,' as he pushed his mouth over mine like a tube emerging in a rush from a dark tunnel.

10

ANOTHER THORPE

Jeremy, this time, and not Thomas: do I read a message in my attraction to the same name twice? Howard's biked off to his dealing room—I repeat it again—'It strikes a man more dead than a great reckoning in a little room,' as I lie in a bathtub churned a dense, oily green by an emerald dollop of Pine Needle Oil. Immersed in this green meniscus, my anxiety chills, and the moody hum coming from the building's core is my point of sonic awareness. I try to refocus on what's happening in W.S.' life, and his oleaginous quango, and according to Howard W.S. only uses Charles Street when he's in town for business and boys, not excluding Lucy, who I intend to call and arrange to meet in our best interests. But last night, while Howard boozily slept, I learnt a few useful but scary things after using codes to access the dark web, or digital underworld. In fact, I did it on Howard's tablet, the one he uses exclusively for porn, after Kit had supplied me with codes and instructions to access the cyber-pit.

As far as I could make out two unnamed financiers, who I suspected were associates of Howard's were evidently attempting to defraud criminals on the dark web by masquerading as money launderers. I started to wonder about Howard's input into a scheme partially exposed as a black market network offering to help drug traffickers' funds into fake accounts. Whatever the honeyed jackpot there was a whiff of Howard being an accomplice to something uniformly corrupt about these quasi-legal transactions.

What I hadn't told Howard, like most things in my apparently youthful timeline, was my involvement in another time with the disgraced politician Jeremy Thorpe, who serially exploited opportune teens who were homeless and on the game, chancing their luck in the confused neon milieu of Piccadilly Circus and Leicester Square. On the menu were people like me, only my intuition and facility for self-reflection was a lot brighter than the runaways he picked up, in working out the configuration between sex and money. Thorpe and his accomplices in their Jaeger jumpers and Hackett blazers—Jeremy owned over 100 neckties from the racks of Liberty, Harrods and Turnbull & Asser, were mostly sideline dandies with an ulterior motive—recruiting young flesh sold on selling sex for drugs, or the basics to live. Thorpe hung out at the Reform Club and the A&B, he knew the mapping of gay subcultures sunk into Soho, Chelsea and Earls Court and trawled bars and the rent epicentre at Piccadilly Circus for casual pick-ups with whom he was brutally acquisitive in his infractions. But he'd get himself into a sticky spaghetti tangle with the lowlife to whom he gravitated, and kept me as a sort of intermediary to try and intercede with their usual blackmailing demands. He really believed bodies were disposable in his ruthless drive towards power. He never seriously considered that bruised-up, disenfranchised, drugged teens from the underclass would come back on his tail with sordidly candid revenge.

But I hung in there, part-time, streetwise, avoiding his demands for sex, and being paid as a mediator between him and his pick-ups. One of these was M.S., a boy Thorpe had picked up outside Christopher Gibbs' antiques shop on the King's Road—Mike as I knew him—a typical hustler with a dangerous underside of blackmail. As I got it from Mike, Thorpe with egregious aplomb had whisked his pick-up back to his flat, sniffing he was in need of a meal, degraded him by providing him with no option, and fucked him without apology. It was a familiar story, but with a twist. A few nights later Thorpe had picked up Mike in the red and blue neon storm of Piccadilly, and at first didn't recognise the person he'd already used and kicked out like flotsam. But Mike was wised-up and had already discovered Thorpe's real identity, went through forceful sex again, was paid and shared a fry-up in the morning, sausage pops, auroral eggs, scrotal tomatoes and greased bread, before being summarily shaken out of the door. Knowing precisely this punter's celebrity Mike had gone back to Thorpe's flat later in the day, and pushed a note through the letterbox demanding £500 in cash, and gone back to working the Dilly.

I'd called over that evening and Thorpe was under a moody penumbra, drinking Plymouth gin, down in the dumps and disinterestedly trawling the Times. Trusting me, he didn't conceal the cause for long. 'I'm being blackmailed,' he said, 'and you and Bessell are going to do for this bit of trade. We'll put him in the river if he persists. Or shoot him. No chicken is going to put me in a corner.'

Thorpe was a testosterone hazard—he was in love with himself as a retrofuture supremacist—hanging out at the Standard, a pub on Piccadilly Circus known for rent, and the Salisbury on St. Martin's Lane, a theatre pub for a predominantly queer milieu. He was up there on his own inviolable celebrity; he wrote compromising letters to pick-ups on House of Commons stationery, inviting blackmail from the manipulative and leaving his signature thumbprints available for future forensics. His mania grew to be the size of Harrods, but it was a self-absorbed one, like a sex-toy massaging his ego. He was an Edwardian dandy at a time of psychedelia, and he was too self-obsessed to notice the incongruity.

Thorpe liked the idea of a male harem, an assortment he could pull from at anytime due to money and power revving his arteries. That he couldn't use me, but at the same time wanted my looks—there had to be someone he couldn't exploit, unlike the serviceable meatrack he picked from at the Dilly, only further fascinated his purchase on buying into youth. And of course he owned a copy of the Sonnits, a biffed, lived-in edition, Jonathan Cape Ltd, London, 1925, with an Ex Libris label pasted in. The book's previous ownership was Henry Upton, a friend and lover of Thorpe's who'd mysteriously disappeared at sea off the Sussex coast in a 15-ton motor cruiser, with Thorpe undoubtedly playing a significant role in having Upton thrown into the sea.

I'd found concealed in the book a photo of the blond Upton in Poona, with an unnamed Anglo-Indian boy, his arm draped over the boy's significantly muscled shoulder. It was this chance finding on a randomised, disordered bookshelf, in his flat had me dig deeper into the patina of grime coating his deviated affairs. What Thorpe wasn't was modern, even his pattern of crimes were a throwback to a colonial sensibility skinning slaves like beef, that he converted into a system of hush money for abusing pretty boys selling sex in the capital for lack of any other commodity. Thorpe was a habituated fraudster, a raincoated predator with a diamond-sharp wit lit by a hologram of self-regarding vanity that culminated in tabloid scandals.

Lubricated by green pine oil in Howard's off-white and jade marble bathtub it all came sloshing back to me like thought-waves conducted through the water. It was the unashamed need of money, and of being elevated to a role of unimpeachable trust in his life kept me in his pay for five years as London exploded into psychedelics. I wasn't his procurer, but more his facilitator to try and prevent boys from talking about his indiscriminate promiscuity. I think it was hoping to get caught partly motivated his picking up lowlife in public places. Piccadilly, as I knew to my cost, was policed with almost forensic acuity, but Thorpe showed no least impunity in hanging out in its lurid amusement arcades and conspicuously under the arches. His reckless celeb was processed there under the street, and in rooms he rented by the hour at the adjoining Regent Palace Hotel, its peeling cream façade concealing a mobile brothel.

Back to the Sonnits and Upton's bashed copy that I loaned out of curiosity, with him telling me to keep it. He was drunk at the time on gin and some new conquest—Alex—what sort of name is that? I couldn't then get Upton's backstory, but today I'm nudged by his Wiki entry.

Upton was it seems the blond sadistic heir to Viscount Templeton, a rapacious pervert who swapped boys with Thorpe like fencing stolen goods. There wasn't it seemed any boundaries to Upton's depravity, and he found in Thorpe a willing application to his own dispensable quotient of vulnerable rent. They pinked off twinks, carved into them and often refused to pay. Thorpe it seems joined Upton in Poona and assembled a slave-ring of local teens, boys with no rights of protest, arrogated over by old-Etonians acting like sexual butchers. From what I'd discovered, Upton—and to a lesser degree Thorpe, was admitted through a local guru into the rites of the notorious Thugees cult. This was an organised mafia of Muslim Indians who for six hundred years operated as group assassins, or more literally thugs. The methods of robbery and killing employed by this residual cult clearly established an empathy with the cold liquidation of enemies Thorpe was to pursue in the interests of silencing any payback from his blackmailers. I could already observe the ruthless disdain for the underclass growing in him when he brought rent back, leaning on their status as rough trade to consistently degrade them through arrogance. 'Do you know who I am?' he'd say with a deferential sneer, his invincible conceit used as a tool to help humiliate boys cowered into having no comeback. But of course, a few did, those who were more chippy, streetwise and realised they too had rights, even though Thorpe's word would always prevail over theirs in terms of the law. Who, I ask you, is going to believe a street tough over the Liberal leader, and his close party members. Bill Shannon came back and so did Bunny, a.k.a. Norman Scott.

I got to sort out Shannon, because he was vindictive, rather than intelligent, scheming rather than perceptive, and believed Thorpe's minder Peter Bessell would authorise a contract killing if he didn't shut up after payment to secure the return of highly incriminatory letters. Thorpe was too cowardly for confrontation, so Bessell was always the elected hitman with the steely pathology of a Harley Street dentist. Shannon like most rent was a compulsive shoplifter, and his numerous convictions were part of Bessell's offensive for fucking over an opportune teen. As I'd learnt from personal experience, selling to rich men makes you want to be equal to their growth as coefficient revenge. Shannon like a lot of disaffected rent was a compulsive shoplifter, with a police record, and his convictions were a part of Bessell's comeback on an opportunistic teen got out of his class. Shannon didn't of course return all of Thorpe's indiscreetly phrased letters—and why should he?—he had his own designs on their impulsively romantic poison, but part of his educational curve was to learn that the rich punter always wins over the poor runaway. Thorpe, as I quickly got to realise, shopped for boys like discounted goods. Already ruined, he gave them a hint of privilege; then slapped them harder, back to the rain, street drugs and homelessness. In his St. James' nut-brown homburg he stood out like an awkward troll in the Piccadilly milieu, a debonair mismatch with perversity written all over his face. He simply couldn't get modern on street lingo, and most of the Dilly boys thought he was bad news, although those who sold him sex found an element of kindness attached to his put-down of their status. And there were likeable points; he left me alone, paid for my tiny Chelsea flat at Worlds End, but of course nothing comes without a price, and I had to negotiate with street toughs, boy pimps and hulks living off immoral earnings who curated the rent schematic. In getting people off Thorpe's back, they fastened on to mine, and if you paid them, they swore blind a week later that the money was counted short and more was needed. You couldn't win or ever extricate yourself from the deviated underworld logic. And all the time his incorrigible megalomania had him believe he could go on repeating the risk without any payback, as though as perpetrator he was anonymised.

I covered for him, carried envelopes of cash to placate spotty teens or their thuggish procurers, but there weren't any Dilly angels, and negotiations were often verbally rough. I brokered the costs of moral indiscretion at Burger King, under the statue of Eros, in the White Bear, the Golden Lion on Dean Street, places where homosexual transactions took place, fearing always I'd be bashed or arrested as an accomplice to Thorpe's notoriously serial double life.

I listen out in the bath to the building's insulated quiet, no noise from W.S.' apartment, no Lucy waiting outside on the red carpet with a handgun, just the empty anonymous hum of a high-end shell, with few of its occupants in. I adjust the thermostatic tap and the emerald water steams with pine resonance like a drizzled Jacuzzi. I'm confident that my book's going forward, its subversive vector pointing into the red-zone, its disrespect for mainstream, optimal. Underground writing has the power of a rogue drone to smash through a Boeing's cockpit and explode. Why else did I read Burroughs' *Naked Lunch*, Ballard's *Crash*, or Pynchon's *Gravity's Rainbow*, contemporaneous with applying entrepreneurial muscle into disentangling Thorpe's criminal activities that I suspect are minor to Howard's facility for open-door money-laundering with Russian mafia. The hot stream hikes my cock erect, a trophy I pat favourably on its round circumcised head, before pushing it down under the opaque green water. For some irrational reason I have this gut feeling my life will end collateral with finishing this book. And oddly the thought doesn't scare me, as it did, when out on Thorpe's oil and tacks trail, nosing into Playland's pinball arcade with leering punters breathing over runaways dressed in XS white singlets and lived-in skinny jeans, 14-17 aggregate.

I remember Johnny was there with a questionable street-tough, Bill, waiting for the cash buy-off I'd come to facilitate. He was on a winning streak, slamming the plunger's spring-loaded rod into a metallic landslide of coins, and his creased minder said, 'Go for it Johnny, I've fucking fixed the machine,' as another surge of cash crashed into the money chute.

I almost walked out, sensing the latent contention ahead, like a sniff of underarm acid. The place was an underage meat market, and Johnny the worst combination of naïve in the know and rude ignorance sharpened into cunning. I got that just by looking at him, Johnny the runaway they all wanted to fuck, the rough diamond that was straight, and only playing at rent for the drug money or whatever he did with a bit of evaporating bling. Intuitively, I sniffed he lacked any form of pleasure-principle, he was essentially a cold sociopath who exploited sleaze—a highly manipulative kid who thought buying a scooter placed him on the rich list, and that sex with Thorpe was the pathway to a retainer for the rest of his habituated life. I saw right through him like light. Anyone that got to him was in fact bankrolling Bill, who looked like his fist could argue with concrete. I watched Johnny topple the jackpot again, the machine disgorging money and Bill grappling to scoop it ahead of Johnny, with the frozen face of a truck.

I'd already mentally walked out but was still there, locked into the rigidity of my fear. I was the surreptitious courier of a celeb politician's rent addiction and I wasn't sure, despite my insider's track, of how to carry this through. I lacked empathy with dysfunctional, and Johnny was clearly non-verbal and Bill quasi-psychotic. The two were a fusion of meat and murder and I lacked access to both brutally alienated states. All of my instinctive siding with the subculture to which I belonged evaporated in the face of these two lowlife hustlers doing a scam in Playland, while men in suits, tentatively surveyed what was on offer in the aisles. It was a place I'd always avoided for its tacky associations with underage boys going through the blender with the likes of suave old-Etonians pretending disinterest in the predatory market.

I knew Peter Bessell had supplied one hundred pounds in an unmarked envelope as hush money for two letters and there was no room for bargaining. I couldn't really see the money silencing these two, or Johnny for that matter coming to the realisation that he'd go permanently missing if he didn't sell sex for this nefarious bruiser.

After what seemed an indefinite time, Bill swung round and looked me over. 'You Thorpe's boy?' he asked, derisively, muttering, 'another fucking twink,' and poking Johnny in the ribs to demand his attention. 'E's here and he betta have the dosh.'

When Johnny turned to face me I knew I'd seen him before, both under the Regent Street arches, and once transitioning from Thorpe's apartment as I arrived. Johnny seemed a sad throwback to delinquent imps who sharpened their criminal potential to saturation at the Dilly, not only to exploit, but also to rob vulnerable punters. What struck me as incongruous was the gold filling in his left upper front tooth and the cheap gold bits he wore, a neck chain and two distastefully clumpy rings. I could see at a glance he was working to buy street drugs by his film-coated eyes and his constant drift of focus to lateral.

'I can get your sugar daddy into big trouble, mate,' Johnny came out with, as though I was a bargaining post. 'Tell im from me, this is just the start—there's other boys too want payin. Aren't you on the game too?'

'I've got an envelope for you,' I said, keeping neutral, as the best defence, 'and I'm told it's a one-off only.'

Bill elbowed his way a step closer to me and leered with slow-burn anger. 'Giz me the envelope,' he said, not aware it was Smythsons ivory, and he roughly tore open the seal and counted the notes crisp from an ATM.

'It's ten short, mate,' he said, 'and don't fucking argue. I spose you've trousered the other tenner.'

'I know it's correct,' I said. 'I saw it counted and sealed in the envelope.'

'Don't act smart with me,' Bill said, lifting his shoulder bumps for emphasis, so that his whole beefy musculature rocked on his spinal axis. 'I told ya, there's a tenner missing, guv, don't fucking push it.'

I felt powerless and trapped, as though I'd been set up by Bessell, but I knew he was lying, the hush money was exact, I'd watched ten tens spread like a fan of cards before being fitted crisply into the envelope.

I could see Johnny had his attention divided between Bill as his spokesman and the pinball teens, mostly losing, or posing as eye-candy to punters. Zippered black leather jackets or just white-tees to emphasise a skinny torso were standard rent boy kit, so too an attitude of availability with danger attached—there were no easy makeovers at the Dilly, only a tricky immersion in getting one over on the punter by hacking into his compromised vulnerability.

'They counted it out in front of me,' I said, growing impatient. 'Look, I know all about these scams, and this isn't one. I know your end of it Johnny.'

'You telling me, I'm lying,' Bill said, shifting forward without completing the action, by way of renewed threat. 'I'ze told you, we're a tenner short.'

There were large boxy raindrops streaming down outside, twinkling hexagonals, as momentary distraction that brought more punters into the arcade. Johnny wasn't really quite there, he couldn't focus for long, and there was a conspicuous zigzag of scar tissue on his left cheek, where I suspect Bill or a client had cut him.

There wasn't anything I could do to placate Bill who appeared to belong to a reptile house. 'You tell your geezer, faggot, what's he, right hon scumbag Thorpe, I want not only the missing tenner, but the same again tomorrow, right, anover hundred smackers, you poof, before you get the letters.'

Johnny had gone back to pinball wizardry and suspiciously scooped the jackpot again in a lurid blaze of digital lights. 'You better dhow u tomorrow at 3.00 with that extra cash, or you'll be in trouble like. Lotsa boys like you go missing at the Dilly, mate. You know what I mean. It's a big world. Nobody's gonna go looking for you. You get what I say?'

I did, only too right. Playland was always the worst of the Dilly dealing rooms that left a moral patina on whoever hung out there, or went to a closed room upstairs where the likes of Charles Hornby and his brother were rumoured to know the lowdown on rent. I didn't hang around, I left the lowering Bill to pimp Johnny, and dodged outside into the rain, and the sequenced programming of neon ads blinking red, blue and green eyelashes in squishy puddles.

When I got back to Bessell's apartment at Clarges Street, with the news, I could see his mind was driving at a brick wall. 'You've got to do something. You've got to stop this, or their demands will increase; and fuck it, they've still got the letters. If only Jeremy would show more discretion and not write incriminating love letters to rent boys. He's left his dirty fingerprints everywhere.'

I looked at Bessell's charcoal cashmere cardie and pink and white candy button-down, as the casual coding Thorpe's circle adopted, half-way modern, but afraid to go the full way: a same-sex tribe radically separated by class from the boys they inveigled into their threatening bullet-nosed quango.

'What if you're deceiving me?' Bessell put in with a sly twist. 'Rent boys know every dodge in the catalogue—I mean you may have the returned letters and have struck a deal with Johnny. How do I know? I can have you strip-searched now, on Jeremy's orders, but you may be telling the truth. I hope for your sake you are. We're generous to you, but your retainer can be taken away.'

I sat there uncomfortably, reviewing my entire deviated past and condensing it into recognised patterns, and W.S. was of course there thumping on my pulse. I heard someone knock authoritatively on a door Bessell had kept shut, and a tall, dark-haired man in an uncreased grey suit came into the room and ordered me to stand up. He posted me against a wall with force, his hands gripping my shoulders, and said, 'Right, off with those jeans, I need to search you. Make it fast.'

There wasn't time to argue or refuse, this man was clearly trained security and brutally, professionally cold. I popped the pewter fastener on my jeans, having surrendered my hounds-tooth jacket, and his hands went into me, pulled my black briefs down, left me to reunite with them, and searched through my jeans' ejected scrambled coins, keys, a silver foil of benzos, and nothing else. He did the same with my jacket, searching for a re-sewn interior, retrieving minimal assets, my debit cards, pens, condoms, more keys, and gave up on his search with perfunctory cool. 'He's clean,' he said to Bessell, 'at least in these clothes.'

Shaken and humiliated, I watched the man leave the room as ruthlessly precise as he had entered, got back into my clothes, stared so hard at Bessell he was compelled to look up from the document he was reading, and walked out slamming the door, so the noise vacuumed into his face.

I got out into New Palace Yard, but before I could cross the wet yard to the security gate, the man who had so militantly searched me, got out of an opaque windowed black Mercedes, flashed his ID at me as CID, and told me in the same impassive metallic voice to follow him into a security door, without giving any explanation.

'Follow me,' the man said, 'or I'll have you in for questioning.'

I knew immediately this was a case of mistaken identity. If Johnny was a one-off lucker, then I knew Thorpe was being persistently and serially blackmailed by Norman Scott, a rent boy whose collection of highly compromising letters kept Thorpe on the hard edge of being exposed to the media, in a way that would scandalously precipitate his personal ruin as an MP. It would be curtains.

I followed apprehensively, pleading misidentity to the vertical wall of his back. 'Just step this way,' he said, using a keycard on the biometrics, and the stink of a subterranean, brightly lit passage was thrown in my face. 'These are the real corridors of power,' he said, coolly, referentially. 'This is the seat of Parliament's brains, Norman, isn't it? People disappear down here, it's all steam central heating, gas and water networks, and the power supplies that keep the building running. Plant rooms, electrical cables, monitoring panels, fans, ductwork, sewer ejectors. It's like your world, isn't it,' he said, turning round to face me, with a grey, full-on stare. 'Just thought I'd show it to you. Boys of your type have been given a guided tour before—the two sewer-ejectors discharge into Sir Joseph Bazalgette's London sewerage network, just thick black sludge.'

'You are going to own up Norman, aren't you, and be a good boy. You're causing a lot of trouble.'

'I'm Will,' I said, starting to feel frightened. 'Mr. W.H. I'm nothing to do with Norman Scott. I just do errands for Jeremy Thorpe—I'm a go-between to getting letters back and negotiable.'

'I know you're not Norman,' the man said, 'but your type are all alike. We'll run you all off Piccadilly Circus, and restore the place to public decency. You've got no rights, soliciting is also obstructing the public highway and a violation of law. That's why I thought I'd show you the infrastructure of a giant sewer; it's where your kind should belong. And remember, I'm on your case. You make any wrong move and I'll have you for blackmail, not Norman. Right.'

He led me back through the labyrinthine industrial complex. 'Don't want to stay here for the night, do you, Norman, I mean Will.'

I was too shaken to reply, and when he used a wearable barcode read by an iris scanner to access our exit, getting us back into daylight, away from the driven hum of the plants, I was close to collapse from the fetid tunnels. He left me there in the drizzled river haze of Parliament Square, saying, 'Do you think I'm going to give you a lift back to Piccadilly.'

I stood there in the thickening damp, my mind scrambled by implicitly homicidal threat, ready to crack, and regretting ever having got involved with Jeremy Thorpe's greasy criminal underworld networking out across the capital. Everything about the man was duplicitous, entangled; but I remembered too the aspects that made him so dynamically attractive, the concealed kindness, the panache, the genuine heady idealism intent on trying through humane policies to reform a dead older generation sold into Angus Beef and carcinogenic blood.

I breathe in again the deep silence of the bathroom at Charles Street as the geographical determinant of my comparative wellbeing. All of Thorpe's criminal subterfuge came back to me in the bright green sheath of hot water puffing into whorls and dispersals of steam. My karmic travelogue has helped protect me, no matter the risks I've invited as the fugitive dedicatee of the sonnits. I'd rather have been in the Sex Pistols, but individual destiny is mostly given rather than chosen. If Johnny Lydon was the beef, I was the asparagus, the historic loiterer, Mr. W.H., with no conceivably provable identity.

It all streamed back to me like a cold memory call. Thorpe's cramped flat in Marsham Court, Westminster, his Gieves and Turnbull & Asser boxy carriers littering the kitchen, the orange frilled scapula from spanking an egg in the drizzle, the Fortnum's Royal Blend tea tin on the kitchen table, and once or twice when I was over on weekend mornings, a recalcitrant rent boy with what looked like a drugs hangover emerging from the bedroom with cowed attitude. Later of course, I learnt it was devious trouble in the name of Norman Josiffe or Scott, who clearly felt resentful and humiliated by conceding to Thorpe for cash handouts. Dark, long period hair, a skinny twenty-five in tee and jeans, he looked internalised, as though anxious about anxiety, a student of his own distress, who'd got into a way of life he clearly regretted, but couldn't let go, like so many rent boys who'd got to be dependent on impulsive cash helpings for sex and to shut them up. When Norman spoke, he kept his eyes turned down, apologetically, and it was mostly about horses, and how he missed the life of stables where he'd started out, and what he called the kindness of animals. He'd got a flat in Draycott Place, Chelsea that Thorpe was funding, but didn't look comfortable about living at the epicentre of a major youth culture movement rocking the sixties. He was clearly messed up by sexual confusion, he was gay and he wasn't, and often looked on the edge of tears. He certainly didn't look the type who could maintain a straight relationship, there was a wobble in him, an equivocal debate it seemed, not only over his sexuality, but his actual lack of strong identity. There was also a social inequality that Thorpe was clearly exploiting on top of Norman's ontological insecurity.

These I recall were my first impressions of Norman, the sneaky blackmailer, who'd hoarded a pile of Thorpe's letters addressed not only to him, but also to other disposable goods in Thorpe's rent demographic, that was starting to become socially obtrusive in ways that criminalised his elevated status. There was no way looking at Norman that Thorpe could pass him off as a friend, he was categorically a male prostitute, broken up inside, and if it wasn't for patronage, would doubtless have been homeless. I'd met so many Dilly boys who were neither gay nor straight, but in-between, but once they started selling sex tried to prove they were straight and only working for the money. In that way they could claim they were sexually abused by punters, corrupted, raped, as Norman claimed in an illegal subculture that worked off danger as its incentive. Everyone assumed a fake identity, police, punters, prostitutes, pimps, the whole conglomerate were as creepy as the Thames sticking its grey tongue out under the bridges.

Norman presented himself like a loser, whereas I always projected a winner's attitude—I don't need you but you need me at a price, and I'm not taking. He simply didn't have it, his nerves were a liability, and Thorpe in his indiscriminate rampage for trade had taken a chance on someone possibly borderline and most certainly depressively suicidal.

All of the malware in both persons was to co-evolve as the relationship got stretched over a decade, and I was to be intermediary, unable ever to establish trust with Norman who'd been so rolled he didn't know how to reciprocate on any level. He couldn't easily climb out of self-pity as a gestural resource, and in turn the strain of viciousness he cultivated against anyone professing to help him, dumped him in a still lonelier corner. He hated Thorpe for helping him, and hated himself for receiving help. His antagonism was complex, and in my experience insoluble, and he grew dependent on being medicated for the parallel processing of depression and anxiety. There was no way of knowing where you stood with Norman, as he'd got used to seeing kindness as a threat, and hostility as normal. But he liked money and saw Thorpe as a limitless provider of what it could buy in a capital that to him was Martian in terms of alienation. He couldn't find a way in or out, but remained frozen on a traffic-gyratory. Norman was one of the hopeless runaways who gravitate to selling sex because they don't fit in with education or employment and just fall into the empty shell of boredom, waiting under the arches to strike lucky, or buying pills on the street. Nothing to do all day but wait, eat burgers and get ill.

Thorpe would say to me, 'Sort him out; get him a job in the country, as far from London as you can find. I can't educate him even to passable standard. There's some boys pass protocol. Norman's toxic, and he'll never learn. I can't take him places, like the Reform, the Ritz, the Ivy, without him looking like rent. And he just flops out, like he's dysfunctional. It's obvious to anyone I'm grooming him, and that he's underage and jobless. I'm in a right fucking mess. Sort it out; surely you can make him see sense. Get him on a farm in Wales.'

These were invariably my ultimatums designed to get Norman out of Thorpe's suffocating tangle of gay intrigue, in which he continually rehearsed his own downfall, right to the bottom of the concrete stairs. It was like all the vitamins had floated out of his party dynamic, and he'd stranded himself in the ammonia smell of a London thunderstorm about to break over Westminster. And Norman of course, perversely wouldn't go, because he'd grown to like being bankrolled for his potential to blackmail Thorpe and other senior politico-aristos who'd come his way looking to turn a trick. He was also disagreeably likely to throw hysterical tantrums if I pushed him towards another stables job. His brief attempt at marriage had failed, he couldn't do straight, and this became still another vicious recrimination he levelled at Thorpe, blaming him for what he considered to be perversion of his sexuality. Norman wouldn't admit to being gay, instead he saw it as a pathology injected into him by the likes of Thorpe, a contaminated virus that had inexorably corrupted him. He was dangerous and repeatedly told friends, but not me, he was going to shoot Thorpe and commit suicide.

My other deep problem with the tangled relations between Thorpe and Scott was that neither possessed the capacity to forgive each other. Both argued wrong as right, and for me the rebuttals from both parties was like standing in the slipstream of a taxiing aircraft. Norman knew his worth, but only in the negative sense of what he had on Thorpe, and part of him got a twisted satisfaction from the suspended threat of outing Thorpe to the media. Blackmail for him became like a donor organ, an implant he wasn't to give up willingly. None of the persuasions I offered to give up his letters, a quantity of which had already been read by the Metropolitan Police and MI5 ever worked. One-off cash payment, the procurement of jobs, a private stay at the Priory, all coercive incentives were turned down by his smug refusal to budge from the jackpot he sat on. 'Tell him Bunny will think about it,' he'd say. 'Bunny needs a bit of time.'

I'd go back to Thorpe's flat, the dark green clank of a Booth's gin bottle squat on the table, and he'd be fussing with tongs, hauling ice cubes into a chunky tumbler like the design of a Russian freeze. The flat had the smell of his vapid Englishness, Penhaligon scents, Quercus or Sartorial, a hangover of slightly burnt toast, one blackened slice still left in the stainless steel pop-up toaster, and that big indomitable odour exuding from London's dirty concrete skin. He'd be skimming the *Times*, and a slew of tabloid headlines for mention of his name, and twitchy like an air-smoker, trying to connect with the comment feeds in his nerves. Before I could even speak, he'd say, 'I hope you had sex with him, he's wonderful in bed,' as if I cared. To me he was just another rent boy with a blackmail file, a lubriciously sleazy portfolio on an MP selfishly hardwired to the political gold rush and the offshore patrons the position aced.

'No letters again,' I'd say, as he floated me a drink, quadrupling in the hope of seeing me compromised. 'If you don't get them soon,' he'd say, squinting with left-eye reflex; then Peter's got the final solution—a bullet. We'll hire a hitman. It's no different to shooting a sick dog.'

'I'll get them,' I said, 'or I'll see him off his game and that will ruin him. Viral negative feedback amongst punters will have him kill himself. Far better than the scandal of dirty fingerprints for the forensic team, J.T.'

'You get me wrong,' he said. 'I'm into the thrill of danger, real blood on the floor, and not giving him the luxury of real suicide in a greasy bedsit.' He simultaneously unknotted the noose of a Liberty's burnt-orange silk tie and reviewed his own squeezed mind-set that I imagined had Norman as a central focus with a red wound in his head.

'Whether he lives,' Thorpe continued, 'depends entirely on you, and I mean that,' he threw at me, cold as MI5 speak in going wet. I could see gin was exacerbating the divisive in him between lucidly proposed reason, and pre-deliberated homicide, with the axis tilted towards potential murder. He dolloped what looked like a triple into his still half-filled fizzing glass, submerging the crescent slice. 'Fucking little shit,' he said, 'if he gave the letters back I could buy him again when I wanted, and bump up his pockets. He's always broke, he can't stick at anything, he's got a personality disorder, as well as ADHD, and they're the worst, you can't reason with a basis that's consumed by revenge.'

I looked away, irrationally conceiving that if you made a fusion of the two pathologies, Thorpe and Scott, you'd have something like the classic oligarch. The grey matter of two brains joined into a cement cake, was how I saw it.

Thinking to distract him, I threw a bit of rent gossip his way to feed his punter's need for salacity. 'You know Jamie from the White Bear—you had him a few times—he got his drink spiked at a celebrity's flat, last week. A big floor in Knightsbridge. Anyhow, he woke up in the morning with someone you know in his bed. It was the Commons Speaker, drinking fizz at 9 a.m. Sunday morning, a cocktail cig jutting out of the corner of his mouth.'

Thorpe exploded with laughter. 'Go on, tell me more,' he said. 'I want to know the lot. So Tommy fucked Jamie, and I'm jealous. It makes me appear innocent.'

He loaded his glass again and seemed at a hysterical edge. 'I hope he gets blackmailed too,' he said vindictively, 'or some virulent STD.' He slammed his glass down, involuntarily, and appeared to savour the idea he had something on someone else, and perhaps could shunt him for a favour, in the way Norman was exploiting him.

'You know,' Thorpe said, 'I really feel like some pickled cannibalism. What about a rasher of Norman's skin garnished with Fortnum's Gentleman's Relish. It's time a Dilly boy was eaten, and my appetite is sharpened. Have another drink, Will,' he said, tangentially. 'It'll cheer you up before you're carved into rashers one day and eaten.'

It was like that; the heat was on and there was already investigative police files on Thorpe's illicit homosexuality, something seen as potentially compromising to his office. His natural arrogance led him to believe he was untouchable by class and position, and that his assumed unimpeachable honesty would instantly annihilate accusations from street boys the *Evening Standard* regularly captioned 'vermin.' Only, I was superior vermin, because I was a go-between for Thorpe, an emissary petitioning rent to keep to the loosely accepted rules of the game. Those were implicitly supposed to be no robbery, no violence, no blackmail, just exchange for exchange: sex=time=money, and a taxi back to Piccadilly Circus if that was your starting hub. I'd done it hundreds.

He was drinking through the day now to know a distorted reality. 'Why don't you spend the night with me?' he whoozily drawled, leaning across to stroke my thigh proprietorially; and I knew it was time to be going. Thorpe drunk was a case of reverse thespian into avuncular, sentimental sugardaddy, a carpet-slippered sleazebag you didn't want to know, as he oozed gin and fake romance.

'Peter's hard on the case like you Johnny, I mean Will. He's tried hard as you know to find Scott a job abroad. He even met the Social Services minister to try and resolve Scott's national insurance problems, and even been to the Home Secretary to ascertain they're not yet on my case. Just get the letters back, right, and I'll upgrade you. How do you like your eggs in the morning, if you stay over?'

I made a reasoned exit, staying cool, and said I was onto another sensitive case for him and meeting the incipient blackmailer at the Standard. Thorpe smiled, and said, 'Good luck, flatten him like a tank rolling over a bug.'

I left, reflecting as I did on the modality of networking authoritarianism, the image-management that groomed the publicly inscrutable like Thorpe, all aspiring to raunchy six-figure salaries, and walked from Marsham Court down Whitehall under a pink miles-wide carbonised sunset, headed towards Piccadilly Circus, intending to give Norman one of Bessell's retainers, and cajole him over the lubricant of vodka into parting with more of Thorpe's indiscreetly phrased letters that pointed to a series of cheap sexual encounters at the Regent Palace Hotel, the room-service condominium of laissez faire for rent boys.

As I soaked in the renewed thermostatic heat of the bath-tub, huge blocks of the Thorpe affair returned to me like scrambled video. I notice too the obtrusive box of prescribed Citalopram that Howard is prescribed, doubtless to do with the exhaustive robotics of a job saturated in the white noise of global make. He'll never properly speak to me of his vi-olently oscillating mood swings flattened at night by drink from the stratospheric stress of financial analysis in the arena of character assassination in the workplace. I notice too the multiple boxes of Viagra spilling from a cabinet, the blue granular diamond that helps sustain his new propensity for chemsex addiction. As far as I've learnt from Howard there's no update on our ambiguous neighbour, W.S., who is still away it seems, doubtless compartmentalising his life into neat unquestionable slices. I keep all these timeframes in my head, as neural databases, and keep my looks, always the same stun-ning posterboy, like a cryonically maintained Dorian Gray.

My unchanging youth wasn't the result of surgery or in-terventions like botox or the substitution of revitalizing hair follicles for loss of fat cells called adipocytes that are lost in the ageing process. I did it all virtually by a process of telemorphed gene-repair never losing my Bowie-like characteristics of ele-vated cheekbones and grey future-roaming eyes that seemed always to live in tomorrow, rather than today. In fact, I often have to make future appointments with myself to ascertain what's really happening in my life. Howard calls it distraction, but to me it's a totally normal perception of the world as it's already happened in the future.

The Thorpe affair, as an exaggeratedly overblown scandal of its time accelerated precipitantly into a state of lawless des-peration. You probably know the story of aborted murder, and Scott's hysterical comeback on Thorpe as a serial predator of juveniles scooped from lowlife. Thorpe defences down over blackmail didn't care how Scott was killed; a gun, a shovel, or cemented into a motorway pillar. I was offered money by Jack Hayward and David Holmes to negotiate a last time, and to diplomatically rough Scott up psychologically into parting with the original letters. I met him at the anodyne Richlieu at Green Park, where the cakes are wedged like fridges with coagulative cream. I knew Norman's soft spot, even though he was still modelling Regency-styled velvets and Liberty fabric patterned shirts. 5'11", chest 38, waist 30. I'm a 29. I already had an inch on him, and I could see he was zonked on downers, Librium and Mogadon, he told me, matched by brandy.

Norman looked wrecked despite his designer, as though his face had dropped with the drugs to the altered look of somebody fifty years on getting squeezed by habituation to heavy maintenance meds. He appeared right down. He'd been kicked out of his Earls Court flat after a crunchingly sadistic divorce, he told me, and needed another sugar daddy like J.T., and did I have anyone on offer?

I told Norman outright that 25k wasn't on offer and that 2,500 was for the originals and all copies made of them; there was no bargaining. The package would also include my personal intro to a rich needy man in his seventies who wanted a live-in friend at St. Johns Wood, and a retraction on his part that Thorpe had effectively raped him.

Norman looked interested, but wasn't buying the package, as he dug into black forest gateau, preening each mouthful with a spoon, rather than a fork. He seemed dangerously on the edge of collapse and peeled off a Librium gel from a silver foil, as though feeding a habit that had got him by the throat. He wouldn't compromise for less than ten grand, and wanted the same amount to supply a statement to the effect that he'd lied about the whole thing due to mental confusion at the time of a breakdown.

I decided then to lean on him as I had a case on him blackmailing a Sony AR man, who I knew, and what's more

I was in possession of the letters, and arguably in a position to counterblackmail. He was sufficiently smart to realise he was caught in a sensitive network sticky as sperm. His way to was to turn defensive, shut up, and play delay tactics with his sluttish cube of gateau. I realised then there was no conceivable resolution to his type of sordid extortion, and no end to the dirty tricks he sourced as self-empowerment. The letters returned, Norman would revert to an anonymous face on the tube, looking out for his next small-time encounter, or nothing at all, but the ozone stench of the escalator up to another rainy street at Baron's Court. And part of me genuinely feared for him, and didn't want to see him taken out as Thorpe's fall guy in his manic presumptive rush to power.

'Look,' I said, 'these guys mean business, I mean Thorpe's dodgy gofers; do yourself a favour, and take the deal. You can't go on doing this all of your life, you're making yourself ill.'

'But I still love him,' Scott said, mouth full of chocolate sponge. 'You don't understand, victims bond with their rapists, boys as much as girls.' Then he laughed hysterically, suddenly out of control, hands flapping wildly, his anomalous behaviour having everyone turn and pointedly stare.

'I LOVE JEREMY THORPE,' he screamed, and as instantly reverted back to character, introverted, nervous, and compulsively popping another pill. It was terrifying to witness, this involuntary outburst stored somewhere in his nerves, and as I suspected, likely to occur again, like a repeat handgun.

I couldn't tell him outright that Thorpe had a contract out on him for £10,000, and that a pernicious ex-pilot called Andrew Newton was to receive that blood money for blowing his head off when he next returned to Devon, or could I? Or could I? 'Look,' I said, 'I don't like authority anymore than you do, but the one thing I know is that if you actively oppose them they roll over you. Let's just say, Thorpe's got his hitmen, and they'll find you out, Norman. Be clear on that.'

'I'll risk it, and hang on to the letters,' he said defiantly. 'I'm not parting for less than £22,500,' and suddenly right in my face, 'the arrogant fucker ruined me. He's a pervert and a liar. He raped me and denies it. MI5 have the whole story on file.'

'That's the problem,' I said. 'That's why there's a price on your head.'

You know the rest; it's documented history. Norman's beatings, Newton's mismanagement of the contract, he shot Scott's dog Rankin, instead of Norman, the media explosion, Thorpe's implacable tissue of lies maintained during his trial for attempted murder, and the whitewash resulting in his acquittal. The corrupt are invariably endorsed by the corrupt that judge them. They're the sleazy interface called the ruling classes; even pissed on, uric acid won't erode their incorrigible defences.

I get out of the cooling green bathtub. The black marble floor feels like a sarcophagus. Howard's squirted me a text to say he's flying out within hours to the Cayman Islands, and won't be back for three days. The usual airborne pursuit of the offshore laundered gold trail. Howard's also got a jam sticky finger in the former Mayfair office and studio of a late restaurateur, now four fabulousy plush Mayfair flats with predictive postmodern finish for ghost owners, like his Saudi royal clients, who will take up virtual residence with their domestic AIs in waiting: an entourage of white robots as geek minders of high-end Belgravia shells.

I'll go out to Hop Gardens and do what I do, write what you're reading, if you've got this far. Most novels are abandoned 30-40 pages in. But writing for me is still an inveterately transcendent act, the chance to put myself into language, as my peripheral. Language is the ultimate robot; it's always there to be read, or just stay squat like a meditation class on the line. I dress, and quit the house like it's already tomorrow today.

11

LIVING WITH BUSINESS CLASS

Howard gets slung around the world like a chunk of ice furniture thrown out of a Boeing. His sex hangover and accumulatively built jetlag often leave him apparently displaced in time, so that like me, he lives in his own window of reality. Howard's brain, and I can hear it, hums like the white noise from an inaudible fridge. Sometimes at home, he walks like he's navigating an air-pocketing aisle to a stainless steel Boeing toilet up there on a blue curve to Singapore. His job bravura has him insistently follow a carbon imprint of kerosene exhaust across the airways to the network of treasure islands, as partially gated tax havens.

Howard's travel doesn't involve anxiously staring at the update on flight status screens, but Heathrow's No1 Traveller, for instance, with showers, nap pods, afternoon tea, treatment rooms, on-site spas, a whole amalgam of privileges that place him in a meta-state between champagne bars and long haul. He's recently returned from a Tokyo digress to the Hakushu distillery, the scale of the concrete site, the space-age tech, white-suited technicians, and security guards patrolling in turquoise uniforms, white gloves and kepis, having him feel like he'd encountered an 007 time-slip. He'd brought back a bottle of Hakashu 12, a smoky event with licks of grass and pear, an egregious blend of cherry-picked cultures given a distinctive Japanese aesthetic, gifted him by a bespoke client. He'll buy T.M. Lewin shirts at airport concessions, wear them a week, and throw them away.

He's in another spacesuit compared to me in terms of time-travel. I don't need to cultivate alien by listening to freak broadcasts bounced in from 1420 mergahertz, I do my time-slips on the only alien planet—Earth. We don't know it as a species, but we're mostly unreadable to other intelligences in the choking gas clouds of the galaxies. Our biology is largely non-adaptive to object travel, and my advantage is in knowing this, together with my facility to time-slip through the tissue of successive remakes. To Howard my concepts of reality would be sci-fi, in the sense of navigating successive pathways with the singular identity of Mr. W.H. And I've taken to seeing Kit again on a casual basis, knowing that Howard is ruthlessly promiscuous and keeps me only as a trophy of wealth and power. I sometimes try to imagine what it will be like when he's done for fraud or rigging Libor. Knowing Howard he'll fall out of a tower at Canary Wharf after denting the bar with a run on Perrier-Jouet. He would never be able to renounce his hedonistic excesses, his Charles Street floor, the Christmas bonuses, his addictive sex tourism, and the thrill dealt his nerves by fraud, crypto-currencies, laundering, and the floating deodrant cube of corruption orbiting his brain.

With Kit it's different, his discontinuous purchase on his past makes him, like me, anomalously weird, decidedly post-human in our contemporary designs. Kit's moved on from the immensely successful plays by which he's historically identified—*Dido, Queen of Carthage, Tamburlaine, The Jew of Malta, Edward the Second, Doctor Faustus,* and now writes, so he tells me as a push-on from J.H. Prynne, with an aesthetic formalism in which his diction foregrounds itself as a play between concretion and abstraction. He tells me self-disparagingly that poetry works like quantum particles—it exists in two separate places without a physical connection and nobody sees it, nobody but other poets reads it. It's there, but it's invisible, like imagining someone you're going to fuck as a free-floating fantasy, which suddenly becomes real.

London, as I see it, is progressively re-landscaped into a post-apocalyptic modality. Its skin is like re-sutured tissue over a hideous scar that was there in 1590 and will always remain. It's the city's core, its hub, its torched navel, its smog drenched in particulates of nitrogen dioxide, its replicants, zombies, AIs that are all headed for the giant orange flash. Kit tells me he can feel it too, the past reposting itself as the future, only with coefficient nuclear tech, rather than blade skirmishes and GBH in muddy ditches on Hog Lane. You can sniff apocalyptic end time in its urban jungle, and see it in the faces peeling out of the tube into still another grainy day that could be any day only it's dated, and probably raining big pear-shaped drops.

I'm headed down drizzly Shaftesbury Avenue in the direction of Hop Gardens, when I see him, and my brain goes into overdrive. It's unmistakably W.S.—I know it by the propulsive thrust of dark energies he emits, as he's maybe just approaching the Japanese restaurant Shibyua, dressed all in black, hair scooped under a black wool hat, and there's no way I can avoid him, it's more that we're on a collision course and I can't turn back, or even cross the road, but compelled to walk directly towards him. I tense up as the gap narrows between us, and on spontaneous impulse freeze a cab, throw myself in and just say, 'Leicester Square, please,' as the driver gets off an amber in rapid diesel surges. Even though I post my eyes out the opposite window to avoid his, I go right for a split-second and he's there frozen on the pavement, his shocked projective stare bouncing off the window like a tennis ball.

The cab gets a red at Cambridge Circus, and I have this irrational fear he'll come running after it and try to force the powerlock. We take a right into Charing Cross Road, and decide to get out at Leicester Square, still jittery with suspicion he'll show up as the conspicuous man in black in the crowd. W.S. with his Stratfordian accent, his indigenous rural walk, his exploitative energies, no Londoner would believe he's back after centuries cutting a solitary figure in the crowd. He was as I remember always awkward in the company of patrons, developed a marginally apologetic air, appeared unnaturally hesitant, but was ruthless when it came to business. His marriage didn't help either, he was ashamed of Anne, and believed he'd married too early and too low, and that the baggage inhibited his gay life in London with the Southampton and Pembroke circles.

I think of all this as I make my way through St. Martin's Court to nichey Hop Gardens, as my concrete workspace, as public as it is private. Some protean graffito's left a fluo-rocoloured surge of lurid pink on the wall on which I sit to write reading MAKE SPACE FOR TWO BLAIR TO JOIN THATCHER IN HER COFFIN. I sit opposite this graffiti sandwich of named oligarchs, and still apprehensive that W.S. will show up again, searching the West End, maybe simply to establish eye contact and move on again until the next time, certain it's me, but not quite, as though he's right on the fron-tier of self-realisation as to our true respective identities. .

It's become history, like a vaccine, that Thomas Thorpe pirated the Sonnits without the author's permission; but it was me who pioneered it through the loan of the manuscript to Thom. He was always breaching publishing rights by ac-quiring circulating manuscripts of what he considered to be literary merit, and got a cult reputation for publishing cut-ting-edge books. Nobody reads them now, but he published John Marston's *The Malcontent*, Ben Jonson's *Sejanus*, Kit

Marlowe's censored translation of the first book of Lucan's *Pharsalia*, George Chapman's *Byron*, as predictable slow-burners, like developing a taste for something dark kept in a cupboard. Only thirteen copies of the original Sonnits have survived the centuries, unlike almost 300 copies of the 1623 First Folio—I know this stuff off Google as I'm the subject of a book that keeps on reprinting or being downloaded as a text for courses. And it comes back on me all the time, the coding in it, the deliberate sexual ambiguity and London's part in the ultimate solution that he helped shape through occult cachet, with the future complete as a red glowering radioactive cone.

And for me, as personal history the lights have gone out at Piccadilly Circus on my old neon drenched rent arena, replaced by a new curved, ultra-high definition 4K resolution screen aiming to futureproof the space, while retaining the familiar patchwork aesthetic. Bigger than a full-sized tennis court, its focus has replaced the old retrofitted six-screens shuffling the familiar ads—Coca-Cola, Samsung, Schweppes, maintained for decades by Land Securities and programmed into the retinal library of every sex-tourist and ex-Dilly boy. The lights are out for nine months, as I write into this space, or rather naked hub, in that its geophysicals attract, pull people in from all over the planet to stand there creating their own configuration of the Circus, as something that has either gone, or is in the process of arriving, like the future is already there, only we don't properly recognise it. The neon/LED screens were like sci-fi boards, industrial complexes built into the sky by imagining their potentialities, rather than their display realities as retroactive consumerism. Stoned, and hanging out there, I'd seen the screens as psychoactive jewels, rubies, sapphires, emeralds, interacting above the streaming highway. There's been no shut down of lights there since WW2, so I stare up at the electronic shells of a dead system, as though time itself has stopped, and will only resume when the lights come on again offering live video streaming and lifestyle updates, real-time social media feeds, ensuring the space stays at the forefront of innovation after a necessary period of tech rehabilitation. Deleting the Piccadilly boards is like rubbing out time and wiping a big part of my life spent there, face spotting to detach a stranger out of the commuter traffic.

Hop Gardens by contrast, is a minor offensive, just an alley without personal associations, and dead to anything but casual pedestrians slicing through to Bedfordbury for a time-gain. That's as much as an alley can do divorced from history, and workable as a timesaving cut-through. I sit there and write, my head naturally full of the return of W.S. I don't think the small fame of a poet meant anything significant to him in his last climacteric years, soaking up damp English winters, rheumatically, smoking drugs and putting a block of ice, big as Antarctica between him and Anne, eating shepherd's pie, like Keith Richards at the knotty rough-grained kitchen table. And whatever Kit's writing now has to differ by his awareness of cyber potentialities and the realisation that somewhere in urban dystopias end time awaits a double-click. In the past Kit's inventiveness was to straddle known geography, declare his status as a proponent of the capital's underbelly, but also as the elevated courier of poetic info to be moved around. I've gone and pulled up those lines from Faustus—'Ill be great Emperor of the world/And make a bridge through the moving air,' and so on. You could do that then, make bits into geography like an apple, with the audience spitting it back in your face. And neither faction was big enough to care. Try telling them that in Waterstones.

I get a text from Lucy Negro, wanting to meet, and it's important, she says. W.S. is sniffing around and she don't like it. Asks if we can meet in Foyles fifth-floor café after a Russian assignment. She's told me repeatedly that there's been three guys hanging out on her Knightsbridge block, who don't belong. And I can guess which they are—Frizer, Poley and Skeres in their new skins, shipped back in time from murders they've already committed. Over the weeks Lucy's told me things about W.S. he always kept secret from me, in that after the birth of his two children, the twins Hamnet and Judith, he clean disappeared, seeing the obligatory fucking of his wife was over. Lucy says he was all sorts of things, a trainee lawyer, a pharmacist, a sailor, a hippie on the road, an actor with a touring company, a retainer in a country house, and maybe in all these roles, a spy with 'the secret protects itself' written into his nerves. And whatever we believe in wears out, like the knees in jeans, or the oxidisation of Bob Dylan's voice from smoke and scorch-marks of whiskey. And I think of five centuries shuttling the arteries, like slower-than-light ships boiling into space, as a-national pirates launched from the Moscow suburbs, sometime so far back in history, it's a snap-shot of the present.

I leg the blocks over to Foyles, my favourite book con-dominium with its retro-future Warhol silver foil industrial fixtures in a digital café that's like one collective display of cos-mic apps. If these spacegirl students from the global village, working on tablets there, knew Lucy had fucked Shakespeare repeatedly as a sex-worker in Shoreditch, they'd undoubtedly spook. And if I told them I was his male whore they'd do quantum stuff in their brain processes as exit doors.

Lucy doesn't look like anyone else in this Tea Pigs con-cession. She's wearing an anomalous platinum wig, and sci-fi paperback orange eye shadow, a leather-zippered biker jacket and pressed navy skinnies. I get it all inclusively in one take; I'm that clothes conscious, not of fashion, but individual peri-od-quirk. She's no-decade designed, a crypto-fashionista with fist-clenched attitude. The café's Asian digital natives don't even know she's there in the lustedgreen design to evoke the elements of bookmaking, like the typewriter key signage and the letterpress inspired serving counter, where I pick up two speciality teas and a raspberry frangipani for Luce or Lucy; today I prefer Luce.

I join her on the corner of a workbench of UCL students, a lot of them Chinese, dressed in jumpers, deconstructed jeans and knee boots, all concentrated into their specific discipline, an exhausted cappuccino at the elbow. Lucy's eye craters are neon orange, and she looks upset, but nonetheless resolute. She apologises for whatever she may be interrupting in my day, and immediately insists I take a tenner for the teas, extracting it from a green Cartier wallet in her bag. 'It's him again,' she says, starting out. 'You know trouble, W.S. He must have followed me from my block into Harrods, I do the Food Hall once a week, largely to pick up punters, and when I went back out without striking lucky, he was waiting for me. He wouldn't go away and insisted forcibly on walking me back home, despite my repeatedly telling him to fuck off. He's got this hold on me, this power and I even let him come up to the flat as I was so sold on what he might have to say.'

'You're joking,' I said. 'You did what?'

'I couldn't break the spell,' Lucy said. 'I was afraid of what would happen if I didn't let him, and afraid of the outcome if I did. Stupid bitch.'

'But he only beat you up badly a few weeks ago, and you let him in?'

'It wasn't sex he wanted, this time, it was something else, I knew it.'

I looked out suddenly at rain streaming across the rooftop garden, and the transient silhouette of a Boeing finning it through a luminous corridor between rolling clouds, as Lucy picked at her frangipane.

'He told me this extraordinary story that probably only you would believe. Not only that we were both his sex partners in history, but that he'd committed murder back then, and that the man he'd murdered was in his sights again, and he felt compelled to kill him a second time. Told me he was seeing a psychoanalyst out of town about the problem, and that he'd left his wife and moved a bit into the country near Stratford on Avon.'

'It's a lot to take in,' I said, coding the facts into what I already suspected, as though I'd shot a film of it before it happened, as a second silver dazzle shower doused the West End and went off on an arc into more rain.

'You never knew Kit Marlowe,' I said. 'He was a close friend of mine and was reportedly murdered at Deptford Creek by undercover. I've always suspected W.S. did it. But there's three other men around, the ones I suspect you've seen hanging out on your street, who are equally dangerous and implicated in Kit's murder.'

Lucy spontaneously pulled up Kit on her phone, and said, 'He's gay of course, like everyone associated with W.S. A real pretty boy, if that's his portrait. Red hair, black eyes, I can see the appeal, if you like that sort.' She chewed on another bit of her cake and suddenly looked alarmed. 'This guy, Kit,' she said, 'Deptford you say? I remember now, once when W.S. visited me, there was blood caked on his shirt, a red crust of it. He made light of it, told me it was something happened months ago, and that someone had attempted to mug him on the street.'

'Go on,' I said, feeling the past and present collide in the quantum rush of a dissolve.

'I don't know why,' she said,' but could this Kit be the person he claims to have murdered?'

'It's sort of playing both ends against the middle,' I said, 'but you're near enough right. Kit Marlowe if you want to know was both an agent and an agent provocateur, what we call a purveyor of both information and disinformation, someone who carried info you shouldn't for your own safety. But he was also a rival poet and that's where W.S. comes in.'

'Dunno about poetry,' she said, fingering her cup with burgundy talons. 'All I know is I'm frightened of this whole thing, whatever it is. I feel squeezed indoors and out, as though someone's about to get me in both places. I've read of cases of possession and that's what I feel, choked on the inside, as though someone or something's broken into me. Do something for fuck's sake Will, or we're all going to end up dead, if we aren't already.'

I sneaked a share of Lucy's cake, wondering if we weren't really the living dead, time-confused replicants invading a space in which we were aliens saturated in immersive flashback.

'If I told you what I really fear, you'd probably think I was mad,' I said, again focusing on a diagrammatic parcel of rain-drops clustering like pear drops on the window. The sky over St. Giles was a debilitated grey, and other lives, other people out there under the rain were establishing their own realities, independent of mine, and everyone else's in the roughed-up capital.

'I still see a lot of Kit,' I said, as though needing to deeper confuse her. 'I can't tell you what he does; only what he did, if that makes sense. I know you have your client confidentiality, like I do. Kit's like us, a time-slip person, whatever that means, only we somehow remain the same through the centuries.'

'I sort of understand,' she said. 'You mean we remember chunks of our past, like we're reliving it.'

'Yes, it's something like that,' I said, my eyes distracted by two Asian girls sharing phone clips like they were mixing a new version of reality.

'Do you believe in the devil?' Lucy asked, 'because I think I've met him and so have you. And you know who I mean.'

I looked out distractively into the increasing rain and re-alised I had too, and that the devil to my mind adapted to the times by slipping into the collective skin. Both of us apparently suspected W.S. as the individual threat to end time, rather than thermonuclear resources, someone who secreted the programme into three pounds of grey matter, with the internalised potential to blow up the world. Lucy's mind was clearly split into obsessive phone checking for clients, and our real-time physical presence.

I realise nobody stays in my life, but everyone significant returns on the unresolved cycle of Shakespeare's tricky history that burns like the compression drive of a pirate starship into the fabric of time. My novel is my ending, and I couldn't care, a few more months sitting out in Hop Gardens, randomly anthologising street life, with its raw ammonia drive, and it'll be done as another novel whirled into book orbit like space junk travelling so fast it burns up on re-entry.

Lucy clears off to cab it back to Knightsbridge for the fuck assignations queuing on her phone. One of her clients, she told me last time, was offering to patent her statistics for the creation of a black sex bot to be marketed in China. It was the gluteal tissue of her bum he wanted to clone to the exact figurative centimetre.

And me. I've got my own assignment with this guy I met at the Porchester Spa in Bayswater, the update of what was the Turkish and Russian Vapour Baths, a hot room complex for man on man solitaries leaving their signature on the steamed green-tiled space. It was only his eyes I liked, their brightness like zirconian crystals showing out of grey irises. He's serious at Tate Modern, so I've checked, and has a flat at Cornwall Gardens, one of a warren of high-end Kensington apartments I've visited in the past for the paid qualia of sex. I've done my research; he's 54, divorced, Cambridge, Courtauld educated, family property in Wiltshire, independent curator, art historian, and currently has a curatorial post at Tate Modern. I've noted the clothes, expensive casual. Grey herringbone jacket, probably Cordings, plaid Burberry scarf, soft roll-collar blue button-down, most likely Ivy League, Tommy Hilfiger jeans, I caught the logo, biscuit suede desert boots—I mentally snapshot it all as detail-specific to my sort of type.

I tube over to Gloucester Road, secretly smug with the knowledge that my assignation is probably unlike anyone else's in my carriage, the suits, the Thai nurses, the eclectic harassed workforce dispersed across the network with stress written into their faces. Each surge of oxidised track heightens the adrenalin rush I get before surrendering to a stranger in a suitably affluent apartment. My life is rich pickings and I've no apology for it. This guy I'm on my way to, I'll invent a name, Stephen, I've told him I want two grand for the look. How can you put a price on an individual signature, like mine, as ambiguously amazing as the young David Bowie. I may up it to three grand, depending on where it leads. In my world one rich contact ideally leads to another, like a process of intuitive sending. The game never kills the risk, there's always the mental shadow floats over my consciousness like a jellyfish that something bad could break out of me, or the punter, in the loose binding of the verbal contract. I've heard stories of boys hysterically trashing apartments, robbing or looting punters, getting into fights, littering teeth over the carpet, getting abducted, or just plain disappearing. Somebody at the Dilly used to keep a black book listing missing or murdered rent boys, all the unaccountables.

I get a text from Howard, on the way, ignoring me, and biting on gold investment demand as totalling 0.4 tonnes last month according to data from precious metals platform BullionVault. Howard typically states Trump, Article 50 and European elections as the key drivers of demand for the safe haven asset. He's incurably obsessed.

On arriving at Cornwall Gardens I depress the annunciator marked 3, and Stephen lets me in. Being punctilious goes with my profession as an escort. I take the navy carpeted stairs up to the third floor and the door's half-open as an implicit gesture of trust. Stephen stands welcomingly in the hall, as though I'm a long-term friend he's expecting, rather than a transitioning escort he hardly knows. People wonder at the mystique surrounding rent, and my demystification of it is that much of the moves are stereotypical heterosexual strategy, only that the transaction is same-sex. I'm offered the usual tea, coffee or a drink, what more do you want; a jade silk cushion into which I collapse my back, while Stephen re-settles into a lived-in rubbed blue corduroy armchair next to a drinks tray, as all too cushy, art catalogues littering the floor, Bacon, Hockney, Hirst, the works. As I look him over I realise he must have been subjected to bashings, hurt, abuse, bottoming out in stairwells, and licked it over with house paint to put a veneer on scar tissue. He knows I know his submerged backstory, and that the subsurface cuts go deep, the revelatory nature of which can only be experienced from the outside. I focus my attention on the room as arty mess inflected with personalised style. Stephen (he could be anyone) uncorks, and pours each of us a glass of, is it Chablis, from the way it splits on the tongue as so lemony French? I've done this so often before for it to be happening in the present; it could equally be an excerpt from a previous decade, or life sent into the present, with a re-set clone substituting for me sitting on a rubbed taupe sofa talking preliminaries, semantics as the inevitable prelude to sex. It's like time's been dosed with Valium in the slowing down into banal sedation. Each move is like a preconceived signal creating a predictable frequency. It's all of course leading one way as rehearsed mildly apologetic sex on a John Lewis or Liberty patterned throw. There was something of the trancy reality of it reminded me of queuing on a rainy runway for the BA boarding steps to the cabin. Stephen was deliberately hanging on to his drink, and the idea of sex, rather than the reality. I knew more or less how it would go, and that the obligatory sex would be damped down in the interests of speed. It's always like that, having sex before sex keeps the act more routinely minimal in my trade.

Eventually Stephen says something real to me in real-time. 'You're very different from the rest, I don't know quite how to put it, but you're probably psychic or telepathic in some way, I mean I can see you've got a curious angle on time.' And I say, 'Yes, the sex we're going to have has already happened in my way of experiencing time. It's like it's over for me, but just starting for you, and we've no way of living in each other's personalised time.'

Stephen laughed, but mixing serious reflection into his response, and went straight-faced. 'I must say in my limited experience of escorts, there's certainly never been anyone like you.'

'Oh, I've been around in the right company,' I said, 'soaking up knowledge of what really makes people work, and I've absorbed a lot of it. It's probably this that makes me a bit different. I don't like types. Probably any more than you do.'

Stephen had a soft round laugh like fuzz on a peach, and used it endearingly. I've never truly fallen for a punter, but the unlikely option is always there, and I quickly shut it out and refocused him as money. I knew intuitively he wasn't exploitable, but nor was he a soft touch or he wouldn't be where he was in the arts world. I've known so many soft or hard Maltesers in my life, the compact chocolate coating on the coercive or marble fist for a heart.

He appears to have all the time in the world, but of course, he doesn't, and nor do I, as I'm here maximum sixty minutes into sex outro. I can tell he's nearing the point where the subject of sex has to be raised, as I'm not a social visitor, but an escort/alias rent. I get a sense of someone else in the flat, an e-body ambience telling me he lives with someone he's cheating on, who is probably at his workplace opening a Pret a Manger pack of hummus and salad sandwiches, as veggie discipline. There's a smell, an aura of it takes two baby about the place, a different psychic imprint as symbiotic to Stephen's own. I get that sometimes, a paranormal tingle, an extrasensory shiver of virtual infecting reality. (I can imagine a fucking mainstream conglomerate fiction editor reading this in flattened one-dimensional reality, and giving up here); and me, I just don't care at all.

Stephen knows I've intuitively sniffed something, and instinctively closes up as a subtle defence mechanism. He wants me to think he's a solo Londoner, too self-sufficient as a bread-winner to need anyone but me, as his occasional privileged escort in high-end Ken. I can see the vacant leather club chair opposite him has lived-in creases, the mapping of regular use by what is probably a partner, so I ask him, 'do you live alone here, or do you share?'

By way of reply he smiles in a way that tells me he's found out, and will attempt to ghostbrand his partner into a casual friend. 'Why do you ask?' he smiles.

'Because my profession is strictly one-to-one,' I say, 'and a second person in concealment could mean trouble.'

'Oh, it's nothing,' he says. 'There's nobody here I can assure you. Robert stays over sometimes at the weekend, that's all. There's no real commitment. We've been on/off for twenty years. It gives me a bit of personal security.'

I trust him, although I've been sprung before, being taken into a closed bedroom where a second man is waiting in bed for an announced threesome, and I've been out of the apartment at lightspeed. Slammed the doors like I'm bolting up history and run. Stephen's 1970s underframe though is reassuring, like he's still got the decade's mix of idealism and brattish punk as an enviable resource. In a different context, I would probably like him, but he's alien, and total dissociation is my method of earning. Whatever the subtle energies at play that allow this exchange to happen, the cold exploitative reason behind it is money on my part, and on his the fantasy of conquest.

When we finally make it to the bedroom the St. Giles blue walls are stashed with artwork excluded from the living space. The chosen colours are anxiolytic blues and greens, a smart television, disordered slews of books on and by the bed, otherwise minimal and with a whiteout blind for exclusion.

Like most serial fantasists Stephen doesn't want to fuck, rather he wants to prize my body, and chew my cock with slow salival massage. If he fucked me the raw physicals of the act would degrade the illusion; I'd be meat rather than a manipulatively elusive image. I can feel the quantum window he's opened, and the divisive between us, like I'm more in his head than on his tongue. He points me up from the balls to the tip of my cock, sensually, learning the flavour of my skin, working slowly from bottom to top like rolling a fetish on his tongue. I don't fake excitement; I leave it to him to work towards his own orgasm through the prolonged thrill of having me in his mouth. It goes on for maybe another fifteen minutes; it's not that I deliberately repress orgasm; it's more that indifference dictates delay. I can't help but be erect, but it's not because of him, it could be anyone male or female giving me head. I can hear the undulating surf of white noise outside, a mix of air traffic and the ambient dynamic of the capital.

Stephen's wanking himself to an end, and I make the concentrated effort to torch-up and cum, and we're both in rubbers, so there's no sticky excess, as a giveaway to his partner, if I'm right about his status. He flops down next to me, one arm thrown over my torso, and doesn't attempt the clichés of 'how was it for you?' or 'that was fantastic,' but just subsides into his own reality. I've already been paid, payment always comes before sex as a stipulation when you're hired, and I'm not going to unduly hurry him by the fact his allocated time has expired. He's my only assignation today, as I needed a bit of spending money, and too the exhilarating dopamine rush my job provides as habit. Stephen trances for ten minutes soaking in bodily release, then disengages and heads to the bathroom. Even though I was rubbered I can hear him rinsing mouthwash, and slapping on expensive cologne I'll instantly identify at a flash. When he reappears he's already back in the same casuals and with a look as though it never happened, and I follow him back into the living room for another glass of vivacious Chablis, like we're sort of quasi-acquaintances meeting to talk an artist over drinks. I have this air-pocketing time-slip feeling like the sex never really happened, at least not then, and we're still waiting on it with a drink on hand again, or something like that.

Stephen makes no mention of blowing me, and reverts to casual inconsequential talk, Bacon predictably, and his assault course on canvas to explode shapes into figurative atrocities—wounding the canvas he calls it with facial lesions, as though the canvas could feel pain. He doesn't know what I had going with Bacon, near the end of his life, when he was wheezy asthmatic, arterially blocked and soaked in booze like a sponge. I follow his art speak curve about Bacon's transgressive take on beefcake physique, his designer clothes, his forays into Harrods Food Hall, and I know it all, and don't let on as crypto-currency. And all the time I'm mentally imaging Francis' split lips, his mashed eyes, the blood leaking down his cheeks after he'd paid to be beaten up in some dockside yard. It was his own face he used as the fabric of an S&M crash test dummy, broken up in a grungy room somewhere with a fist and bottle, and the cash paid for the beating soaked in blood. I knew that, as Stephen glossed Muybridge into context as the influence lived under Bacon's skin.

I leave Stephen, richer by a generous cash tip added on for sex with the escort nailed to the bed once by William

Shakespeare. As I pop into a corner minimart to buy a Kit Kat, what I remember mostly is Stephen's Paul Smith socks, a neon pink, green and orange stripe on a navy basis.

With Howard wiped by airmiles from my immediate concerns, and probably tequila blasted in a hotel bar with an oleaganously tough client, keeping several drinks behind for clarity, I check my contacts, and note Bill has sent me a triple suggestive emoji as coding he wants time with me in his apartment at Peninsula Heights, the Jeffrey Archer tower at Albert Embankment floating its airborne infrastructure over busy river traffic. Each assignation I tell myself is part of the book I'm writing, and part of my narrowing in on the enigma who started it all—the inexorable W.S. with his celebrity stranglehold on the globe. I call Bill, and he's up for it, and his real-time response tells me it's genuine; he misses me, as I know he does, as he's the one I get closest too emotionally, in this game of tripping clients' feelings like fuses. What I aim for as my coercive signature is to have them want me back with the feeling that what they missed out on the first time, maybe theirs the second, third or fourth, and so it goes on, six, seven, eight, in a pattern of repeat losing, but never so badly they abandon hope of forming a more durable relationship. My mind's rammed with this as I hit the underground again, and the tube's excoriating thunder over fried track.

And wasn't that what W.S. wanted all along, to substitute me for Anne, and in a weird way to so identify with me that he'd confuse his own looks with mine; the usual polarised attraction in the age gap between old and young. And it didn't work. It wasn't his body I loved, it was in a perverse way the pity I felt for his attempt to win me, his opposite, that became a kind of fascination as to why I was doing this to myself, having him idealise a love that wasn't his, just the empty shell of the sonnits. The fucking sonnits in which I'm both overvalued and undervalued by his subjective reasoning and my ribs broken by cold technique.

I look across the aisle at the ubiquitous phone readers, and left, close to the exit, immersed in his distractive reading, I swear it's him, the redoubtable W.S. It's like the shape of him has jumped out of my head into physical reality, the black on black clothes, the black woollen knit hat with the pompom, the total self-absorption and un-shareable mix or arrogance and scheming, the mechanistics are all there, like he can't quite contain what he's thinking and it might have him ripped to shreds. I'm partially obscured from his vision, I can see his fragmented profile as strips of black pixels, like holo blobs, and opposite a suit from his phone is sizing me up statistically, like he's rolling a condom on me, and I blank him with a mental force that swipes his face. It never ends, this process of assessing meat for its potential sale. In my panicked confusion I try to configurate what I'd say to him if confronted, and how I'd condense five centuries into a small quantum rub. In my mind I imagine him getting up and stabbing me with a kitchen knife in front of the shocked passengers, simultaneously with the doors opening at Ken High, and he loping off through the squeezed crowds to the exit. It's my rushed paranoid scenario, as I contemplate getting off at the next stop, only he does it for me. I watch him step out into the crowd like he's in the wrong century, a time-slip escapee, like an unnamed astronaut returned from a private 1970s Mars mission in the 23rd century.

Arrived at Vauxhall, Bill knows me only by the abbreviation W.S., he's never questioned further, and why should he in our particular exchange of money for flesh, or a largely absent body. But at the same time he's the only punter who really cares about me—I know that intuitively—and can read his concern and worry when he comes back from the kitchen with the gingersnaps and shortbread, and the frames of his designer eyewear have slipped to expose the worry lines. Bill got rich on fashionable menswear, a mod generation's commitment to the look, and total dedication to every nuance of self-appearance, as his edgy updated selling point. But inwardly, he's ordinary in terms of basic human needs—supermarket, the Sainsbury's giant mall at Nine Elms, domestic polish, concern over the health of friends, London politicos, the grind of the ordinary made into something purposeful in his floor overlooking on one side the MI5 fortress at Vauxhall, and on the other, the footage of Whitehall, over the moody, loopy Thames driven by angry green tides.

When I arrive Bill's trying to be on top of a bad diagnosis, and whether the positive is in him, or he's trying to be that, I don't know. I notice a teardrop brushing his left eye, but he's quickly immersed in making tea and peeling Gingernuts from a Sainsbury's pack on to a bordered plate. I stay with him in the kitchen, and then follow him into a streaming blade of sunlight that dazzles in our sitting place, with a police tug in view bouncing downriver and a tourist ferry churning up under Lambeth Bridge.

Bill just wants to pay for my company—his PSA levels are on a dangerous hike from increasingly aggressive prostate cancer, and the injected drug he's on, Zytiga, has stopped working. He tells me there's no right time to die, it's always too early or too late on the curve, and it's hard to imagine simply not being. 'I've got nothing important left to do in life,' Bill says, 'but I don't want to lose whatever it is I'm doing.' And of course it's always like that, the little and the much, and we cling to both, as all we know, unless like me you've got a psychic way of tricking time. 'It's the indifference of the world,' I say, 'how nothing out there seems to care, that puzzles me. I mean, there's no appeal.'

Now that John's dead—they were lifetime partners—Bill says he's got nothing to live for, but his daily domestic routine, only he's attached to it as a functional go-factor. I can see Bill's in the ontological crisis of wishing he wasn't here, but afraid of the process of dying. He'd probably like to have it all behind him already, painless as a screening, and in some quantum way of post-human identity be reunited with John. That's my assessment of his thoughts and not what he's telling me.

Bill hands me a sealed envelope of money, despite my resistance, and insists I take it, as in my game time is money. He's come out of business and knows the value of cash, the tactile exploitative purchase power of red fifty-pound holographic stripped notes. He tells me his oncologist, who is a personal friend, has an expensive US drug lined up as a method of pharmaceutical counterterrorism on warring cells, and as a weapon to extend his life at astronomical cost, should NHS drugs fail. And although the drug is not available on the NHS, Mark, his friend, will make an exception if need be, or failing that buy it wholesale for about one-sixth of the retail price. It's a little bit of optimism that floats in his mind like a moon-launch that might never touch planet. Bill's eminently practical.He's in and out of the kitchen fetching more tea, just ordinary M&S English Breakfast Tea, and to incite taste, chocolate digestives. And I think of the diverse shapes of my profession, where it places me, in situations I wouldn't otherwise encounter, sitting for instance a floor below Archer's designated gallery with the Warhol pops, talking up Grade 3 cancer with a friend, who is also a patron.

Bill's doing his best to remain bright, but I notice each time he goes to the kitchen to fetch his mood drops down the colour index to cloudy, but not quite monochrome grey. Inwardly, he's got an obstacle like a refrigerator in his brain he can't think around. Bill's thinking out loud as he re-crosses the room to me. 'You know, John was the first pop celebrity to buy a Rolls, lipstick-red interior, drove Princess Margaret to a club in it, while she was fucked on the backseat by a toy boy pouring champagne over her tits. Don't know what made me remember that; it just came up now. Those were different times,' he laughs.

I re-imagine his sixties clip, Margaret with her skirt hiked up, drunk, being worked up and down behind smoked glass at the Knightsbridge traffic lights in the psychedelic stream of the sixties by a teen with his hair on his shoulders and a head full of acid. I replay it to Bill, and he laughs, 'something like that, I'm sure.'

'This drug I'm on wipes out sex,' Bill says. 'I've been given Viagra, but it's so desensitising it's like the erection isn't even mine, so I don't even bother, but I need you to come over still, as a friend of course.' And outside, the green river pushes in inexorably, as the city's fluid muscle, and police sirens chase up from Vauxhall to Lambeth in a blue light attack on their targeted mission.

'I've never told you,' Bill said, 'John in his manic designer years. And he'd go into an altitude higher than the Shard, took a third mind into our life, Frank, and I loved John so much I adapted to the triangle, knowing in time we'd revert to two. He met Frank at the Turkish Baths in Jermyn Street—they were 24 hours, and it all started in hot steam.'

He looked away upriver, tracking a yellow tourist ferry rolling on the undulating swell, and looked both sad and relieved he'd given a slice of the Carnaby Street epoch that chanced into his immediate memory.

'The problem was they were a drinking combo,' Bill recollects, 'brandy and mixers and the real works, got so smashed they couldn't find the flat when we lived on Jermyn Street. I'd look out late at night and see them totally lost for our address, when they were right in front of it.'

I like being part of Bill's reinvented biog, the retrieved facts and added on fictions that package his memories. Part of being an escort is to be entertained by other people's lives; the punter often creates a fictitious persona to try and validate respect, and the escort brings to it his own monopoly of lies that have become truths in these fabricated realities.

From Bill's widescreen viewing of the river, I look out at London's soaring skyline, like we're already space colonised, skyping aliens in offworld architecture slung up and bolted up above the city's matrix, up with industrial overhead cranes with their red aviation warning lights blinking through a soufflé of indigo clouds massed into an airborne continent. It's so much a quotient of big city alienation, our window framed into the disconnect of millions who won't know each other anymore than signals bounced in from 1420 mergahertz, the most promising channel for alien broadcasts. It's like that. And Bill senses it too, in his own way, ontological separation, and probably the way illness excludes him now from normal life, and that his oncologist's floor at St. Thomas' Hospital is located somewhere out there in the clustered schematic of lights.

'Why don't you have a few things that were John's,' he says, cracking a ginger nut. 'When he was having an episode, he'd go to the big auction rooms and bid on so much stuff, vases, statuettes, carpets, you can see the place is cluttered. I'd got a letter from his psychiatrist so we could send most of it back to Bonhams or Christies; it was crazy. The random aesthetic at work in John's obviously serendipitous purchase on antiques was clearly accidental impulse, and I tell Bill another time I'd love the big decorated Chinese pot on the marble table outside the bathroom, for the big pink chrysanthemums splashed life-size on its enamel. Bill says he'll have it packed for my next visit, as he seems set on my having a piece of John. It's the chrysanthemums I really want; I can almost smell the damp, musty Chinese autumn in their spiky pink petals. John's a psychic fingerprint on the universe now as I imagine it, a bioluminescent pulsar of consciousness glowing on the fabric of inner space. And I wonder if Bill will ever find him again, like searching for a raindrop in the rain, a teardrop in the monsoon.

We're locked into the filter for boarding after leaving the gate, at least that's how it feels in the options of hope given Bill, and in the sensitive dialect we build around the fact. We have of necessity, as I know, to ramp up imaginative hope, even though we both know it's fake. Bill's been told he has a year maximum, unless the new drug adds an extension to his biological timeline. He's a walking archive of what it was like to be on the heartbeat of London's sixties fashion hoopla, and how a Soho backstreet with no apparent commercial potential became a gold highway to its inventive pop retailers dressing mod as continuous update on the fashion drug.

I extend my sympathy time; I'll genuinely miss Bill in the smoke of the capital's crematoria, and when I go out it's coming on rain off the river, big dazzling silver whorls that make me suddenly present to the present. In fact, I delight in the rain's sheeting impact, and stand on Lambeth Bridge and face it full-on in its driving vector, and shout into it, 'I can never die. I can never die.'

12

FUCKING WITH FRANCIS

They've all got their angled stories, including me, on Bacon, the street toughs, the rough trade runaways, the financially rewarded, the scam opportunists, the paid muscle who beat him to a pulp in piss-drenched Soho yards, the Colony drinkers, you name it. Most people in Francis' life collapsed into ruin like the faces he exhaustively bullied into exploded pigment on his canvases, beat-up atrocities worked into baseline distortion by his warring aesthetic to annihilate beauty into a new postmodern assault.

Today, you get the facial mash in military kit photography, Richard Mosse's thermal imaging of strikes recorded in shockingly close detail by state-of-the-art military hardware used to focus atrocities. I'm of course in my niche at Hop Gardens swiped by ambient white noise like the rush of radio. It's his exhibition as a conceptual documentary photographer at Barbican Curve points back tangentially to my intermittent life with Francis, as still another species of time-travel, sitting out in powdery gold light, wondering too if I'll be sprung by W.S. as a knife-carrier for the recreation of a 16th-century street stabbing. Mosse's use of a thermal camera reads temperature and is blind to skin colour, turning the face to hot black and the hair to white, like an object to be annihilated.

His photos skin his subjects viscerally, like Francis did his, peeling them into sexually radioactive pulp. I can't ever get his excoriating images out of my head, as I write, munching another EAT hummus wrap. I've got an assumed timeline in my blood, like nobody else in the people mechanics of this pollution washed city. I can feel centuries of exhaustion in my veins like a rocket escaped the solar system. What I like about Richard Mosse is his mix of tech from all epochs amalgamated somehow into modern, like he's shot Saddam Hussein's palaces with a Victorian bellows camera on a tripod; child guerrillas in the Congo with decommissioned air force infrared film, and sometimes employed highly classified cadmium telluride sensor, of the kind used by the U.S. air force for targeting smart bombs and by other nations for border protection and war zone surveillance. His art is one of confronting the military with the classified tech they implement to singularly affect horrendous asymmetrical warfare atrocities. It's like victor and victim sharing the same gun in a disorienting time-slip. It's in part a symbiosis like the one I share with Shakespeare as mutant time-traveller into the unreadably morphed future.

I'm going to tell you a story of Francis Bacon, the person I experienced in what was the last decade of his furiously hedonistic life, in which his booze input was like fuelling a Formula 1 racecar. Francis' sexuality was a complex infrastructure of brutal self-debasement and aggressive sadism— the two colliding like a head-on car crash. Bodies and bottles got littered in the process, eyes came out, bits of jawbone, crowned teeth, and champagne doused the lot, as liquid debris. Francis would habitually stand under a pear-shaped naked light bulb bleeding from the mouth and his popped eyes, as though the carnage was justified by his having invited it. He'd take a handful of sleeping pills and only be more alive to his existential crisis of wanting neither to live nor die, nor occupy any platform of compromise in between. I was there sometimes, but mostly I left him to it, went home after drinks or Charlie Chester's casino on Archer Street, and re-engaged the next day when his manic tempo had dropped.

Eighties London, all those orange post-punk unisex hair-dos integrated into the New Romantic, boys will be girls etc., and the Führer in a skirt arbitrating from 10 Downing Street over an extortionist, collectively fat cat demographic of laundering bankers; the price hike on Bacon's paintings escalating to sublime optimum, the same old London of winners and losers grimed on the millennial system, and finally erased biographically with an anti-bacterial wipe.

I was there, same me as 1590, only reset DNA with indestructible telomeres, and now this book as one amongst the skyscraper stacks of bibliomaniacal deposit, and me hoping it will shine like a hard diamond tooth in an incinerated skull. What we remember of a book isn't its language, its individual phrasing, but the idea of its schematic that somehow got programmed into grey matter like hearing your own pop in a foreign country.

Bacon was something else, not as he'd like to think a re-life of the sixteenth-century Earl of Verhulum with his boundless awareness of science, but an explosive phenomenon living in an anarchic shattered studio with trial marks of paint bannering both sides of the door and up the walls like blotched psychedelic arabesques. The studio floor was a layered raft of mashed books, torn-up images, paint tubes, discarded shoes, cashmere jumpers stiffened with paint, the whole exuding foot-mauled litter of decades of painting accessories trampled into debris as his personalised signature of a memory-bank stored in Reece Mews. He didn't tolerate people in his creative space, he was more like a garage band tuning with paint as a weapon. On the few occasions I went in there it was like housebreaking or accessing a zoo cage, and even though I was invited in I felt like I was crossing a frontier into a war zone.

Francis would be so compulsively wired in there, attacking the canvas like he was engaged in a fistfight, his obsessive regard for self-appearance nonetheless maintained, his heartbeat audible like a descending bass, his eyes liquid with hot adrenalin, his impetus screaming up at the red line like a biker with the fuel tank under his armpit.

'You're too pretty to model for me,' he'd joke. 'I'd skin you like a cow and all you'd see is innards and offal. Then I'd put you back together again, with a mashed jaw, a flattened nose, an agonised rictus for a mouth, a mutilated torso, and you'd be like a post-biological survivor bleeding on the canvas. I take the credit for reinventing survivor anatomy, literally slicing it off the skeleton like an autopsy.'

He'd talk at me like I was Bacon 2 and not me. I didn't live with him, that would have been annihilative, but we came at things without commitment on either side, as something that wasn't intended to fully materialise and observed definite boundaries. It suited us both, as Francis was with John as his emotional investment, and I was at the time with an older man who sold insurance and put money into independent movies, so we were both partially committed in ways that put a constraint on our friendship—should I call it that, as the underside of fully knowing each other's grease. Genial, warm, Francis became something else when his brain became saturated in booze, the repetitious monologues, the existential dilemma churning on philosophic enquiry into futility, the whole sordid process of queer ageing, the systemised rivalry with contemporaries, the bad mouthing of friends, it all came up under raw light bulbs, as though he was standing on the edge of the world with a bottle in his hand. I couldn't have sustained Bacon the night stalker, the nocturnal outlaw who wore darkness on his skin the better to be absorbed into it.

Mostly his life was routine. A chronic insomniac with alcohol orbiting his veins Bacon was up at 6 a.m., booting empty cans across the studio, building his energies into attack even if his subject matter admitted calmer space, rather than gesticulatively figurative agony, with blues and rich pinks flooding his colour hormones in his untiring drive to identify as totally and tirelessly creative. He was both ahead and behind himself in that last exhaustive decade of his life, snatching at times at a briefer serener vision out of the old implosive documentation of flesh, while being pulled back into what he knew best, the body as distorted shattering. He was asthmatic, wheezy, toxic, beating himself to death with paint. It was like he wanted to be his final painting, rather than the painter, affect that last reverse into solid degradable Dulux.

I'd meet him when he needed company in the hazy longeurs of the late afternoon in the West End, sometimes at the Colony, at Wheelers, or deliberately ratty bars in and around Piccadilly Circus, where Francis would sit wrapped in heavy black glasses, already stoned by booze, reflective, stinging, sick of it all, but unable finally to let go into dissolution. He wanted the lot and he wanted nothing and the two were the same.

Even in lowlife pubs he'd drink champagne and throw looks at skinny boys for size. He was always the focal exhibit, the exuberant resource of faded energies burning up and burning out. He had the idea you could somehow break into death like a bank, do a heist and steal the data you needed not to have to go back.

One afternoon when he wanted to slum it at the Golden lion, before he was going on to the Ritz, he told me rather fantastically George Dyer was back in town. He said that bad luck or wrong karma manifested itself in his belief in ways that re-trod tragic events. George was back in Soho with the apparent intention of squeezing him out of life by a confrontation; and that if they met George would murder him, as a life for a life. He told me that George was living next to the Regent's Canal in one of the skyscrapers on City Road, and hung out in the pubs on the Hoxton waterfront. With my experience of repeat transitioning time-slips, this news oddly didn't surprise me, nor the fact Francis was shaken into drunken panic by the reality of George's afterlife.

Francis sunk his fizz like life support, his nude foundation starting to crumble on the sides of his nostrils, his pudding face warped by nights that dissolved into drunken red dawns, throwing paint over the studio walls, and crunching trash into the floor like he was pulverising layers of dead memories.

'You're certain of this Francis?' I asked, attempting to test his booze frontiers that were rarely delusional even if soaked. You couldn't ever entirely liquidate the hard diamond of his intelligence in drink; it shone through no matter what the state of intoxication.

'He's back, I saw him in the crowd, I'm telling you, he was cutting into Jermyn Street, where I used to take him to have shirts and suits made in the sixties. He was even more obsessed with self-appearance than me. And worse, he was wearing one of the charcoal suits I had made for him, and the blue, lapis lazuli to me, tie, he knew set it off. I'm not hallucinating; it was him George Dyer, who we buried in 1970, got rid of him finally in London dirt.

'I don't doubt it,' I said. 'I'm quite sure that half the people we see in this city are officially dead. They come back some-times, in what I see as a sort of fluent exchange, or maybe it's impossible in their cases to break with old habits. You've probably been dead many times in your life without being fully aware of it. I have, it's a bit like jet-lag and being alien for a day.'

He looked at me full on, like he totally understood for a moment and doubted the next. I could sense the facility within him psychically to happen on this sort of paranormal encounter. What he was telling me simply reconfirmed my experience in believing that London really was the city of the dead, the locus for zombie crossovers, bleached aliens, time-slipped humanoids, or my type soaked into potentially final ends by the Shakespeare conspiracy theory.

Out of a green Harrods carrier, Francis with a twinkle pulled a scarlet flask lettered Hong Kong Gaij, and stood it on the table. 'I stole this flask from Manetta's last night, when I was drunk,' he said. 'I left it in the taxi and the driver actually drove back to mine with it, knocked at the door, and it ended up with him blowing me for an extra tip.'

'Do you want a sip?' he asked.' It's a strong spirit with a fantail of overripe mango and aniseed aromas. And believe me shots cost. You can pay anything from up to two hundred pounds for a small glass in China Town. I've probably got about three grand's worth in this flask. They wouldn't dare accuse me of theft for fear of losing my custom. I spend more in a night than the worth of this fucking flask.'

I took a tiny sip of the heavily fermented tasting liquor, with its plum finish and felt my body jolt quite literally from a shot, as though I'd swallowed a bullet. Francis, on the contrary, drew heavily on it, imbibing without gagging, shooting volatile spirit into his bloodstream. 'Fuck it, it's lethal,' he gasped, refocusing the room. 'It hits the champagne like a bomb.' He took a second more prolonged swipe at it and twinkled. 'There it is. I needed that to wake up to reality from celebrity.'

The floor was starting to thicken with leather boys and their counterparts, skinny rent, looking to angle lucky and pretending indifference. It was the stereotypical schematic of chooser and the chosen one, with neither anxious to self-iden-tify, and both pretending disinterest. Francis threw acquisitive looks at the packaged meat and returned to me as central fo-cus—the pretty boy without rival, the Shakespeare pet. And for a moment I considered blowing it and telling him my story as the legendary Mr. W.H., and I had little doubt in view of his George Dyer sighting, that he'd believe it. And do you, whoever you are reading this, have you taken on the idea of me as a tourist back from the future? Don't really matter to me. I'm writing this book in a different time to you reading it. If words weren't fixed, you'd get wobble like an aircraft cabin all over the page, or device on which you're reading it.

Francis hit the flask again with renewed vengeance. 'Fuck it. It's the last thing I needed, George around again, and in what sort of capacity I don't know. Is he really George, or some sort of copy who dematerialises when he's caught shop-lifting in Harrods? We had that in the past. I'd bribe security when he got caught by telling them he was schizoid, and he was. I read his prison hospital diagnosis, the psychiatric report on his suicidal tendencies, and his pathological identification with gangsters. And somehow we ended up together, two psy-chos forced to live with each other's insane realities. You know, he even planted dope on me and called the Drugs squad.'

He held up the empty champagne bottle and said, 'Cheerio. I must have downed half a million by now. Just go downstairs and blow them a kiss and another one will show up. Cheerio.'

I went down, signalled to the earringed bar staff and another bucket appeared on our table. Francis seemed able to downsize a lake into his bladder, and seemed in certain soft profiled angles to lose forty years and to morph into his enthused, vigorous thirties. It wasn't just the fifties biker boy grease quiff, or the slimness he maintained, it was more how he threw shapes at life as the individual qualities he shared that always seemed young, challenging and ultimately reckless. And I mean you couldn't get into him mentally, couldn't work out where it all came from, the neurotrophic motor at work within him, hippocampus and amygdala, remote as planets outside the Goldilocks zone. I was sitting talking to him a light-day away in a Soho bar, me who'd been Shakespeare's rent, and he who was probably heading east by the river later on, to be beaten up in a marshalling yard. It didn't make sense, but it was happening. 'George'd say, I fink that fucking pink paint's awful; I look like streaky bacon. It's vile, the fing looks like a palone got slapped up the carsey.' He deliberately exaggerates his take on polare, and what he tells me was George's speech impediment, and how he came on hard at the Colony as a pretend gangster, and drank champagne with obvious displeasure like it was the tapped beer he preferred in pubs.

Time with Francis was abnormal time, because it never seemed real, as though you were meeting the idea of the person, rather than the real, de facto man, and that what was happening in the present was going to come back to me in the future like a diverted flight. A meeting's like reading a book, it's only a few megabytes, but we can't memorise the contents, can't lift it outside time into another window and remember the lot. And because Francis was so much his own creation, he'd get loopy, recursive, self-referential, so that I and everyone else were excluded from his soliloquised drinking. He'd be talking drink to drink, which is alcoholic dialogue. 'Barbican,' he'd break off and rumble, 'bottles 90-year-old Italian Barvera from a 20-house hamlet in Alba. There it is.' And as though reading a menu, 'Dovetails beef tartare and white truffle from the grower's cattle farm and forest.' Then he'd get back on the shine, his look slicing the room open like an orange in his sexual urge for bulked muscle, the rough trade that seeped into his distorted anatomies.

I'll time-slip back to the present soon. I mean, it's weird writing backwards when you appear to be living forwards, while neither state creates any platform of stability. I'm speaking to Sumin in Hop Gardens, while I'm relocating Francis in eighties London, and she's talking phone tech, and how the P10, which has a 5.2 screen and the larger P10+ with its 5.5 inch display, both have two cameras on the back. She points out, checking a black nailed finger that's got chipped, that there's a 12MP colour sensor and a 20MP, is it, black and white one, both made in partnership with high-end camera company Leica. 'It means also,' she says techily, and as a camera enthusiast, 'that while the two sensors work together to improve res, you can also shoot with just the monochrome camera for grainy, atmospheric black and white shots. The format she adds, that currently interests her. She's so nice, I get lost in her voice, black hair arrested by a purple band, her tech-savvy existing independent of her generic roots in something simply human. She doesn't really want to go, we create a sort of candy coloured softness together; but she's got school and makes tracks after her Starbucks quota in the direction of tubing to UCL. London's like that, 10,000 people per square kilometre and the chances of happening accidentally on the same person twice, minimal, only I know where Sumin works in the immersive jungle, should I wish to make contact.

What Kit's provided me, as a point of confidential security is an ultra-secure smartphone from DarkMatter incorporating extra encryption and two-stop authentication. Kit emphasises its four levels of security protection—the phone, its operating system, applications and a cyber-command centre. It's a weaponised humanoid brain, preloaded with apps such as encrypting voice calls and a messenger that automatically secures photos and expires after a time limit. 'Eventually,' he says, 'we'll download the human brain into a phone as smarter co-efficient to our own, an exchangeable download that doesn't oxidise like human software and serves as a potential futures implant.' Kit tells me M16 are using human implants in e-butlers and espionage bots. The multi-race girl sitting apparently innocuous in a hotel lounge bar, pretending to be waiting on someone is as he says a thing of the past, a Bond feature, like men skydiving out of planes.

Someone sitting writing on the street in London is both a pixe—an isolated nano-blob and a human fortress. You can't break into my imaginative bandwidth, but you can deny it any financial resource. Paid writing feeds the state by its reserve, unpaid rips the lining out of the arsenic sugared cookie called economic camaraderie. Nothing to do with my rogue invasion of the capital's system, writing next to crackheads and the unchecked overspill of a leaky downpipe.

Kit confides in me that on a security level he's not overconcerned about an international biological attack. Epidemiologists he says predict genetically engineering a synthetic version of Ebola, the smallpox virus or a super contagious and deadly strain of flu travelling as a fast-moving airborne pathogen that could theoretically kill more than 30 million people in less than a year. It's all relative; according to intelligence, and even if most London was wiped, W.S. would still remain as a signature in the ruins, acting out his plays solo in deserted peeling West End theatres. He would always be the last man in the capital, the spook declaiming on top of a mound of radioactive bodies in Trafalgar Square. What do I care? I'll time-slip my way out and relocate another time, it's all the same, and it'll be raining still in Leicester Square.

Howard's still away on his tax loophole treasure-island itinerary that provides bonuses and boys, none of them as pretty as me. What he lives in denial of is the endemic E. coli risk to meat-eaters with possible contamination due to faecal matter as likely pathogenic bacterial deposit. Think of Morrissey and me chewing edible roots in the middle of a green meadow in rainy Berkshire, our arteries clean from lack of fatty cholesterol, while Howard's gut claws at the hormonal rigour of Angus axed off the bone.

I know it too from Kit's hacking his phone that Howard's implicated as a regulator in waving through an 800m bank transfer to a convicted mogul as the proceeds of a corrupt oil deal. Howard's near enough got coagulative black gold in his veins. He'll end up morphing into an oil resource piped to JP Morgan through whom two payments of 400m each which were wired by Howard's associated clients. It's a story that's commonplace in Howard's deviated network; half the money gets converted into bags of bribe cash via off-shore bureaux, with tens of millions it seems wired to buy a private jet and armoured car in the U.S.—the whole thing aided by two ex-MI6 officers hired by Shell as business and investment advisers. Howard goes to bed with these sort of deals happening in the deregulated finance ionosphere; it's no different he'd say to putting a condom between buyer and seller so that at no time could either make direct payments to the criminal mogul. Add some lube, and you're there, money laundering evades indictment, it's like the pull of a black hole that info can't survive. If a payment gets rejected, the tranches will be called in somewhere else as the laundering network where jackals drink oil. Howard's learnt how to operate those modules like the International Space station, those global regulator labs where the movers smell like new cars, and their biometric passport photos resemble Gestapo instagrammed back from the future. With Howard's type, and why shouldn't I be kept, greed is metastasised into full aggressive combat. He'll come back, hair re-blackened, pills for hypertensions versus Viagra, a stripy (orange and white, emerald and white, black and white, blue and white) Ralph Lauren button-down open at the neck, a diamond-filling showing vulgarly in the front, cram vodka and collapse. Wrestling with money was as much physical as mental and burnout wiped Howard's type as a form of viral payback.

That's me now, and I'm still telling you the best and worst of Francis Bacon, resituating him in the meta-realities fiction assists, knowing only too well I can't pull the eighties back from a dead signal zone where physics doesn't apply. What you get is language substituting for real, the fiction soap opera dealing nothing but lies.

Francis was irremediably convinced for a time that George was back, a reconstructed George who'd died in the bathroom of a Paris hotel in 1968, or as Francis thought psychically dovetailed into the body of a copy as one possibility, or become a frozen download with re-set DNA, my own thesis on this George phenomenon, if he really existed as a suicide tourist. Francis put it that suicides aren't properly dead; they've evaded the process of natural death and live suspended in an intermediary state, and to me a sort of replicant evolved as a proto-self-replicator through quantum whizz. Theory doesn't account, but Francis' story hooked me.

'It shook me right up,' he said, 'and I've seen enough blood on the floor, I can tell you, mine and others. But George—he's come to get me—it'll be the walls of his fists and a knife, nothing as clean as a gun. Francis was sweating, and there was a conflict with his makeup that he always denied wearing, nude foundation that flaked by late afternoon, as not right. The room was crowded now with the predatory, boys getting eyeballed and punters immersed in doing body scans of trade. He seemed suddenly displaced, as though he'd used up his airmiles as a visitor from tomorrow, and was now that worst of all things confined to ageing in the present with all the oxidised erosion that brings.

'Anyhow,' he continued, 'George insisted I came with him one day to a room above that shop on Rupert street, a convenience store, that sells unusual imported liquor. He'd met a psychic at the French House and wanted me with him for a sitting he'd booked. Of course I was sceptical about Iris who claimed she had a special message for George. Are you sure you want to hear this?'

I was fascinated and told Francis so, and tangentially by a guy with coloured service award bands striping a designer jacket who I'd once seen at the Dilly selling drugs from a Rowntrees sweet bag, as though they were candies.

'Well, we go upstairs, both of us drunk, or rather fall upstairs, and go into this dark room full of occult paraphernalia. Iris is sitting there in some sort of red robe channelling messages intended for George from a spiritual guardian. She tells him, when he's got his eyes open, she can see a big black hole in his life, and Chan her spirit guide is trying to walk George round it to avert some disaster. At which point George starts smashing his fists down on the table like he's possessed. I don't know if it was the drink or susceptibility, but George goes into what looks like a sort of trance and starts freaking. He's convinced the room behind Iris is the entrance to the black hole and starts kicking at the locked door and using his shoulder to try and force it. It was madness; I tried to pull him off and he resisted. Iris helped me, and slapped him hard to get him sober and aware. Even after we'd restrained him he ran at the door a last time and head-butted it. Eventually he collapsed and Iris did something to bring light to his bruised karma, and of course paid her double for the sitting. She told me as a parting shot he was a troubled case, distressed, dysfunctional, you name it.'

He broke off into real-time, the rolling car suspension of the present moment, the sound of choked car horns on Shaftesbury Avenue, the circulatory whoosh of unspecified noise, the elusive re-sequencing of action which always involved others rather than oneself driving the whole configuration forwards to the edge. He looked momentarily exhausted, like he'd burnt his fuses in telling.

'Anyhow, George went back there of course, broke in when Iris was at the French and kicked the door in of her secret shrine. After that, everything started to go wrong for him, and he attributed it to fuckin' Iris. "The bitch has kersed me," he'd say. "Bleeding old witch needs a slapping, Francis."

'He went back another time and Iris called the police, and I had to sort it out at Vine Street, convince them George was seeing a psychiatrist and sometimes acted out of character on his medication. I blamed it on the pills, said he'd probably dosed up on too many, and with a backhander from me, Iris dropped charges of assault.'

Francis was suffering from cardiomyopathy and fatty liver, but he clearly didn't care; he was exhausted from work and the personal assault course of his life, but he was still looking to push frontiers with paint, work his fingers into the fourth-dimension before he exploded into death.

I said to him once, 'You're speaking to me in 1984 and I'm writing this is 2018, and I can travel there now, and you can't.' And it was raining outside in swirls of dull phosphorescence over Dean Street, and it was in the sub-display in the base of my iris—a thirty-year shift in the city's upgrade into digital natives, vat-grown hearts, an immersive e-reality and AI autonomy, a collective inured to sensory deprivation, no neural-input into the organically real, like Francis deployed pigment. Sling a rainbow over Shaftesbury Avenue and nobody even notices its iridescent urban glow slowly vaporising like a contrail over the concretised capital.

And I'd say to Francis, what's the difference between a painting and a poem, in that one fetches escalating Russian investment from financiers, and yet you can't give a poem away across the street, and yet both belong to the same family of neurons, the same creative clusters that polarise the visual image as optimal dialect. And he wouldn't argue object or artifact, just investment. 'It's like banking,' he'd say, 'it's a worthless fucking investment—a bit of Dulux on canvas; but it's a seriously bankable commodity to the art market. Nobody's ever tried to do that to the written page, sell it like meat in the auction room—words on a bit of paper; but you can't alter the system, there it is, corrupt as maggots.'

Francis was starting to go down, and he both knew it and didn't in the reckless bravura he showed towards getting wasted night after night in central Soho, with the usual series of falls ending in A&E, or his private doctor being called out to the Colony to put his eye back in.

But Francis still wanted his pick of trade, like handling goods—and I was there on hand to help filter, pass on, talk up Francis' extreme fetishes that were often refused despite the serious money on offer. Boys sniffed at it and walked away because it was too hardcore. Most wouldn't do GBH or want to use a doglead on an asthmatic—they didn't give a fuck what he was, just a punter with perverted tastes and a fat wallet. They called him pudding, rich pudding, and he spooked your average Dilly boy looking out for his regulars. But Francis' invulnerable energies were impervious to street rejection; he was most of the time too anaesthetised by booze to care, bouncing from one drink to the next, like it was a way to cross the universe. Being old and gay doesn't usually fit, and that's where John Edwards came in to help cushion the long drop into the bottomless stairwell. For Francis it was like being sucked into a giant black hole in the middle of the Milky Way and being decrypted atom by atom into a downloaded loser. He'd periodically suffer meltdown crises and smash an indifferent bottle of wine through a bar or restaurant mirror, the clunky shattering missile a substitute for his incandescent cirrhotic rage. Francis was king inside his glass, but obstreperously obnoxious when confronting the degrading issues of age. When I was in tow I'd pay another pretty boy to throw eyes at him, express interest, and nudge sellingly into our company. Attentioned by youth he'd re-float his boat, and talk sex instead of death, tomorrow instead of yesterday. 'Picasso had to go, because I became too big for him; there it is.'

Francis was so great he couldn't take the crumble. He'd pay me to write lies about him, invent my own Francis mythologies and disseminate it to those in the tribal know. It was in a way my first writing, the start of the build to revenge I'd always wanted on W.S. for using me up like plane fuel in the sonnits—the SONNITZ—that inerasable slab of stylised literary graffiti thought to be directed at Henry Wriothlesly's looks. I'd write on bits of paper, near anything, while Francis gulped and waited for John Edwards as his pillar to restart his dampened morale. 'Nobody loves you when you're old and gay,' Lou Reed sings as period.

Take a break from Francis. London underground is on germ games and other biohazard preparedness exercises and Donald Trump's platinum hairdo goes a storm as newbie tweet-politics after destroying the corrupt Clinton/Bush fake camaraderie—the arms dinosaurs in their arsenals of wealth promoting democracy and waterboarding. I argue Trump with Howard and how I like the Warhol hair colour, the downsizing of America's global load to an i-Phone's characters limitations; the smart modernism and speed overwriting tedious debate. Howard's ruthlessly up on a sheik interested in purchasing Endless City, a 958ft skyscraper proposing an entire ecosystem as the brainchild of SURE Architecture. He wants to purchase the virtual configuration even if it doesn't find physical realisation. 300 meters tall, a space-saver super-skyscraper dissolving the break between street level and tower and between the skyscraper floors themselves with interweaving ramps that wrap around the tower, as a city in the sky, a colonisation of the grey London cloud ceiling. This colossal architectural hike fits into Howard's entire spatialised brainspace, I can tell by his hysterical messages that arrive like neuroimaging the schematic as cash. He doesn't mention boyz, the multi-race pursuit he buys and then kicks back into the corners of their lives like a white supremacist. What he gets for his trouble is hypertension and the mirror confrontation he has to pay money he'd rather reverse into his digitals.

Whatever brushstroke of romance existed between us quickly faded into a contract; he's the czar and I'm the pretty boy paid to be pretty, as the extension of his assumed power in the gay demographic. As I told you, it allowed me to write, and maybe when this book's done I'll walk out of one door into another. It's getting near to the end of our appetite for the book as physical object, anyhow, soon it will be streamed by the writer's smartcells to the reader through smartlenses in wraparound sunglasses. You can read it as it's written, no revisions, no edits, no rewrites—book as it's happening. Hop Gardens suddenly fills with sunlight like lemonade—I'm there ordering physical detail into words, while some u-class Chinese space hauler churns towards a mineral-rich asteroid, its red exhaust plume like the first hydrogen grammar in the stars. Hop Gardens as a transit-zone is all about mobility, whereas I'm stationary, and suspicious for it. If you stand still in London you're a suspected criminal. And they're there again, the trio—Poley, Skeres and Frizer, or am I hallucinating their menace like dropping a 3-D pill into a glass of water? They don't follow through on looking at me, but hang on the Bedfordbury entrance to the alley, like a solid wall of deviated snoop. They're the sort of operatives who wormhole into people who end up in the city morgue. If it's really them, then they've time-slipped centuries with my facility to reset the past in the present. Time is composed of a tissue of meta-realities, large-scale spatial dimensions that most humans can't access. That I know. Imagine what a spherical ball looks like observed as it passes through a 2-D sheet, (can you?) as a circle whose radius expands and then contracts in time, sort of something analogous to that. One time drivers raced to jump the gap between amber to red, but now Audi enables traffic lights to talk to cars to tell drivers how long they have before the colour changes, and time-slips are a bit like that, you get cellular news that the organisation's starting to go down, and you quickly reset your executable DNA, if you're up to how, like me.

London builds into the clouds, there's no burial space in the toxic sink now, so death gets digitised, or the moon's sterile regolith appropriated for celebrities, moguls, rock stars, oligarchs, Blair and Cherie buried in a solid gold coffin in the war criminal zone of the Theophilus crater of the moon.

Howard's back to me on culinary microbials—what's it this time in the cannibal bucket—buttermilk chicken in baskets of pine cones, haggis with Korean gochujang mayonnaise, ox-cheek cannelloni, olives stuffed with rabbit sausage, bear-hugging Angus with orange curd? His tastes are calorific voodoo spells, visceral gunk that's like ingesting your own gut walls in beef red wine cure. I'm sure in my mind he'd barbecue a Moroccan boy's foot if he could garnish it with black pudding, or beef dripping keema naan.

I'm whatever I am to him—this green immune-modulating vegan chewing on rocket, spinach and watercress, for subtle passage through the arteries. Shakespeare guzzled sides of beef during our brief partnership, call it that, or youth flattered by an older man's attraction to his looks. One of the St. Martin's Lane Hotel cigarette-break waiters looks me over, and says, 'are you writing about me?' as though I'd waited all my life to intersect with him for power inspiration. I want to say, 'fuck off will you,' but I block the impulse in case he shows the welling aggression that lives in every pressurised Londoner's skin. Aggro has become a subcutaneous river networking through the collective and it explodes at the least impulse into callous stabbings—youths leaking blood down the road like red paint before collapsing in doorways. I've lived to see the 16th and 17th centuries recycled in terms of knife culture and the cheapness of killing. In Tudor times without forensics a blade cut and a pair of biker boots kicked the slashed body into the river. Now sticking a knife is like guzzling a burger, meat on meat. You can do it in Macdonald's or out, it's all the same.

I write my time into this cut-through, wired by the gut tension danger induces. You can't be a body on the track to time—you have to go its way down the digital river. When I worked the Dilly I abstracted time into colour coding, I thought of a blue pigment, a green that promoted psychic self-defence and soaked into the colour, waiting. In that way I thought of blue or green people and gave punters one colour or the other, as they came out of the traffic haze, as though they'd just been invented that moment.

Francis of course, just wouldn't give up on anything in his recklessly hedonistic pursuit of death as a potentially marvellous encounter. And the more he imagined an end to his life the more he burnt out like a torched car. His philosophic dictums, stripping down of Greek tragedy, degenerated into petulant irascibility or downright slaughter of whoever dared oppose him. I'd have to get him home or sort of out of the debris—he hardly ever won at Charlie Chester's casino, and often for no other reason other than he played to lose. Totally plastered he'd give me all the cash he still had when we finally left—'There it is,' he'd say. 'Winners always lose.'

Most often, he'd get fixated on his rejections, the tricks he couldn't turn, the teen runaways who hung out in arcades scratching for drugs and loose change. He'd got hung on one called Danny who'd take, but wouldn't give. If Francis offered him money up-front, he'd pocket it and scram. It became a game—he'd be slipped a fifty and laugh, stick his tongue out derisively and run back downstairs into the underground having excited Francis' masochism. Danny was a streetwise droog, elusive as rain, someone who'd deal your identity if he could, sell it on so you were left without a composite personality. 'Just a dumb fucker,' in his street lingo; a cash, hit-and-run twink, when the east end was still east of west to its own detriment. Anyhow, it was the last serious mess I sorted for Francis on the Piccadilly radius.

Francis wanted it to get nasty and reach crisis point. He'd allude to it in drunken parentheses, and I could tell his tangled emotions were stretched to breaking point over Danny. The boy sat in the window of Burger King with a group of skinnies when he was on the game. They'd sit there eyeing and being eyed, pretending straight, and maybe some were, except totally straight guys wouldn't do same-sex acts unless they were disposed. Danny wore standard kit; hip-length black zippered jacket, white tee, faded blue jeans, scuffed sneakers. Nobody knew his name or anything about his personal details. He could have been anyone; he was like fog dissolved into fog. You got the feeling he could morph into abstract if you tried it on, he somehow personified the art of dematerialisation, the boy who was only real because you thought he was there. I'd say to Francis, 'You ever tried fucking the rain, that's Danny, if you really want to know.'

One day Danny was on a particularly strong wakey, and I arranged an assignation for a way over the odds £500 which was like sitting on top of the sky for rent. Money meant nothing to Francis—his cash flow was ten grand a week and it went to the winds. He threw it one way and it came back the other into his teeth. I warned the boy that this wasn't normal and might involve him having to beat up his client. He just shrugged because substances were waterproofing his veins, but I knew intuitively it was going to be sticky and I wouldn't personally like to be him. In these instances once Francis was resolved there was no possibility of turning him round. He'd have battered a concrete pillar with his head rather than be persuaded to desist. It was a foggy September day, and I'd done the cash deal, paying only a tenner upfront in the underground toilet at Piccadilly Circus, and knew this time Danny was interested and wouldn't pull out of the purchase price. He'd got so skinny and lesioned standing there dubiously under the fluorescents I thought he was a virtual. He was more drug than blood, and so hauntingly beautiful for the wasted state, I kissed him brutally as the room was momentarily empty, and it was like slipping my tongue into fog. That kinda confirmed the deal, the lowlight ambience, the incentive to have a throw of cash lasting for weeks, the neon alert to the brain that this could also be a case of rolling the punter, but ultimately it was money, cash you got before digitisation feeding smart cells.

I communicated back to Francis that Danny was up for it. That he'd been brought captive after months of trying in the lugubrious Dilly corridors. I suppose I feared Francis having a cardiac arrest or being killed by a kid deregulated by bathtub drugs got cheap on the street. It was obvious to me that neither party could win and that the money was confetti on Francis' part and crystal on Danny's. Pre-mobile it was arranged I'd take Danny not to Reece Mews, but to the back of Soho's Ham Yard off Great Windmill Street, and to my mind, hang around in case things got bad and they did, and after that I moved away from Francis, who was even more going down London's bottomless stairwell where ends were final.

By 10 p.m. the yard was empty in its potholed dereliction, as a badly resurfaced bombsite, and it was mostly homeless people used it, or junkies shooting up back of Piccadilly. Francis of course knew every yard and alley in Soho's still ungentrified ventricles because they could be used for brutally raw sex.

The fog had come back in blue atomised puffs damply settling on the red light quarter, as I walked Danny there from his racketing under the arches. He'd forgotten the assignation or whatever he was on and told me the police had moved him around all day on the Piccadilly loop. He looked even more wasted, but Francis liked them rough as he could get, scooped off the heap, because fucking he said, was like painting, a manual assault on a surface that resisted. When I mention the five hundred on offer Danny came alive as though money was the best drug he could do. His deconstructed jeans were ripped, and he shivered in the chilled air, his thin body shaking as we rounded the corner into Great Windmill Street, looking for the moment like somebody who is trying to signal from one side of the city to the other to someone they lost too long ago to remember.

When we slipped into the yard Francis wasn't there, so we huddled deep into the dark and waited until we heard someone's footsteps crisply approaching. It was Francis of course, wearing his black ankle-length Gestapo coat, and drunk although he never showed it because being drunk was normal. He threw Danny a look, as though stripping him of all worth, dragged into his pocket and said, 'Here's half of the cash, you'll get the rest later.'

Danny trousered the cash and faced Francis down, with me still too apprehensive to go. 'Don't get nufin pudding unless I get the whole lot upfront. I've bin around mister, I know your sort, get what you want and refuse to pay. It's upfront or I'll smack yer, see.'

'That's what I want,' Francis said, 'smack me hard as you can,' and simultaneously Danny split open his lip like a tomato. I was so shocked by the level of violence I almost threw up. 'Harder,' Francis said, feeling in his pocket for a stump of cash and getting another slap from his anorexic junky. Blood was rolling down Francis' chin from his teeth, and his head dropped down and he extracted a fist of notes from his pocket, a crumpled ball he didn't count and shoved them into Danny's hand. The boy crammed them into his pocket. 'I didn't mean to hurt you, at least not that hard,' he said, his voice genuinely shaken by what he'd done in breaking Francis' face.

'Now get down on your knees and blow me,' Francis ordered derisively, 'or I'll kick your fucking balls in, scum.'

I moved over to the side of the Lyric pub, stood up against its peeling façade, and left them to it, keeping an alert eye out for police. Ten minutes later, a white-faced Danny slunk out of the yard, and seeing me waiting there said, 'He wanted to be hit, I only did it coz you told me he liked it. I didn't mean to slap him that hard, really, I didn't,' and he hurried off fast, back into the immersive Piccadilly neon.

Francis was adjusting his clothes when I went back to find him and suggested we go to A&E to stitch up his shredded lip. He laughed off the suggestion, saying he'd done this all of his life, and requesting I get him a large brandy from the pub to get him right. I brought him back two doubles and he sobered into cold reality on their impact, like someone stepping out of a bath. I knew I had to get him back home in a cab and then insist on calling his private doctor. He'd lost colour and was wheezing asthmatically and his face was swollen like the deformity of one of his slaughtered portraits. I got a taxi dropping off at the Lyric and went back with him to Reece Mews, cleaned him up a bit, and called his personal doctor, who used to this sort of incident promised to come over right away. I left when he arrived, but not before telling Francis it was an end, and that I couldn't cope, or rather didn't want to be involved in this sort of assignation where licensed GBH was the determinant. I went back out into the wet South Kensington night, pulled a cab for myself, and never saw him again.

13

THE PLUMBER SAID IT WAS BLUE

Howard's offshore so often now, his business class airmiles make him an airborne global expat to my specific London reality where increasingly people are partial bots rather than physicals in rehearsing a post-apocalyptic 1984 for its arrival through the junction gates in 2084 with the furious aurora of nuclear thermodynamics.

Of course I imagine urban end time and its red mushrooming plume of exhaust as I walk down Broadwick Street to the Carnaby Street intersection where I'm to meet Kit in one of his identiless adaptogenic roles of hacking into someone's system like a virus. It's definitely Christopher Marlowe; my poet friend knifed to death in 1592, by my prime suspect, William Shakespeare. Kit's grown slowly into a fully formed identity directly relatable to his historic past, as I knew him, confirming my belief that time is a psychosis and not a linear movement with the arrow pointing forwards. And Kit's getting a bigger purchase on his past by reindexing memories, learning to fit it like a light bulb in his head and not be frightened of the red glow it emits, or that's how he describes it to me. For me in my math it's closer to the concept of information coming back from plus infinity and propagating back through time. It's partly a matter of realising, I tell him, that there are more large-scale dimensions than the up-down, left-right, in-out we're all used to as preconceived expectations of seeing.

Kit looks so cool by trying not to. Reflective Ray-Bans with smartlenses, a green and white check Ralph Lauren shirt—I spot the pocket logo—scuffed jeans, green Polo sneakers; he's really got the look of style without intent, casual without purpose, no least espionage giveaway. He springs it on me we're going to meet Lucy at the Patisserie Valerie on Marshall Street, the one that's on the site of William Blake's birthplace on what was Broad Street's muddy highway. I know about Blake, he fitted the cosmos into his head rather than fitted it into the cosmos—his vision was so big he carried London in his brain like a virtual city lit up in lurid red and gold. There's a sixties block, a concrete brutalist tower on the site, a place where humans live in their own ecosphere—344 square feet per capsule at an asking price of 450k, windowing UV radiation.

Kit is so inwardly focused he needs to talk distraction, while remaining polarised to his optimum. With Howard it's food and with Kit cars as his automotive fetish. I guess it's the Bond legacy—retro-ritzy spy glamour with alloyed wheels and martini lunches. He tells me little or nothing of the poetry he's writing, only it's abstracted from semantics, he tells me, with a gin splash of Ashbery in the mix. He alludes sometimes to the fact he's a cult: 'Poetry,' he says, 'nobody bothers; it's like pissing into your own piss. One time it stuck like glue, now it's like fake news, careerism—who cares?'

I look up at the concrete decanter that's Blake House and imagine Blake as a rogue pilot returned as a tourist from the future steering the nose cone of a 777 through mid-building. I get these thoughts and visualise them internally as real happenings. Kit's wised up on the post-truth society falsifying public policy. Kit says his AIs are smarter than fake algorithms with their dubious online content propagating statistical errors. We're already in a digital hole, he says, peer reviewers are at the core of the trap, layering fake with fake.

Lucy's got a window seat on the curve of Marshall Street and is sitting there eyeing the air and not her phone, picking at a shaven pink mille-feuille's flaky collapse. Her MAC Russian Red lip signature precedes all other facial characteristics—it's a red attractor with every look. It's like she's scarlet lipstick on a single muscle to my way of seeing.

We join her and I try to believe we're ordinary people in a popular chain, and not three infamous time-travellers with a history that would be the reverse negative of most people's idea of linear reality. Most of the time I adapt except in these crises of self-awareness when weird floods my veins, and the centuries fill in like liquid memory. It's then my brain cells flash up like the galaxy until the light goes off again. I transition out of the time-slip and sit down with Lucy, while Kit orders from the young Polish waitress with saturated mascara. The place is packed with Euros, sort of non-specific race types who nomadically roam borders and seemed bleached of genes. Could be anyone as an emergent for 2084.

I watch Kit tentatively snick the foil on a fake Valium, an Indian benzo strip of whites from the same source I'm using, and with my trained eye for non-generic I've observed the imprint as wrongly coded, like false number plates on a Russian car. We neither of us care providing there's Diazepam traces in the chemical's mixed ethnicity. Benzo's not a drug, it's a way of life; a metabolic river that shapes what you see and feel different to others, like I know Kit and me aren't seeing what Lucy sees.

Through with familiarities, her handbag positioned on her crotch to cover what her black leather mini reveals, Lucy comes straight out with it. 'He came round again, the mean fucker, tried for a reconciliation, and I didn't give a fucking inch, you know, he told me he could give me a child who'd be the ultimate genius. Satan's brainchild or something, he called it. Said it was the only way his genius could be cloned.'

'That figures,' I said, smiling, 'he's always considered virtual IVF as the only way for him, rather than having a company grow your clone in a tank and reset your downloads in a secure memory.'

'I don't know anything about death-tech,' Lucy said, exposing a length of nyloned leg that ran the length of the A5, polarising the Chinese guy opposite into the co-efficient of eye-sex.

Kit threw a surround look on the room, as though he was always coming back to that one room at Deptford where he was murdered. Maybe he had a sensor on someone in Pat Val showing up in his lenses that kept his inner awareness so singularly focused. Lucy looked mindfucked, as though her encounter with W.S. had really messed her up again, but present, millimetres behind us, but there.

'You're going to hear soon that he's arranging a meeting for all of us,' she said, 'to escape the loop, whatever that means, he keeps talking about getting back into real-time soze we can all die.'

Kit locked into the conversation. 'Yup,' he said, 'it's like we're astronauts fallen out of a ship and floating endlessly through deep space, only we're human, or at least I think we are.'

'Where does he propose meeting?' I asked, feeling the apprehensive chill in my nerves, as though I was suddenly frozen in time.

'Senate House, that place back of the BM,' was what she said. 'Don't like the idea of it myself.'

'An empty study or events room in Senate House, given it's so faceless, has to be right,' I said.

'It's the best place to kill someone,' Kit said with clinical authority. Who'd ever know in that honeycomb of conference rooms. There's also a secret panic room in there, you depress a button and this huge steel wall slides down from the ceiling blocking off all access.'

'God, we don't want to get trapped in there with him,' Lucy said. 'He's a psycho.'

I more than anyone knew all about the compulsively driven psycho in him, the insurgent ego infected with a monomaniacal drive for power he'd somehow got from the start and nurtured. Retrospectively, his name had dominated world theatre for over five centuries, like building a global solar panel with his writing hand. By appearing not to care about his writing—he famously never corrected proofs—he'd got to the top of the sky, like a diamond sitting on top of a skyscraper.

Lucy sat there constantly rearranging her pins like luxury goods, as though she had some input we didn't, something come through. Kit apparently seemed incorrigibly up on the infrastructure of the Art-Deco-designed Senate House, a nineteen-floor fortress, housing the deep resources of the University of London Library, which according to Kit was in excess of 3 million books archived between the fourth to the sixteenth floor. It was an eerie monolith I often passed on Malet Street to the west, or Russell Square to the east, a brooding fortress capped by a syringe that I knew was allocated The Ministry of Information in WW2, and had read a fictional account of it in Graham Greene's novel *The Ministry of Fear*, in an old beat up orange Penguin, sitting out in Leicester Square.

'I googled it,' Lucy said, 'and it's an events venue it seems, conferences, film shoots, intimate meeting rooms, why's he want to go there?'

'Simple,' Kit said. 'It's not only a warren of loosely aggregated rooms, but it's a place where people disappear, and believe me, I know. They simply dissolve namelessly out of existence.'

Lucy looked shocked by the idea of the place and checked her lipstick on the reflective screen of her phone. 'I meet all types in my work,' she said, 'but he's the worst. Nobody's ever slapped me up that bad, and it happened in the past too, now that I remember, beatings, kicking's, refusals to pay.'

'It's that past we're all trying to put an end to,' I said, 'otherwise none of us can be free. We all remember lives we shouldn't with such clarity, it's scary. Imagine if we really told people who we are as the unbroken continuity of who we were—we'd be treated as zombies. They'd experiment on our bodies, like all those accounts of abducted humans.'

'There's also what I call contactless murder,' Kit said. 'It's possible for instance to shoot a futures tourist without it registering in real-time, and likewise do a time-slip kill by dodging into the future and back to the present with murder on your hands.'

I thought long and hard on that one, time travelling into the future to kill and then reversing back into the present, like the dead could arguably live their lives backwards to birth. Or somebody dead, killing the living, as quantum homicide. All I was sure of as a displaced person was that W.S. was a dangerous hybrid, an arguable interloper from the fourth-dimension. If time really went both ways then murder between the living and the dead was a supportable theory that might have been going on forever. I didn't like the feel of it on my nerves, particularly in relation to W.S. who possibly transitioned between parallels with alarming facility.

Lucy was throwing eyes, even though this wasn't the place for the sort of high earners with BMWs she targeted. She'd removed the coverage of her handbag and she was all nylon with virtually no skirt, her banana curves fluent as two pencilled coffee eyebrows. She made compulsive phone-checks, but I knew intuitively she'd made contact, and there he was at a throw of my head, seated behind us by the door, W.S. in familiar black, dissolving between physical and virtual, as he exited the door heading down Marshall to Beak Street in Soho's monochrome haze like a postmodern Tudor spook.

'He shows up all the time,' Kit said, coolly, as though he hadn't bothered to tell me about this red high-priority icon showing up on the grid. Lucy instantly started to relax down now that he'd gone, as though he'd sucked all the air from the room into his own personal biosphere.

'What does he want?' I asked, stunned, more addressing my own point of enquiry than the others.

'To kill all of us,' Kit replied, 'that simple. It's obvious, we're the only people alive who know who he really is, and he's the only person who knows who we are. It's a bad equation.'

'And what if we killed him?' Lucy asked, 'would his real identity be known?'

'He's unkillable,' Kit said. 'You'd have to access his quantum window to do that, and arguably you might never get back. You'd be lost in unquantifiable space. But in my job there's a freak way of doing it without the risk.'

I could see that Lucy was out of her depth with quantum weird, and the idea that ends could take place before beginnings, so that the finish was the start, as a process of evolution in reverse. We were after all in a central Soho chain, where ordinary people were focused on tablets or just chilling over coffee. I felt sorry for Lucy being sucked inexorably into a zone where information kept coming back from a time she thought she'd left behind, long ago. She of all of us couldn't get on with her life for fear of this recurrent invasive housebreaker into her psyche.

I too of course felt creepily unnerved by his having been seated behind my back with the same sort of elusiveness you get masturbating over the recreated image of an attractively fetishised stranger seen earlier in the day, that sort of contact-less feeling of being used and using. That's how I felt about the sonnits, and there was sure to be a copy at Senate House amongst the 120,000 volumes printed before 1851 that Kit had described to me after he'd been tracking someone who used the library for meets with a Russian spy.

Lucy was submerged in her phone, doubtless attempting to harness clients wanting a black sex-worker in a high-end apartment. I could see outside the window it was raining again on the unredeemed streets, ubiquitous London rain, its airborne sparkle wiped on atomised contact with the street. Squeezed into this little corner in time all we had to live with was the imagined future as a purchase on time. It's all anyone has, liquidated and liquefying time.

At some point Lucy got up to leave, saying she had busi-ness, and in the process drawing gobsmacking attention to her unstoppably fabulous legs on lipstick red heels as she sashayed defiantly out of the sixth-floor café.

Lucy gone, I leaned in on Kit, watching her go. 'My prob-lem is,' I said, lengthening the thought, 'is that I'm ahead of time. I see things happening that aren't here yet, like Harrods blown into the sky, it's already happened, but won't take place in real-time until 2040. 2,000 dead is it? I process big events like traffic data, predictively; and it all goes back to those fucking sonnits.'

Kit looked over a young guy come in who was detail-spe-cific gay, like the boy was the physical materialisation of a sexual fantasy. In reality, he wasn't even a choice to me, but to Kit he was a possibility, like I remembered in backstory pubs, his coded signals to boys who'd have run him through if he'd put so much as a hand on them. Something of that lived on in him, the slight inhibitive impulse-the check on spontaneous desire that showed in small actions, like this, that carried no follow through; not even a hint to me of his attraction.

'What I've got to do,' Kit said, 'is work out what time he's living in, is it ours, do we cross over with Shakespeare, and who if any of us is the alien?'

'Yes, who is the alien?' I asked, supposing it to be me, and terrified of the concept. What if it was me who lacked real human affinity and was totally humanly contactless—it would be like being a species of one, solo in the universe. A spaceman who didn't know he was a spaceman.

'I'm sure he's got some purchase on our time,' I responded; I mean he's my neighbour at Charles Street, for all that means, but yes, his disappearances to the country could be something completely different and outside time.'

Kit was off another line of thought, paid the bill and I followed him out to a clearing sky, blue attentive to grey. Soho's busy, punchy dynamic was on the damp air as its buried soundtrack. On a sudden impulse I looked round, back of me towards the Nuburgh Street split with Marshall, and they were there, the three of them, slung together as a group with obvious menace. Skeres, Poley and Frizer, the inexorable trio. They were staring directly at us, and we at them, through wavery haze. Two of them were in black leather coats and the third a putty-coloured trenchcoat, and people had to step round the trio to bypass them. They were literally obstructing the highway, all eyes pointed towards us as their polarised focus in the crowd.

'That's the Deptford contingent,' Kit said. 'The ones who set me up at Eleanor Bull's. They're around, because he is, they're a team, and they can't figure out why they or I are still alive. You get me?'

'Are they in real-time or parallel?' I asked, feeling the tightening of muscle in my gut.

'They're in our time, right on,' Kit answered, as though pushing a button on alert. 'They're the three, they've been tracking us for months, only you can't see them for the light, rather like you can't see the stars by day.'

'Where do we go?' I asked. 'Casual or run?'

'No worries,' Kit said. 'They know I'm armed with an e-gun that shoots backwards as well as forwards. They hacked me before I got invincible end-to-end security.'

Kit pushed me with him round the corner into Broadwick Street, and there was a green saloon he abstracted, bundled me in, remoted the tech accelerants and screamed into a U across the tyre-licked highway, slamming the wheels into Poland Street, mounted the pavement to overtake the driver in front, cleared a pathway into Oxford Street using a simulated police siren from an automated sensor, and cleared a seguing pathway through traffic as a forcible getaway. At some point Kit abandoned the stolen car, left it parked up, and we got a cab back to his place in Devonshire Mews.

'You bet they'll be at the proposed meeting at Senate House,' he said. 'They're Billy Boy's agents, let's code him Billy Boy, and get rid of that ridiculous Shakespeare.'

Kit poured out two dollops of Soho gin with vapour trails of fizz and collapsed back into the sofa exhausted.

'Fuck it,' he said, we're in a time-sling, and we've got to find a way out to be free of them. The hard one is to try and crack their rogue reality, whatever window that is.' He swallowed a third of his glass in one gulp, like the transparency with him didn't count, and didn't. This was the infamous roaring boy of the 1690s inheriting a booze gene, an alcohol chromosome, and staying with it to alter reality into something more liveable.

'It seems like a quantum puzzle,' I said, throwing a look at his bookshelves packed with 16th- and 17th- century paperback editions of the dramatists, himself, Webster, Tourner, Marston, Kidd, Greene, Nash, and his own books chewed up from repeated use. At a look I surmised he'd gone into them repeatedly as part of the process of reconstructing his identity.

'It's a bit like being chased by aliens,' he said, 'and not knowing if it's really you chasing yourself.'

'But we've got to find a way out of the trap,' I said, thinking for some reason of the way manufacturers tint a soft drink pink to compensate for having reduced the sugar level. You drink colour imagining it's sweet. And maybe that's the way we perceived this spookish Shakespeare clone.

Kit sat on his thoughts in silence, downing gin. He looked ageless, like he'd just come out of a tank in his late twenties that was always going to be his late twenties.

'We haven't got much time and I've got to act fast,' he said. 'Don't worry; I'll crack it, independent of networks spreading false information across the net.'

I left him subjectively immersed in trying I assumed to reconfigure our first meets with William Shakespeare. Walking fast into drizzle I cut across Marylebone with its back to back high end and lower, and headed for Soho, as the secure locus I knew best for its apparent illusion of an urban mirage. Everywhere I go, people throw looks at me as though what I do lives on the surface of my skin. It makes me reflexively defiant that people attempt to abuse me in this way, hoping to reprove in me what they so dislike in themselves.

Waling means breathing in the city's complex ecosystem, inhaling and exhaling history as it oxygenates the blood. I cut it quick, no messing round in my direction. It's like walking into a real-time movie, this transitioning across a capital, fingerprinted by millions in their forward drive. I reach Soho and the pressure drops now I'm in my milieu. There's the usual stream of faces up and down Old Compton Street like footage of themselves endlessly rebooted into the same. That's life.

I go hide out a while in a café in Greens Court just to get the quarter on my pulse. With Howard being so regularly away, I've got into the habit of being an escort again, not for the money, but to keep on proving my desirability to others. It's not my fault; I'm so unusually attractive both men and women come on to me as though they've been looking for me all of their life, and I encourage it by passive provocation. There's a rehearsed way of making my eyes catch someone's playfully, inadvertently by rolling them middle-distance to create the illusion of dreamy availability on my part. It doesn't amount to very much these vicarious cancellations, but it's all part of the game, an ambivalent enticement ending in fuck off before you even start.

I'm sitting there in the window, looking cool, and I suddenly see the three guys I've got to identify as Skeres, Poley and Frizer, standing outside debating something in the alley. I get a nano-second slice of their existence that I could almost believe I've hallucinated, but I know for sure it's for real. They're headed in the direction of Brewer Street on roaming alert for someone or something, and I'm convinced it's me.

I stay on in the café, deflecting the opportune tryers on in this space and their dull homogeneity, but shaken by the knowledge this residual hitsquad from a shared history are out there in the rainy Soho ambience probably invisible to everyone, but me. I wait my time, which probably isn't theirs, and go out cautiously, expecting a predictive recurrence of the rogue posse, but the alley appears clear both ends. I take the Peter Street exit of the indomitably oppressive passage, and almost immediately bump into an unwelcome ex-Dilly punter, as a residual hangover from the recent past, who opportunely recognises me, picks up on my unchanged look in a series of unnervingly startled blinks and hurriedly crosses over the street.

'It can't be,' he says. 'I hope you remember me, I'm Jack,' he says, declaratively, as if I could care, but I quickly place him in my dealing-room. He's most likely still a psychiatrist at the Middlesex Hospital, with his air of off-duty alcoholic displacement; and a downturned loneliness rolled like a pancake stuffed with existential filler.

I look him over with a tweak of compassion for his clearly stuck life, ask him disinterestedly how he is with a tone of half-recognition, and decline his offer of a drink, as the beady rain starts up again. I go into my phone to exclude him, and Kit's text informs me the reckoning at Senate House in its labyrinthine honeycomb of bespoke conference and meeting rooms has been set for the day after tomorrow which in my time is really today. I feel suddenly totally isolated, as though I'm separated from all humanity by my individual role in an endgame that in my imagination could precipitate the end of time. I go and hang out at Bar Bruno on the lip of Wardour Street, and there's a big red crescendo of a sunset over the quadrant like a gas giant reddening to attack.

Wardour Street, site of David Bowie's 'London Boys,' can't go back with me into personal history or advance further than I can imagine it. That's the thing about cities, you project their future without you and it's subjectively conjectural hazard. I've been there already, and I haven't, and the present's in between. Howard on my phone is pursuing a billionaire U.S. investor who has chosen to list on the London Stock Exchange to attract British investors, after a failed passive investment in pharmaceuticals is costing his hedge fund 4bn. And me, the zingy Soho rain falls like memory cells outside the window of Bar Bruno where I used to sit in the quiet immersion of ordinary lives after colluding with punters at the Dilly. Now there's a different kind of reality threatens me, like tearing the skin off an apocalyptic sky. Kit's picking me up in nearby Dean Street in ten minutes in his new swapped car—I'm to look for a black BMW 530e, as the latest addition to Kit's automotive fetish, a hybrid petrol electric fusion with enough engine turbo at max, he assures me, to generate the whine essential to his concept of using the carriageway as a runway, rather than roll in silent, electric-assist driver-autonomy.

I go out of the café into the ubiquitous London rain, and I can't miss Kit, as we think parallel, go into Dean Street where he screams to a halt, opaque windows, and as I bundle in the car smells of expensive groomed ergonomics. Kit's in his smart Ray-Bans adapted for driving, and doesn't tell me where we're headed, and I note the booze flask featured as a dash accessory. His breath smells of scotch, and there's a used benzo foil discarded on my seat. But he's chillingly cold sober, in his look of absolute lucidity, like he's brainscanning me all the time he's driving. There a super-glue stick of traffic on Oxford Street due to another moped heist in Regent Street, that Kit clears by activating the police siren customised into his car and clearing a pathway through obdurate lanes of heavy metal.

'We're going to see Thom Walsingham,' he throws at me. 'You know I stayed with him for several months before I was murdered. He was my last protector, patron and lover; he witnessed my last weeks for good or bad, and things have to be settled. You remember or don't, as I think we were out of touch at the time, that I spent my last months at Thom's house in Scadbury, quite close to Chislehurst, working on Hero and Leander and in hiding from government spies.

'Did they come for you there, or did you go to Deptford before that happened? I need to know.'

'They came at night, two secret police as part of the Secretary of State's private security, but Thom threw them off my trail—he had a way that assumed a power that wasn't really his, and of course the Secretary of State, Francis Walsingham, was his cousin, so it wasn't that difficult.'

A silver deluge opened up over Marble Arch, rinsing the hood like a car wash with drilling atomised particulates, making the sky appear tropical with the torrential slash.

'It's end of time rain,' I said, 'the big flaw in global ecology,' and Kit responded by snapping a chip off a blue Valium bit as upper or downer, I couldn't quite work out anymore than with my own habituated chemical response to the drug. It was luck, one or the other, and we took a left into Regent Street ruling the central reservation through our low-fi scary siren clearing a pathway through the wall of rain.

'Thom's essential to the reckoning,' Kit said, totally focused on his thoughts rather than his attempts at stunt driving through gelled, agitated traffic. The rain kept up its monochrome pounding over the quadrant, chased by hot yellow zigzags of lightning, as we drove a rogue clearance through the traffic build.

There was something about Kit, particularly evident now, that I'd noted so often before, and that was his imperturbable focus, so intensely dissociated at times that you feared for his safety, his total removal from danger, as though exempt from personal annihilation, but was all part of his life in real as trained undercover. Either he wasn't there or I wasn't, in this moment of abstraction, shunting down Regent Street in surges as the traffic unfolded in response to our blue light siren.

'There's no licence code on this vehicle,' he said, 'nobody questions I'm official. And if you knew the concealed weaponry in this car you wouldn't come near it. I can get data updates if I switch to video glasses.'

When we got to Piccadilly Circus, Kit said, 'Thom's in the Albany. You know, gated privileges. It's where Ian Fleming, Graham Greene, all those types hung out for books, sex and booze. No questions asked what you bring back. But anyhow, we're meeting at the nearby Wolseley for a drink; it's a few doors from the Ritz.'

Kit put his saloon fortress into an empty slot on Jermyn Street kept vacant for the purpose, he said, of those on a wet mission. We legged it round the back of Fortnum's, up Duke Street, to a rammed Wolseley layered with a high-tea-and-networking-drinks crowd finding their moneyed navel in St. James, like a diamond skull sunk under the pavement.

Kit walked straight over to Thom across the centuries, who was sitting isolated at a private table upstairs from the main sumptuously art deco dining hall, absorbed in a glass of wine like a flawless ruby. Late thirties maybe, as my first impression, black-gelled sideparting, ochre and ivy chequered jacket, a postponement of action in his look. I caught his left eye first, as the pathway in.

'Kit's told me a lot about you,' he said presumptively. 'We met so long ago it's now the future and not the past.' He laughed down into his glass, as though there was a solution there. 'You never got to Scadbury, and now it's a ruin, with the shell of the old manor-complex surrounded by a moat in the park.'

Thom ordered drinks—large martini cocktails and a bottle of fizz and canapés, as we adjusted to and got above the soundtrack of brokering chatter down below. 'What you learn,' he said, 'is that death is history. There's no past or future, it's an erroneous diagnostic, stay in the present and move on without reference to either.'

'I'm sure you know the danger Shakespeare currently asserts,' Kit said. 'Re-murdering me is only one part of his occult bid; the city is the rest of it, ashes to ashes, that's his real purchase on final solutions, understand.'

Thom extracted the bottle from its ice bucket, vapour condensed on its chilled skin, and poured reflectively out of the 1590s into the contemporary moment, like downloading five centuries into a glass.

'I know, it's the real thing this time,' Thom admitted quietly, as though he scanned his thoughts in the process of talking. 'W.S. can open a portal into whatever we imagine the end to be, but will find out in the process. The future, as I see it, is always locked down some place else, but finally it's arrived. Am I right in thinking that, or something like it?'

'Too right,' Kit said, 'people always think poetry's redundant to their lives, that it's got no place in functional reality, but all the time its message is building towards an end more terrible than WW4.'

'And Shakespeare's at its core,' Thom said. 'That's why he killed you early, Kit, because he wanted uncontested fame, not only as a dramatist but also as a singular power broker in endgames. That bendy, twisty influence has got into intelligence like chlorine for as long as the world can remember. He's the language virus they can't kill.'

'Are you suggesting he has now to be killed?' I asked outright, as though this was the undeviating schematic of Elizabethan espionage over modern tea on the hub of the Ritz quarter, with money tucked into the creases of faces.

'It's not that simple,' Kit replied, as though murder was too commonplace to merit thinking. 'It's more, how can I put it, like the murder of the first time-traveller, the homicide of an alien in central London.'

Thom looked away, as though it had already happened, and that we were in the process of catching up with whatever had already occurred at Senate House ahead of the future. And in my mind the outcome was part of my novel that I would go on writing in transient episodes at Hop Gardens facing into a future I needed to retrieve by documenting nuclear drill.

'The biggest problem,' Kit said, 'is he can kill us, but I'm not sure we can kill him, due to a time differential I need to hack.'

I looked Thom over, dressed by Jermyn Street or Cordings at Piccadilly, so conventionally stitched together, nobody would have conceived he was a humanoid slung out of a rural Elizabethan past into the contemporary moment we were all experiencing in another time, another place.

'If you think of it, we're all captives of his dished out mania,' Thom said,' and that's why we can't get free of each other and start again. We're all locked into an immersive time-slip with Billy boy, as we used to slang him, manipulating our ties to history.'

Looking down into the circular room with its lighting thrown from elaborate bronze pendants and concealed lamps I was vertiginously aware of the overwhelming diversity of times and nationalities condensed together in a room so different from the shabby one in which Kit was stabbed to death at Eleanor Bull's in Deptford. This was Howard's set, the international cluster of financiers licking the last crumbs of tatre au citron from its residual smear. The Singapore hottie in the strapless black tube was an adjunct to the coercive financial lap, a slow-burn curve doubtless fed with priceless De Beers diamonds on a spoon at breakfast.

Thom threw an ostensibly erudite eye over the building's interior, as though it was part of his estate, remarking that the red, black and gold lacquer on the doors, screens and panels was still William Curtis-Green's original design from 1921, when the buildimg was constructed as an elaborate car showroom for Wolseley Motors. He was sure of it, and clearly at ease with posh, looking down at the intricately patterned black and white marble floor that clearly this could have been home to him in his confused history of time-travel without any recognisable breaks in the pattern.

'It was also home to Barclays Bank,' he said, negligently, clearly looking for distraction in our surroundings. I could see the underwritten exhaustion in him stretching back to his unsuspecting origins, and wondered how like me, and Kit, he survived it all, this being aware always of the past leaking into the present. I had the feeling too that if we both crashed into normal sleep we might wake up in a different century, dragged back to where it all began or launched forward into a future two-thousand light-years away, but instantly recognisable.

'I've never told you,' Thom said, directing his eyes at me, 'but Shakespeare, or Billy, was also a lover of mine. I mean, he forced it, he wanted to take me away from Kit, and he wanted intelligence. The inequality at the time didn't seem to register;

he probably thought his reputation as a writer overrode it. He made it happen at Scadbury. I felt demoralised afterwards, got up early and disappeared before breakfast into my woods. So you see, we're all impregnated in some way with his stain. He got into all of us physically or mentally. He's the reason, the real reason we all keep on inheriting what seems like a deathless gene for good or bad.'

Nothing really made sense in this richly lacquered room, the hedgefunders; the billionaire Beijing women with inscrutable looks, reviewing London through its brands, the sterility of luxury hotels, and the unstoppable momentum that drives its money markets. In my own way, I felt more at home at Hop Gardens, the place where for me it all happened creatively. What I was observing from our private table now, was already in the future of my book, the one you're reading, and waiting for an end.

'I'm starting to get it,' Kit said, apparently out of a cone of concentration, 'the way to hack into his dimension and deny him access to ours forever. We need to lock him down into the past where he belongs and where he'll die without any comeback into the present.'

Kit looked marginally like he'd nailed it, put a spike through the head of our time-roaming chimera, at least mentally.

Thom was preoccupied with his fizz; he looked used up of all experience like a petrolhead who'd pushed a car to zero and bounced it down the road manually without fuel. 'Shakespeare's pervasive presence has near destroyed all of us,' he said, putting his glass down and signalling for another bottle. 'Money simply gets you served quicker, nothing else,' he said. 'You know, we've never got rid of slavery, even today, tip generously and you'll win a subservient trust. There's zero pleasure in it, once you command the rules of the game.'

I could feel we'd exhausted the place, and that for all of Thom's apparent dislike of class, he still lived off its system, and that if his privileges collapsed, he'd be crunched like a cyclist dragged under a truck at a roundabout.

Thom poured again, mechanically, like the loop we were on. Money didn't matter and the Wolseley was accustomed to sheiks and the harem they took to Selfridges to buy sex with a bottomless resource. It was just one of those things.

'Presumably we'll die naturally at some stage after his death,' Thom reflected. 'I mean, won't that be the first time we've ever done anything normal—die.'

'That depends,' Kit said, 'if our genes can be reset to normal circadian rhythm. Or we could arguably burn off and dematerialise like a body popped in space.'

'We've got to take the risk,' I said. 'I've been self-identified as Mr. W.H. for what feels like several lifetimes of repeat journeys to Mars, or something like that.'

I hit on a text alert from Howard telling me he was now batting in Jersey CI, his first time on the offshore tax loophole, advising a client whose investments were in Russian energies, and paranoid. According to Howard he was being hacked by Putin's cyberespionage and lived in fear of being poisoned by a nerve agent. Howard was gorging on local seafood, and I could feel his gastric juices leaking out of the message like a rumbled gut,

'Those three guys over in the corner of the room, recognise them?' Kit asked. 'Frizer, Poley and Skeres all in the service of W.S.'

I threw a look at the three sitting so close together talking they were almost in each other's face. Dressed casually and over bottles they were intensely focused into conversation, and may have been looking at us all the time without our knowing it, the way most important things go parallel without necessarily being observed, like dark objects on the edge of space.

'It's those three set me up at Deptford,' Kit said. 'I got into the wrong end of lowlife, the Shoreditch bin, and of course got knifed. Did you know it was coming, Thom? Don't lie, tell me.'

Thom looked thrown, and mumbled, 'pressures of State, slapback machinations, they stuck it into me like a wire. Did I or didn't I? I don't know, and I mean that. I heard loud shouting in my library. What I remember was the pounding rain outside and the library becoming an interrogation room.'

'You haven't answered me,' Kit said. 'I want the truth; the cold psychopathic rationale behind my murder.'

'They threatened me with rape for buggery. A boy on the estate I'd fucked—could have cost me my head, and they knew they'd got me over a barrel. I told them where you were expected to be, that's all, they had me shackled to the bed.'

'That's all,' Kit said, glaring hard into his empty glass. 'That's all. You had me murdered.' He slammed his glass down so hard it snapped the stem causing eyes to look up and quickly revert to conversation as a denial of the ugly incident. Kit toyed with the fractured stem, ran it testily over a vein then jettisoned it to the floor. 'You lose some and win some,' he said, 'and both are the same. Ultimately, who cares?'

'It's all so long ago,' Thom said, 'but in our world it isn't, it's yesterday. We're still in the present that should be the past.'

'That's why we have to break out of it,' I said. 'It's insane to keep on the same loop, with this one man in our face.'

Kit had calmed down and reverted to his usual inscrutable cold. 'Sorry,' he said, 'I don't usually lose it these days, unlike in the past. Sometimes you get a bad benzo, Indian fakes. Those three down there, they're evil.'

Almost spontaneously, sensing our interest in them, the three turned their heads towards us, like they were suddenly aware we'd noticed them, while they were probably watching us from the start. It was the implicit threat I felt pass through me, like sudden contact with a cold bath. It was like they'd already killed us once, it was that sort of stare, and now they'd do it a second time, wake us up to real-time, and do it a third and fourth time cool as a mortuary fridge.

'How do we get out?' asked Thom. 'Just overturn their table,' Kit said, laughing, 'the noisiest way out is always the best, something I learnt centuries ago at the theatre pubs—do you remember the Bode's Tavern, when I got into fights with sailors and kicked out tables, then fought with marshals in the street.'

'They won't do anything here,' I said. 'They're just a warning, and again are they real or virtual? I mean are we both in the same time?'

'That's what I've got to work out before Senate House,' Kit said, 'how to collapse them back into the past, so they die off into history.'

Thom discreetly made eye contact with nearest staff and waited on the bill. 'Give it a year,' he said, 'and you'll pay by facilitating smartcells in your irises. You'll blink on the transaction as timesaver.'

The three of us got up and walked leisurely down the short flight of stairs and cut an unflustered line to the door. There was no attempt to stop us, no immediate pursuit as we stepped outside into the late sunshine of the Piccadilly afternoon, its gold rinse squeezed through the smoggy light pollution. 'We're safe,' Kit said. 'I did something to disrupt messages across their entire brain, rather like the effects of propofol. I can't tell you what, it's part of my job.'

Thom left us to walk back in the smudged pink evening light to the nearby Albany, while Kit and I disappeared back of Fortnum's to find our car. I pointed out the block on Duke Street where William Burroughs had lived in the late sixties as a landmark in subculture of the period, but Kit was too car-conscious to take it in, and the full-on Jaffa sunset exploding behind us as a big light in the smog.

Using his cell phone to remote us into the cabin, Kit sat in front of the dash, and I knew he'd got it, the algorithm or whatever it was that he knew could put an end to the wormhole Shakespeare and his contemporaries were exploiting. I'd noticed the girth of the wheels, the flare of the arches and the depth of the bumper scoops. Kit sat in the unlit cabin as though locking the thought down into synaptic storage, and remained like that for a long time, like a jeweller searching for flaws in a diamond. Kit sat for a long time in the digital virtual cockpit before opening the taps to drive off in a surge of grunt, throwing at me, as part of his deviated schematic, 'I'll drop you off in Soho, if you don't mind, there's a boy I'm doing at the back of the Soho Car Park, risky but that's the pull, giving me no alternative but to consent. I got out in Greek Street, and cut across the hectic frazzed out carriageway of Shaftesbury Avenue, and into Leicester Square, where the collective tempo dropped marginally from hyperactive into crush. I sliced in rapid transit through the transitioning crowds and made it back to Hop Gardens to continue writing what you're reading, only you're in the future of this book.

I'd sort of planned on leaving Howard anyway, as I'd grown tired of his fat cat hedonistic excesses that lacked taste. The huge bonuses and global hops reeked of the pedestrian even if they were facilitated by business class designed into stays in five-star hotels overlooking aqua beaches. My personal wealth was secure, quite independent of Howard's hawkishness and I knew I could up and go anytime I wished if I survived the arranged confrontation with W.S. at Senate House. For as long as I could remember I'd always self-identified as Mr. W.H., Shakespeare's capricious bit on the side, and couldn't imagine an alternative reality without my personal history.

I got into the alley and settled into my writing, aka what you are reading, and time altered again in the process of converting reality into fiction. I realised that right from the start of my relationship with Shakespeare I'd lived a deviated life, but that all experience belonged to a general plan in which everything was unconditionally absorbed into the ultimate scheme of things, good, bad, and all their related moral attachments. It was necessary in my mind to experience opposites to have truly lived. And at the end, as I imagined it, you arrived where dualities were resolved into a single unity. And maybe that was my lesson in the cold equation of metaphysics, that like the introduction of friendly bacteria to the gut I needed to reconcile good with bad and bad with good as a holistic fusion.

There's this perceptible pull in London drags you to its core, feet-down right into the vertiginous underbelly like the black Northern Line. I could feel it happening inside, like a plane beginning its rocky descent, this sense of being sucked by apparent gravity towards the bottom of history, and right into Shakespeare's loony red eye. I could feel it all the time, this precipitous descent as though I was ledged above the rumble of massive sewers and tube-whine shuttling through the underground. Just the thought of it crushed me like avocado filler in a sandwich, this being drafted into the city's squamose intestines on which blocks, skyscrapers and towers were built in their competitive legislation of the sky.

I sat writing what you read, and scoring out what you can't in a confused state of existential bleed, as the sky built into suggestions of rain over Bloomsbury's expensively squared symmetry of top-end, and my whole life seemed on the precipitous edge of redemption or collapse. There were people coming out of the Friends Meeting House, with its crude biometrics, sometimes lit up euphorically in the belief that spiritual healing was altering their lives, and going off down the alley into the anonymised day to be absorbed into the tube. It was the amazing diversity of individual lives in the capital always got to me, each with a different DNA signature, a unique biological tag—the millions of street faces in diversified disconnect that to me was like a still inchoate army waiting to be mobilised by war.

I could hear the occasional rumble of a bomb going off in the city periodically, as reminders of radicalised cells holed up in warrens underground, physicalising rather than employing cyberterrorism to have the city's money markets crash. I'd got used to the explosions, as we all had, tending to edit out the soundtrack, and accustomed too to the rogue Boeing 777s painted black that lumbered over without warning at rooftop level, simulating landing in Regent Street, and screaming over Selfridges as a pretend target, before releasing thick broad red contrails as they regained height in the airways.

I finished writing and walked back over central to Charles Street knowing Howard was back and out, the texts from Jersey attempting to mediate his actively pursued double life as a sexual predator. There was an open suitcase on the bed, partly plundered on return, a rich tangle of shirts braided to Armani briefs and Jaeger sock stumps. Nothing seemed quite right. But there was a voluble addition, and I went back outside into the corridor drawn to loud voices inside W.S.'s apartment, one of which was unmistakably Howard's. There was a vehement argument in motion, and curious I switched on the recording app on my phone. They were arguing and I could hear my name being shouted as acquisitive useage between them. Nothing quite added up until it clicked that Howard was doubtless not only informing on me, but was also one of W.S.'s casual sex partners in this mad game of transitioning in and out decades. Suddenly the argument stopped and the room went quiet, and the tempo altered, and I could hear Howard coming on to W.S., in a way similar to how he did with me. They must have gone into the bedroom as their voices receded and I backed off into the flat and debated what to do. Instinctively I rummaged in Howard's Vuitton suitcase under a folded charcoal suit, one of his Paul Smith office numbers, and found in the process a large polythene bag of money, what must have been an offshore bribe, Viagra foils, incriminating coke, at least 5 grammes and sufficient to get him done.

I decided to pretend nothing had happened, and started preparing dinner with a view to noting his behaviour when he returned, and whether or not he showed any sign of guilt at doing it right next door. I poured out a large gin marrying it with bouncy tonic and the Bombay Sapphire hit my head. Because Howard largely ate out and my vegan dictates were by contrast simple, I decided to do a pasta salad with rocket, pine nuts, avocado, pea, basil, blood orange, olives etc., whatever I could locate for the mix, something he'd doubtless see as a starter and altogether lacking the sinewed grunt of meat. I worked on managing taste, the pop of orange with endemane, the fury basil added to pea, the gunshot of black pepper on mint, all of it improvised and intuitively measured, like mixing a rogue cocktail with random ingredients to ramp up the sting.

I opened the kitchen blinds and caught the last of the piled up orange sunset over London's plutocratic mansion blocks, places I'd sometimes known as an escort lubricating a short-term stay by intensifying each expensive transitioning moment. I waited and got into the cooking and heard the flat door peremptorily open. When I turned round Howard was at my back pointing a handgun at my head. He was staring at me searchingly, full-on, like my life was worth nothing, and said coldly, deliberately, 'It's you or me, luv,' and turned the gun on himself, his brains blown all over the white kitchen tiles like red dripping graffiti. He collapsed backwards with the impacted bullet through his brain, landing with the amplified thud of a heavy object exiting gravity.

I looked down at the warm yellow pool trickling onto the floor and realised I'd pissed myself involuntarily from shock. My jeans were stuck to my legs, and without even looking at the body I went straight to the bathroom, peeled off my jeans and showered my body that was shaking all over, steamed myself and changed my clothes. I immediately popped a benzo, came back to the kitchen and found the body gone, as though I'd hallucinated the whole thing as virtual murder. I ran my hands over the kitchen tiles and there was no trace of the pulverised bloody plasma and grey matter exploded there minutes ago. The salad I was preparing was still in process in its hectic citrous colours and I polished off the remains of my robust gin in an effort to get above it all. It was as though nothing had happened and that I'd projectively imagined Howard's blowing out his brains. And I remembered in a flash what Kit had told me—the future is complete, and that everything had already happened, and we simply catch up with it and sometimes experience an event as a precognition of what has already occurred further down the line, or something like that. I sort of half understood why I'd seen Howard's suicide as a reality executed in front of me—he'd shot himself rather than me, and that the act was part of an irreversible momentum he was gaining on that in time would become a physical reality witnessed perhaps by someone else other than me, one of the stable of boys at his disposal due to the coercive power of money.

I foundered around, pouring another gin and feeling it come up on the benzo, as though the two as strange attractors were coefficients to doing things left side of normal. I regained my composure and phoned Kit to tell him what I'd experienced. His rationale was coolly expedient—time was complete, but only to the few involved in the schematic, and that Senate House would confirm that. He told me to go out and leave Howard return as though nothing had happened, if it ever did.

'How do you know he's next door?' I asked, gulping air on my words, only to notice that Call Ended showed as a terminator on my phone.

As far as I knew Howard was still next door with W.S. in real-time, and I'd simply travelled too far ahead into the near future. It was like jumping traffic and coming back from my destination before I'd arrived in a crashed car with the headlights out. I went out into the red crescendo of the sunset suddenly made unreal by Howard's virtual suicide, and made my way over towards the Ritz side of Green Park, aware of my separation from the crowd in the war of parallel dimensions in which I was a key-player. I was tempted to hang on the Ritz forecourt in the chance of a punter, but it seemed too obvious, too luridly cheap in its calling. Instead, I walked up Piccadilly in the kinetic way you do, as part of observing others in their transitioning reality of which they'll never know or have any provable historic identity. People come and go, come and go.

14

SENATE HOUSE UNDER A RED SKY

I reflexively checked my phone and fingered a text from Kit. 'It's tonight. Senate House 10 p.m. Be There. Don't, I repeat, go back home to Charles Street again. You are ahead. Howard will commit suicide tonight in the kitchen at 1.00 a.m. just as you experienced it virtually. Stay over at mine. You are out of real time now.'

I continued walking down Piccadilly in a way that seemed to stop every atom in its position. I went purposely and hung out under the Regent Street arch as a landmark in my past. It was now just historic architecture for snapshots on every Chinese phone engineered in Taiwan. Now I saw the place stripped of its obdurate selling point for rent, and as remodified in the pedestrianisation of big city hubs as anodyne Westminster repurposes. You can never find the city's untraceable core, not even at Piccadilly Circus, it belongs rather to an elusive bassline that can never be traced, but comes on air at unpredictable times, although to go follow would end up by dropping into the swollen green river.

I retrod my past—Glasshouse Street, Denman Street, places where I'd got to meet my sort of people, and made my way slowly over towards ambulatory Bloomsbury, as though I wasn't in any sort of reality that had a consensual relationship with time. Senate House as I approached looked like a giant Art Deco fortress, obscured by clouds, designated like Harrods to be a post-apocalyptic mortuary for the victims of WW3 vapourised in a red updraft of fire bigger than the sky. Kit was as pre-arranged waiting for me in the Patisserie Valerie in Brunswick Square, looking ahistoric over Ray-Bans that gated him into opaqued privacy. The regular three spooks were there, Poley, Frizer and Skeres, and Kit was indifferent, informing me not to be put out, as they weren't in real-time, but rather in a locative that couldn't intersect with our own species of reality. They're connected to weird unquantifiable stuff, Kit alluded—I mean laundering dark energy from the invisible elephant in the universe according to quantum physics—I guess you call could it spacetime vampirism or something like that over which W.S. presides.

'Another fifteen minutes to go and we'll walk over,' Kit said. 'The days of handling guns are over, now it's weaponised implants or the use of nerve agents. Think of it, do we create them, or do they create us, and will the extinction of one result also in the death of the other.'

I did a necessary reality check in my mind, wondering still if I was imagining it all, but then it wasn't only us, we were involved with others—W.S., Lucy, the three Deptford suspects, Skeres, Poley and Frizer, Thom Walsingham, all of who were interactive with our daily lives in this extended narrative stemming from the 1590s to what I recognised as the present, the immersion in transitioning now.

'What's the proof we really are visitors from the future?' I asked, feeling my mind flip. 'I could blow you in the toilet,' he said, 'and maybe then you'd find out. It was actually one of the last things Thom Walsingham did to me before I left Scadbury for Deptford, in a block of missing time, which is either today or five hundred years ago, and in quantum rub, they're both the same. So that's your answer.'

It wasn't an answer of course, it was just speculative propositioning, and he looked at his link and said, 'Another ten minutes.'

The Brunswick Centre personified anonymity. In the variant racial mix it wasn't easy to identify who anyone was or even why these bleached-racials were there in the progressively nomadic trending of urban lives. The square itself had been subject to a fleet of quadcopter drones flying investigatively in autonomous formations only last month, as unexplained aeriel robots clearly operated by an SG network, as part of the end time phenomena programmed into the times. Most people now lived in mixed realities, fusing organic and virtual, a combo that was radically altering human relations into street digitised priority.

We came out of the square into Marchmont Street under a taupe sky flattened by low choked up cloud. Nothing seemed real to me, other than the physical motion of walking over towards the art deco Bloomsbury landmark under dusting drizzle. There was something about the fortressed look of Senate House always got into my nerves like the cold passage of swallowing an ice cube. It looked like architected psychosis, a giant historic book barn facing down central London with its warren of conference rooms honeycombed into a concrete shell.

Suddenly I heard a voice shout, 'hey you guys,' and it was Lucy running in heels to catch us up. 'I told her to come,' Kit said impassively, 'as she's integral to the plot.'

Lucy looked like she always did, loaded with sex, hot red lipstick signature, neon pink eye shadow, black bra straps crawling down her arms, super accentuated skinnies and a walk that charged the air with saturated pheromones.

'She works for us,' Kit said, 'selling sex is the best form of espionage.'

I swallowed this with surprise, as we walked on, Black Luce affiliated to secret service, almost any reality appeared possible in these apparently parallel timelines. The drizzle was thickening into a smeared plume as we tracked the short distance over, an unmarked black police car barrelling past at blue light speed, headed doubtless towards some new terrorist incident in the capital's cluster of radicalised cells.

Kit stopped back of Birkbeck and debriefed us. 'Remember, W.S. and his three associates are leaking through a time-slipped reality. They can't shoot us, but I can liquidate their autonomy for good, freeing us up from their attachment. Let me tell you, even if it's hard to follow, if all events that have or ever will occur are permanently located at some point in the block universe, then the relativity of simultaneous timelines becomes no more puzzling than the fact that two objects in space can appear to be aligned or not depending on where you are standing. Simple as that.'

There were a few students coming on and off campus in the prickly drizzle, otherwise the concrete cenotaph looked like an idealised barracks, a design fortress for special-forces infrastructure. I'd always been chilled by its menace architecture, its lowering retrofuture façade that dominated the quadrant like some squat obelisk still awaiting its functional call for the future.

'We've got a private function room on the 13th floor,' Kit said mechanistically. 'The deal on Shakespeare's part is that to alter the course of our personal histories we have to crossover into his timeline, while the city can only be saved apocalypse by his returning in exchange for real-time. It's a terrible demand.

We went in security-free with Kit doing something with his Ray-Bans as an approved signal. I was so focused I could see atoms in position and the molecular network firing momentarily in my brain, I was that clear.

I didn't see security anywhere, doubtless on Kit's command, and we went into the exaggerated Art Deco proportions of what turned out to be MacMillan Hall, as one of the large flat-floor spaces, hired as Kit suddenly informed us by the upper echelons of the international events marketplace. Like so much sunk into London's architecture I'd never been aware of the building's sumptuous interior and was thrown by the two stunningly ornate mirrors that spatialised the room into its confirmed association with royal chancellorship. There was an arrangement of chairs around a large wooden oval table, glasses and obligatory bottles of Evian; the formal anonymity waiting to be pinched alive by whoever took the room over as dominant. I sat down nervously next to Lucy, while Kit did something with his reflective glasses. I could feel my life viscerally in the pit of my stomach, my pulse beating there like an electrified tomtom telling me that whatever my identity was as Mr. W.H. was about to be exposed in all its historic valency.

When Shakespeare appeared dramatically, after a short wait, wearing a black hood, and flanked by unrecognisable minders, he was taller than I remembered, and authoritatively self-possessed. He was accompanied by an entourage of twelve, all similarly wearing black hoods, who came in behind him, faces partially obscured, to be named by him as master of ceremonies. He called out their individual identies: Ben Jonson, Thomas Walsingham, Lord Strange, Edward Alleyn, Richard Burgage, Sir Walter Raleigh, Simon Forman, Thomas Kyd, John Webester. Philip Henslowe, Henry Writhesley, Christopher Marlowe.

This trancy procession, which presumably included Kit's double, stood in a line confronting us with Shakespeare positioned several paces in front, like a singer come on with a band. I could recognise instantly they were possible humanoids, and that their location in time was displaced, yet for the first time I was able to see him very clearly, the man who'd signatured my life in ways so ambivalent that I still hadn't sorted out the confusion of his sexual exploitation of me, or his apparent genius. I didn't know who he was or why we were here, and he just stared at me with no more feeling than a fridge. I got the idea too that the persistent tomtom rhythm I could hear, issued not from the room's audiovisual tech, but from some internalised space inside my brain.

After staring me down he switched his vision to Lucy, then Kit, with a cold impassive scrutiny that registered no feeling at all in his inquisitive scoop.

'DO YOU AGREE TO THE EXCHANGE?' he shouted, like I'd heard him centuries ago on stage at the Globe, and other suppurating pits in London Fields. The voice hadn't changed, only it appeared to be located somewhere I couldn't place outside our shattered timeframe. 'DO YOU AGREE TO EXCHANGE REALITIES?'

'You've opened a time gate on your past,' Kit responded, 'you're in a space that isn't ours—go back or I'll disconnect you from the future. You'll disappear and never make it back.'

I saw Lucy spontaneously come alive to Kit's command in this impossibly deregulated encounter with the past. I could sense she was as fired up as Kit, ready to resist the black-hooded procession standing there as a pirated tribe, like psychic terrorists in a Bloomsbury landmark.

I recognised the two actors Richard Burbage and Edward Alleyn, acquaintances of his I'd often met in rowdy theatre pubs as integral to the success of his plays, when they were noisily drunk after impassioned performances to the howling mob. Kit tried again to turn them round and back, and all the time I could hear the drum-driven chanting growing louder, as though it was trapped in my head, and what now sounded like Shakespeare's voice co-opted into unstoppable percussive bongo.

It was hard keeping my nerve, even with Kit's debriefing that these visitors from the future lived parallel like weird radio signals detected by SETI from a nearby red dwarf star. It was then that the trio implicated in Kit's murder appeared—the threateningly polarised stalkers I'd seen around my patch and identified as Ingram Frizer, Robert Poley and Nicholas Skeres. I watched Shakespeare, eyes fixed on me, remove his hood and he was still 1593, black eyes and receding hair worn long to the shoulders. The security detail, Frizer, Poley and Skeres moved in behind him, as though they had business laid down five centuries ago and pulled out knives ready for use.

I didn't see what Kit did, only that it was in his glasses, and the irradiated flash appeared to melt time and the assembled group like stripping paint from a door. Only Shakespeare projected through the red fireballs' searing shockwaves in a state of ravaged meltdown, knife in his hand, while his hooded entourage were burnt out of time like liquidated pops of plasma. As a detonative torch he lunged at Kit with a kitchen knife aimed for his head, as Lucy without any warning shot him at point blank range, his body crumpling into a sticky goo of scorched plasma, like a burnt omelette ripped from the pan to shrivel on the marble floor.

We stood there numb from anaphylitic shock in the cold glow of the now empty hall with no least trace of the remains of Shakespeare and the historic quango that had confronted us from some proactive rupture in time. I could hear internalised noises in the building reassert themselves, the metallic chatter of lift doors opening and closing, voices outside in the corridor, the conspiratorial hush condensed into the building's cavernous shell, and the generally diffused ambient white noise of the untiring capital that leaks in everywhere, even into the pores of the skin.

All of us sat down, collapsed back into ourselves, after five centuries of getting there, in the cold shakes accompanying trauma. I realised anything was possible if time went both ways, dropped eggs might spontaneously reassemble, or the dead, like we'd experienced, return to life and live backwards to birth. But for the first time I felt a hint of liberation, as though time might be directed one way for me, and presumably for Kit and Lucy at a local level, so we could live out our realities in the contemporary moment without being conscripted into retrograde past identities.

'Let's get out of here,' Kit said, dispassionately, and we trawled through the building and out into Malet Street, and Bloomsbury was fuzzily silvered with rain, the drizzle helping us come alive in transitioning back to the moment as urban reality. I looked up at a break in the monochrome liquid sky and there were patches of peacock sky starting through smog over St. Pancras way, where the black River Fleet navigates its ambulatory subterranean flow through the capital's sink. Lucy expressed the desire to be alone, to walk and think in the rain, and suggested we meet tomorrow and talk at her place. 'I can't believe it's really over,' she said, 'I'm thinking he'll be back on my bell tonight at 2 a.m., hanging on it for life.'

'Don't worry, he's never coming back now,' Kit said. 'We're disinfected of our core enemy, and hopefully everyone associated with our past who knew him. They've left us for now, but they'll be back as spooky returnees.'

Kit looked at his phone as synthetic intelligence and said, 'I shouldn't tell you this, but someone's biohacked a senior minister's pacemaker, and he'd dead. I'm wanted on the case. I've been watching the suspect and his accomplices for weeks.'

I watched Kit hurry off in the direction of his car, clearly so singularly focused that we no longer counted. And with Lucy gone, I felt suddenly excruciatingly alone, without a past or future, and totally consumed by the divergent present. I decided then and there that if I wished I could change my name and move on. I'd amassed considerable wealth from patrons and buried it in tax holes under the company name W.H. Investments, banal as any other offshore finance modality seeking anonymity.

Not wishing to go directly back home to Charles Street, in the fear I would find Howard dead, or overdosed in the apartment, I hung around the Brunswick Centre, and its busy concrete piazza full of Waitrose shoppers, tourists and Asian UCL students. The drizzle had subsided and a carmine sky faced down over Marchmont Street and Bloomsbury's top-end rectilinear squares occupied by international financial barons. I felt totally alone in the universe standing under Senate House's portentous monolith, its entire surveillance system put out by Kit's counterterrorist facility. I stood outside the entrance to Waitrose, free, jittery and afraid, before going in to casually browse its aisles. As I did, I noticed something glutinously sticky on the left thigh of my jeans, a little squamose dribble of no-colour goo that I instinctively picked at to try and get rid of the stain. When I touched the residual trace the contact burnt my fingertips, like nothing I'd ever experienced before. It was on looking like a malevolent radioactive blob, something to be analysed by a xenobiologist in the lab. I knew instinctually it was a globule of Shakespeare's torched plasma I'd come away with after whatever Kit did to liquidate him and his cell. It was like contaminated semen stuck to me from the wrong century and perhaps in some non-physical way there was a dirty oplalescent dribble, like something you might find at the back of a bus seat or smeared on a black sack awaiting collection from an urban dump. It was like adhesive chewing gum holding on as the last trace of him, like his last rites; his final attachment to me and the city he continued to dominate by way of overpowering literary precedence over all his contemporaries past and future. I recoiled from picking at it like superior alien snot, a sort of congealed circulation, a zombie sign on distressed denim. I had this wild imagining suddenly that if I touched it I'd be torched and burnt to the bone like the wick in a petrol bomb. I was in fact in the Tea Pigs section looking at Moroccan Mint tea pyramids in their nylon parachutes, as well as at their own brand Ceylon and Lapsang Souchong teas as nothing exceptional if you knew the right places to go. I roamed distractively from aisle to aisle just for the sake of it, deciding in the process I'd check into the nearby Russell Hotel overnight, and maybe stay a week in one of their topfloor luxury suites, hermetically sealed from the big city exchanges going on around me; the burning buildings as a regular recurrence in the east, and terrorist cells in the west initialising random terrorist surges on the tube and in the warren of the underground. Right next to me in Waitrose an Asian girl—the violent contrast between her ebony ponytail and magnolia skin pulling me into attention of her short blue and green plaid skirt, was looking at expressions of cheesecake in packed triangular wedges, as though assessing the aesthetic of presentation. I watched her choose what looked like blueberry, adroitly correct an escaped navy bra strap, smile at my attention, and move on out of my life for ever, as simply another contactless London face inhabiting like me, her own inscrutably private reality.

I walked over in the drenched pink light to the Russell Hotel, its Victorian terra cotta cladded façade glowing in the peachy aquatic sunset. I took an available suite high up and fronting the square, chose to climb the monumental Pyrenean marble staircase, rather than use the lift, swiped my key card and once in propped myself up on the bed and peeled off my jeans in the hope of cleaning the little viscous smear off in the bathroom. Before that I took a mini-bottle of white wine out of the fridge, drank it off quickly, uncapped another and carried my jeans into the bathroom. I wetted a dark blue flannel with soap and water and dabbed at the congealed blob. The stain wouldn't wipe, and the more I worked at it the more I felt I shouldn't, suddenly convinced that if the dead existed, I was perhaps trying to rub out a bit of somebody's soul with soap and water, something so weird in the thought I was convinced

I would be contaminated for ever. Was this I asked a blob of Shakespeare's soul that looked like silver mucous clinging to denim? I kept on trying to erase it, knowing intuitively I could never succeed in rubbing Shakespeare out. Arguably, I considered cutting the square of denim out and having the residue analysed by forensics and cryopreserved in the lab, but who would ever take me seriously in my claim to it being a burnt trace of William Shakespeare. I got into a state of panic and went back into the bedroom and sank another drink before returning to the unwashable and unscrapeable stain, like a bit of indestructible plasma peeled off something alien that didn't belong here.

I called Kit, but he was too busy to give it time. 'Don't touch it,' he said. 'Dispose of it somewhere safe and take out any cameras first.' The call was instantly dropped.

I sat there, left with the mystery of William Shakespeare on the leg of my distressed Levi's. The stained site was significantly near my crotch in its accidental placement. It meant, as the smear appeared irremoveable, I'd have to discard the item and bin it after buying new jeans the next day. Disregarding Kit's advice I continued to apply soap to the residual trace, but it was like trying to rub out a star hundreds of light-years away with my thumb. I remoted news on the flat screen to learn that a raging fire had broken out at the Globe Theatre, while a radically revamped King Lear was being performed, and that at least 40 people were dead and over two hundred seriously injured. The cause still hadn't been identified, nor terrorism ruled out as a possibility. I went to the window and a giant plume of black smoke was thickening the air like a new choking occluded atmosphere over the capital. Almost simultaneously there was breaking news of a massive fire at St. Helen's Bishopsgate, the 18th-century church I knew Shakespeare to have attended during the time of our relationship in the 1590s. Other reports rapidly followed, the reconstructed

Globe Theatre at Bankside, the iconic landmark St. John's Gate at Clerkenwell, and almost in direct succession Middle Temple Hall niched into alleys in the heart of the Temple area, all of which I recognised as places deeply associated with Shakespeare's London at the time I knew him. It seemed to me that all of Shakespeare's landmarks were exploding into flame as part of his propulsive psychic explusion from a city he'd written into history with his indomitably driven genius.

The London skyline with its elevated grammar of sky-scrapers was on fire, orange-red cones of flame launched at the clouds as the underframe of a dragging muscle of dirty smoke building to a bulbous summit in the east end. It wasn't WW3 or WW4, nor a pilotless drone attack on preselected sites; of that I was sure, as I heard the divergent cognitive dissonance of blue lights racing across the city. I could smell burning in the way smoke infiltrates every accessible fissure. People were gathering in panicked groups outside in the street, all focused on the incandescent pyrotechnics of the near skyline, like the nuclear sun had finally risen over the city. I knew without doubt this was Shakespeare's doing and his act of final revenge from which there was no come back.

From up high in the Russell I could view it all as the spectator of my now incinerated past happening in the com-bustible contemporary moment. It wasn't London that was burning; it was in my mind Shakespeare who was torching all associations with his past in one giant flameout.

I stood at the open window breathing in smoke and sur-veying the crowds all looking south towards the mushroom-ing build of dense black cloud roofing the city. That police suspected covert terrorist cells of serial arson came up on my phone, but I knew this wasn't the real cause. Building after building was autocombusting without any apparent cause in explosive cones of orange flame.

I knew deep down this wasn't apocalypse or end time, just a massive act of cataclysmic revenge on Shakespeare's part, now that he wouldn't be back to personalise his associative London geography. At least, it was my interpretation of external catastrophe, and the fact the city was burning south of the river like a torched oilfield.

I looked out at a skyline of mirrorglass skyscrapers, cladded towers, squat black fridges, money built into the sky as fluid architecture simulating retro-rocket launches, huge tech objects blasting a hydrogen plume in lift-off. That buildings couldn't do ballistics was for me part of their concretised limitations in being designed for a sky they could never reach. Asymmetric, tapered or linear they were grounded in a concrete matrix as floating architecture that would corrode, oxidise and crash. The sunset, almost indistinguishable from the flames was starting to dip in a dowsed vermilion fireball to be replaced by a southbank in a state of site-specific meltdown. I didn't doubt the fires were manageable at the expense of hundreds of trapped casualties, and viewed it coldly, philosophically, as part of a process of accumulated violent ends worked out in time as part of transitioning time zones in history.

The jeans though: I retrieved them from the bathroom, the viscous dribble still glittering like snail mucous, and looked at the residual smear a last time as Shakespeare's final remains; took them to the window, debated for a few minutes and then let them fall, and watched as they instantly caught fire, crumpled into searing flame and plummeted in free fall into the busy street below.

A PARTIAL LIST OF SNUGGLY BOOKS

MAY ARMAND BLANC *The Last Rendezvous*
G. ALBERT AURIER *Elsewhere and Other Stories*
CHARLES BARBARA *My Lunatic Asylum*
S. HENRY BERTHOUD *Misanthropic Tales*
LÉON BLOY *The Tarantulas' Parlor and Other Unkind Tales*
ÉLÉMIR BOURGES *The Twilight of the Gods*
ADA BUISSON *The Baron's Coffin and Other Disquieting Tales*
CYRIEL BUYSSE *The Aunts*
JAMES CHAMPAGNE *Harlem Smoke*
FÉLICIEN CHAMPSAUR *The Latin Orgy*
BRENDAN CONNELL *Clark*
BRENDAN CONNELL *Metrophilias*
BRENDAN CONNELL (editor) *The Zinzolin Book of Occult Fiction*
RAFAELA CONTRERAS *The Turquoise Ring and Other Stories*
DANIEL CORRICK (editor)
    Ghosts and Robbers: An Anthology of German Gothic Fiction
ADOLFO COUVE *When I Think of My Missing Head*
QUENTIN S. CRISP *Aiaigasa*
ALADY DILKE *The Outcast Spirit and Other Stories*
ÉDOUARD DUJARDIN *Hauntings*
BERIT ELLINGSEN *Now We Can See the Moon*
ERCKMANN-CHATRIAN *A Malediction*
ALPHONSE ESQUIROS *The Enchanted Castle*
ENRIQUE GÓMEZ CARRILLO *Sentimental Stories*
DELPHI FABRICE *Flowers of Ether*
DELPHI FABRICE *The Red Spider*
BENJAMIN GASTINEAU *The Reign of Satan*
EDMOND AND JULES DE GONCOURT *Manette Salomon*
REMY DE GOURMONT *From a Faraway Land*
REMY DE GOURMONT *Morose Vignettes*
GUIDO GOZZANO *Alcina and Other Stories*
GUSTAVE GUICHES *The Modesty of Sodom*
EDWARD HERON-ALLEN *The Complete Shorter Fiction*
RHYS HUGHES *Cloud Farming in Wales*
J.-K. HUYSMANS *The Crowds of Lourdes*
J.-K. HUYSMANS *Knapsacks*
COLIN INSOLE *Valerie and Other Stories*
JUSTIN ISIS *Pleasant Tales II*

FREDERICK ROLFE (Baron Corvo) *Amico di Sandro*
JASON ROLFE *An Archive of Human Nonsense*
ARNAUD RYKNER *The Last Train*
MARCEL SCHWOB *The Assassins and Other Stories*
MARCEL SCHWOB *Double Heart*
CHRISTIAN HEINRICH SPIESS *The Dwarf of Westerbourg*
BRIAN STABLEFORD (editor)
 Decadence and Symbolism: A Showcase Anthology
BRIAN STABLEFORD (editor) *The Snuggly Satyricon*
BRIAN STABLEFORD (editor) *The Snuggly Satanicon*
BRIAN STABLEFORD *Spirits of the Vasty Deep*
COUNT ERIC STENBOCK *Love, Sleep & Dreams*
COUNT ERIC STENBOCK *Myrtle, Rue & Cypress*
COUNT ERIC STENBOCK *The Shadow of Death*
COUNT ERIC STENBOCK *Studies of Death*
MONTAGUE SUMMERS *The Bride of Christ and Other Fictions*
MONTAGUE SUMMERS *Six Ghost Stories*
ALICE TÉLOT *The Inn of Tears*
GILBERT-AUGUSTIN THIERRY *Reincarnation and Redemption*
DOUGLAS THOMPSON *The Fallen West*
TOADHOUSE *Gone Fishing with Samy Rosenstock*
TOADHOUSE *Living and Dying in a Mind Field*
TOADHOUSE *What Makes the Wave Break?*
LÉO TRÉZENIK *The Confession of a Madman*
LÉO TRÉZENIK *Decadent Prose Pieces*
RUGGERO VASARI *Raun*
JANE DE LA VAUDÈRE *The Demi-Sexes and The Androgynes*
JANE DE LA VAUDÈRE *The Double Star and Other Occult Fantasies*
AUGUSTE VILLIERS DE L'ISLE-ADAM *Isis*
RENÉE VIVIEN AND HÉLÈNE DE ZUYLEN DE NYEVELT
 Faustina and Other Stories
RENÉE VIVIEN *Lilith's Legacy*
RENÉE VIVIEN *A Woman Appeared to Me*
ILARIE VORONCA *The Confession of a False Soul*
ILARIE VORONCA *The Key to Reality*
TERESA WILMS MONTT *In the Stillness of Marble*
TERESA WILMS MONTT *Sentimental Doubts*
KAREL VAN DE WOESTIJNE *The Dying Peasant*

www.ingramcontent.com/pod-product-compliance
Lightning Source LLC
Chambersburg PA
CBHW020128120726
47903CB00007B/2153